A CHANGE
OF SEASONS

A Change of Seasons

Published by The Conrad Press in the United Kingdom 2021

Tel: +44(0)1227 472 874
www.theconradpress.com
info@theconradpress.com

ISBN 978-1-913567-89-7

Illustrations by Hana Elahi and Eisha Elahi

Typesetting and Cover Design by: Charlotte Mouncey, www.bookstyle.co.uk
The Conrad Press logo was designed by Maria Priestley.

Printed and bound in Great Britain by Clays Ltd, Elcograf S.p.A.

A CHANGE OF SEASONS

KHURRAM ELAHI

Special thanks to my family

This is a story about heartache…

PROLOGUE

He could hear a bell in the background, yet strangely it was in the forefront of his mind. It was not just one bell, but many. They chimed ceremoniously, yet lacked unison. The bells carried authority and emanated a depressing sombre drone which remained in is mind throughout. A wry smile lit up his face when he found himself visualising butlers brandishing bells, standing to attention. But then, reflecting on how unquestionably inappropriate it was he extinguished any lingering thoughts. This was not a time for laughter; not even a time for tears. This was not a time for anything.

The bells droned continuously, reverberating perpetually in a kind of mad party of bell ringers trying to peak the loudest and take home the star prize of a gold bell engraved on a mahogany stand. These thoughts, on top of others, ridiculed this far from frivolous situation, but he seemed to have no control; seemed to be driving a car with no brakes.

Suddenly, he found himself in a large, endless room... no it wasn't a room, it was too big for that. It was simply a space. A space with similar people to him, presenting similarly distressing and confused faces. A space, but on planet Earth. You could hardly compare it to a bus stop but bizarrely John did. People were impatient, nervous and overcome with trepidation. Others, he noted, were actually trembling. The occasion must just have been too overcoming, immersing them within a basket of fear.

John noticed people in this queued procession, queuing or waiting for what though? The sentiments which overcame him were familiar to him, in fact, to anyone. Though he had never been there before it felt like he was meant to be there somehow, making him feel confused and unaware of his surroundings. Deja vu knocked on the door of his mind, a mentally battered mind; a mind that he could not slam shut.

Then something caught his attention. Something staring him in the face so much that he did not notice. All the people who had been placed here were young, probably around twenty years old, certainly younger than thirty. He was the only older person present. Wait a minute, even he felt younger, but having no mirror he could not substantiate this. There were also no women present. He had no idea. Everyone else was young except him? How did he get here and why? Maybe everyone else were having the same thoughts as he was? He took in a deep breath to try to control and harness his sanity and thoughts. External incidents had created and internal mix of insecurity and apprehension.

His panic steadied somewhat. Traumatised eyes turned to his own self, his clothes. Adorning a white robe, John had no belt nor was his jacket strait. He wore nothing else; nothing except that look of devastation mirrored from the time pieces of other onlookers.

His feet were numb; they wore no protection. Their bareness exemplifying his intractable state of mind. He sensed darkness; could feel an icy cold chill in his blood, yet brilliant white light mirrored endlessly above and around him. He felt disquiet trying to comprehend the nature of these feelings and images. Too scared to run; too pointless to shout, he felt a resigned sadness and helplessness overthrow him. The expanse around him suggested no exit was possible, although the thought had not even crept into John's stuporous mind; a stupor that had already befuddled him. How wrong he was; should have awoken from his slumber.

His disbelieving eyes arose to discover silence and solitude. Somehow, he had been transported from the begs and cries of others a few moments earlier to complete and utter loneliness. He spun around praying for life. Forget hearing a pin drop, John could hear his own breath reverberating in glorious stereo. Although John never considered himself, and was in fact not an agoraphobic, his panic would have set a cardiograph alight.

A fearful, yet somewhat nonchalant glance upwards, discovered a planetarium skyline. But that was where the astrological comparisons subsided. There was an inevitable need to stare upwards, absorbing the fascinating view at hand. Moreover, what John perceived was an anthology of pictures, some moving and some not; a timeline? This was a frightening colourful arrangement, picturesque yet grotesque. Confusion drowned John into a sea of insanity. There was something odd but John just could not put his finger on it. Like an itch that you cannot reach or an appetite that you cannot quite appease.

An image appeared above. He saw someone, a kid, fighting with another aggressively. Jeers and hisses from the periphery helped to show that he was not the crowd's favourite. This was understandable, predominantly due to the fact that he was one and a half times larger than the other. Blood was dotted around the overwhelmed boy. The whole episode only lasted a matter of seconds but John watched perplexed. He continued.

Act two provided John with another moving picture. It rang bells, this time inside his head. This set of events stuck out from the array of images trying to warn him. John figured a woman, no, a teacher, was in her office seemingly dominating a pupil in a vitriolic manner, showering the boy with accusations, many of which were fallacious but being labelled a criminal came with its mud.

'Jonathan, you've gone too far this time,' the head teacher growled, looking down at the ever-present but useless piece of paper in the middle of the table. 'What the hell are you trying to achieve with stupidity like this?' she spurted aggressively. A band of hair bounced down from the woman's side across her cheek, over the corner of her eye. She hastily returned the strands back to their family.

'A grade "A",' he mused, whispering so as to be inaudible to her, yet have at least some childish satisfaction. In his mind it was a tiny victory he thought smugly. Inadvertently, she only heard part of his snide remark, demanding to hear the rest. 'I said I don't know what to say,' he returned, as straight faced as he could muster. It was clear that he had lied before as he acted out his role professionally. The head teacher retained an air of caution throughout the rest of the interview. It had become obvious that Jonathan had committed a crime of some sort, and his punishment was to promptly follow.

'The caretaker may seem an easy target for you, but he is

a member of the school, just like you and me, so I cannot understand what you thought you were doing,' she continued stern and straight. Jonathan's eyes pierced the floor near his feet, seemingly more aware and interested of the carpet texture than this more serious episode. Being is his early teens, he had little interest in obedience to acquiesce, and was one of those kids who stood out like a bad tooth rather than a beauty spot.

He had always been popular with the wrong crowd, and unpopular with the right crowd, depending on your choice of crowd. On concentration, he could make out a horse with the shades of the carpet. It took some effort and squinting, but in the end, Jonathan managed to figure out the horse's head and body. It meant a lot to him to get that clear in his mind. To him, he found it a distraction, but a needed distraction at present. It was a personal victory, and he felt like telling his friends to see if they could also see it.

'Something funny down there boy?' This time the head teacher addressed Jonathan with scorn.

'Sorry miss,' apologised Jonathan, erasing the image from his mind, though knowing that it would still be there on the carpet roaring across the floor as if in an episode of Black Beauty.

A little apprehension caused him to smudge a thread of perspiration quietly progressing down his forehead, cutting the strand in two. It was partly due to the heated room he was in, but more noticeably due to the predicament he had put himself in. At first, he took it all nonchalantly, but was now starting to feel a little regretful as he bit into his tongue in nervousness.

During the lecture (a kind of extracurricular lecture that had been forced fed to him), something discernible caught his attention, forcing him to suddenly look upwards and behind the head teacher. Initially at least she did not notice anything was odd or wrong. In fact, she became gladdened to a miniscule of a degree that he was seeming to take more attention. At least that was what she thought as he at least looked in her direction rather than anywhere else in the room, or more specifically at the bland carpet below.

'The problem with you, Jonathan, is that you never have learned and never will do' she lectured. Now she had his undivided attention she wanted to make sure to use the time wisely. 'We have given you so many chances to show us you want to improve and you will thank us later in life. I have no doubt about that.' But Jonathan was more interested in Trevor behind the teacher as he mimicked both he and teacher, providing graphical insults and expletives. A half-hidden snigger crept onto the edge of Jonathan's mouth, leading to an inevitable jerk round from his superior. Her vison caught nothing other than a few kids playing football in some unused tennis courts a few hundred feet away. It was tantamount to detaining a guilty criminal with no evidence or witnesses. This angered her even more, and her anger alone would surely have ended any hopes of Jonathan being treated with impunity. At this point she didn't care about the evidence. She was now in a mean mood, intent on getting her pound of flesh.

'Placing ink in the caretaker's mop bucket is not the kind of thing advocated at this school. You may do it at home, but not here.' Raging with abhorrence she stood up in a psychological attempt to exert authority. All Jonathan could think of was when this would be over so that he could go back to wasting time. 'As well as that,' she said, 'I believe you have been vandalizing the toilets and damaging the plastic fencing behind me.' As she spoke, she automatically turned to show him where she was referring to. Becoming an opportunity to blame Jonathan for anything and everything, a wish list of things to include, she was mentally ticking them off one by one.

Coincidently, Trevor was now actually near to the fence in question. He was playing football, but was not very good; had about as much footballing ability as a tramp has dexterity. Jonathan glanced towards the fencing still calm and serene, whereas the head teacher had become more fidgety, as if roles had been reversed. Now the teacher was fidgeting like a squirrel with a nut. Yet, Jonathan did not quite know what a fright there was in store for him.

'I have heard there are other undesirable acts you have committed, Jonathan. Do you have anything you would like to tell me?'

Jonathan replied in the negative, with about as much interest as a sloth in a tree. A few moments of silence gave way to an interruption from the teacher.

'I have decided what to do to make the situation better. To make sure you don't carry on this way. Could you follow me please?' This time she exhibited greater calm and tranquillity as she decided to play her joker card. It was as if it had all been planned beforehand. Jonathan was now the quizzical looking one.

Rising with an air of vitality, resembling a queen, she turned her head, strands of brown hair flowing in tune, as she motioned for the pupil to follow her. Inevitably, he obliged, feeling a combination of intrigue, but more anxiety at the prospect of his sentence, words now starting to fail him. On most occasions a simple letter would go home and maybe detention for an hour. This time he suspected that he would have to digest a sterner examination as neither a letter to the parents nor detention seemed to be on the menu.

He caught sight of a strange grin on her rejuvenated face as she headed off in front of him, a giant ogre in full control. The grin comprised scorn and contempt mixed with satisfaction and mockery. It was as if she sensed he was now feeling this anxiety, bordering trepidation. Apprehension glistened on him as his lesson on life was about to begin. In a perverted way though, he felt a sense of urgency to find out what kind of punishment lay ahead.

He reassured himself with an internal embrace, preparing himself for anything that lay ahead. In a sadistic way, a new punishment would in fact make the crime more meaningful, making him ask himself if he would make the grade. Despite the teacher playing her joker card it now looked more like Jonathan was the only joker in this pack.

'Please come in…' she said, opening the door simultaneously. Barely seconds passed before Jonathan realised what was in store for him. What he had expected was a small storeroom with paper, books, folders etc. He also expected a window looking out into the school fields. He had no idea or thought of any kind of punishment. Some kind of solitary confinement maybe?

Yes, probably detention was the ace up her sleeve. It eased his nerves as he had already convinced himself he was right. Detention he was used to, no big deal. What he found was something quite different, beyond the expectations of a school child. He noticed ream after ream of paper, lined and underlined depending on your fancy; but lined up all the same. Folders too, glittered the room, in a spectrum of colours and a shop full of sizes. It was a forest of illusions yet ironically for him, lacking in oxygen. The illuminating feature though, of this unlighted, almost windowless room was an old backless stool with a hangman's noose dangling stagnant about six feet above it. Jonathan discerned that the noose was made of what resembled a thin and undefeatable rope, positioned back-middle of this cramped storeroom. It had probably been used for tug-of-war during sports days at school he assumed, hoped.

Want a game of Hangman, buddy? Come join the fun... winner takes all. The loser, well, he falls!

You never been in here before have you, Johnny? We got a special treat for you inside. Roll up, roll up, place your bets.

No one outside the window, only the three of us now, buddy. Check it out, Johnny, check outside... you don't believe me... check it out. Jingle, jingle.

True enough, there was not a soul outside, unless the tiny window was a portal to another world. Then Jonathan was sure he heard the sound of a jingle, the jingle of a hat. Then just visible from the window, the top of a jester's hat passing by, but from the angle he couldn't make out what lay beneath... some would say thankfully so.

Jonathan then stared upwards observing the ropes length. Yes, definitely tug-of-war, he contemplated, as his head moved slowly upwards like an escalator. This time it seemed he was the one at war. The room was uncharacteristically long compared to its width, and he wondered but could not figure out why. He came to a cul-de-sac that he dared not contemplate, especially as a cul-de-sac had a dead end.

Gazing higher and higher, Jonathan unexpectedly let out a rush of coughs and spurts, his eyes opening and closing frantically. In his surprise and incredulity, he had forgot to breathe (as if the noose had already been placed into position, or maybe it was the lack of oxygen). He was now distraught about what really this noose and his punishment had in common, though was starting to entertain guesses… surely not, he begged himself. Scarier still, the noose looked well used. It looked old, experienced, impatient, enticing and waiting.

That's right, buddy, you getting the idea now? Starting to get the picture? Don't hang around here too long, buddy! Jingle, jingle.

Understandable apprehension now gripped him, causing him to smudge a thread of perspiration which was quietly progressing down his forehead and into a point somewhere between the eyes. His right index finger became dripping wet. Without hesitation he wiped his finger harshly and hastily on some loose paper on the table as if detesting the sight of sweat. It left a dark thick line. Finally, some use made of the reams and reams of paper in there.

Somehow it was becoming colder and chillier. Jonathan could feel it all around his body. The storeroom possessed a dank frigidity, colder than Christmas, though Jonathan only realised this now; he had only just been given that gift. In truth it hadn't. Some rooms are colder than others. This, unfortunately was one of those rooms. He could feel the sensation of cold as if impersonating a naked African in snow. Goose pimples attacked him, stretching for air, searching for warmer temperature, tickling him all over, as if the wind was blowing leaves across his arms.

Becoming increasingly colder, he felt the need to embrace himself and smoother the chill. Rubbing his hands in haste up and down his arms, he felt the need to turn around. Someone's eyes were upon him. Like a spider on a string behind you, or a dog following you home; self-consciousness led him to the turning of his head. His backward glance was met with the wide grin of a vengeful woman, as the head teacher, now mistress, stood almost within breathing distance. He heard screams inside his head as imaginary mirrors distorted his reality, images bouncing and reverberating akin to a network of lights in a call centre. The fright startled him. In his perplexity, he found himself biting his lower lip impulsively. His teeth slowly moved around the sides of his mouth and face searching for juicy skin like a perverted cannibal. A combination of the intense cold twinned with Jonathan's progressing panic caused him to inadvertently bite the tip of his tongue. Only a second passed before the blood began to creep out. Although constant, it only ambled out, leading to that familiar bittersweet, sickly sensation of crimson fluid, warm and supposedly wholesome. Fortunately, the blood flow eased and Jonathan's temporary strange facial reactions conceded to normality. Even his own blood wanted to escape the punishment that would follow.

His dread came true.

Hang in there, buddy…

'Put your head in the noose,' she said nonchalantly. Jonathan's already traumatised features reacted reluctantly but positively to her order. For a second, he felt reluctance then inevitable acceptance. He now felt like a terminal patient accepting death. Still, his eyes switched to the noose, where he observed certain loose threads of string around the base of the loop. It didn't take him long to decipher why. It was old and well used, and he was to become the next customer, free of charge. The thought did trouble him somewhat but not enough to force an argument from him. He was in no position to bargain, as if he was walking down the aisle towards his electric chair. The head mistress was making no special offer, just doing her job forcing Jonathan to accept an offer he could not refuse.

He walked towards his maker, or taker, helpless, with every step lasting a lifetime. His mind was working like a tortoise in a shell. Yet the hammer in the back of his head was beating him up uncontrollably. Thinking to himself that it would all be over a few moments was supposed to calm him. It would all be over in a few moments, he consoled himself as he found himself sweating profusely, though he only just noticed it as sweat was spat all over his face. Yet he still felt freezing. His palms were fidgety, cold and clammy, reminiscent or only vaguely comparable to a feeling during a fever.

Nearly done now, buddy. Get ready to hold your breath.
Necks please!

His head was in the noose as he saw his angel of death, now dressed as a highwayman. She wore a large ridged hat and false moustache. It would have sickened him, should have sickened him, but his sanity was not quite where it should be. He thought he heard the sound of the neigh of a horse, a large black horse. The same horse from the carpet? Maybe. He saw a jester's hat alone on the floor, bell still intact. Wetness just above his upper lip now dripped into his already bloody mouth, salty with sweat. He licked his lips impulsively… finger licking good. Then he tried anxiously to regain some courage. He had none, so he stared downwards in resignation; a captive awaiting the rifle; an African awaiting the drought; a glamour model awaiting old age...

'Right... Aim... FIRE,' he muttered madly to himself.

1. BALLOON

He screamed, his body shooting upwards as though bisected by a wooden shaft. Yet, rather than attending to the top left of his chest, his arms unflinchingly sent his hands to his moist neck where a plexus of nerves convulsed frantically. He rubbed fingertips over this already lubricated area searching for signs, and praying for traces of string. Pulling at air, he discovered nothing, and began to slowly accept that there was nothing there. Mixed in with those emotions was more than a little relief. His heartbeat began to react in a similar way.

Looking around in alarm he sat up erect, trying to naturally steady his nerves, digesting the cognizance that it was all only a dream. It had been a bad one. So many of his dreams of late had been bad ones and that's what worried him. It worried him because he very rarely used to even have dreams, never mind good or bad ones. That's not to say John did not fear. He always had a fair amount of fear mixed into his life, just like you would expect.

He sometimes feared life, death, and even sometimes what came in-between. And he had, I suppose, been thinking more about these things as of late. If there was a sandwich on a table comprising life and death, John would most certainly lift up one half of the bread to see what was inside, no doubt expecting it to be off. You see John had become more stressed of late, insecurity had started to eat at his mind. More recently he had let tension consume him and become greedy to only have his own company, very rarely frequenting other friends. In his isolation, he often engulfed himself, not only with his own company, but also with irrelevant knowledge that bottle-necked his mind.

You may think this stress an inconsequential factor, but you would be wrong. You see, John got divorced five years ago. It was in part to do with his overactive mind and changeability of moods. Yes, he loved his wife, but that wasn't enough as he rarely showed it, often taking life and his wife for granted. His tempers would cause fervent arguments over such banal issues such as washing the dishes and cutting the grass. He always left it to the last minute. The arguments lived on like a disease of his mind, and again they too became commonplace; they grew and spread, taking over his daily life. What goes up must come down; too many cracks were beginning to show; his balloon was getting too large and eventually burst.

When a balloon does burst it disappears but can disperse fragments of rubber; damaging others nearby. His marriage was a balloon which got blown up far too much. The divorce was the exploding rubber with the shrapnel release having irrevocable aftereffects on John himself who had been suffering ever since. On the other hand, his ex-wife Kate, well she had fared much better after the breakup, finding someone more suitable and appealing for her somewhat extroverted lifestyle.

He had never been the same since his balloon had burst. Everyday had become a battle, a battle which he always seemed to be feeling the bullets from. Fighting it got harder with each punch, an equally more awkward a process. On the bright side, he had got away from that no man's land where he and his wife would just sit there for hours not speaking and only hearing voices in their heads.

Thoughts of this degrading divorce experience shot and bled at his soul like a non-coagulating wound. It blended a mixture of anger and jealousy that vexed his confused head with hate and misery intertwined in there somewhere. Vitriolic cantankerous thoughts cancered him, burning away at his mentally severed body. Worst of all, he was the one doing this to himself. Although hate was the cause of it all, he was still the one who had dwelt on the issue for the past five years. It was a problem he had not yet managed to overcome. In his present state he did not expect to, yet somehow knew he had to.

Numerous battles and arguments had littered their marriage. As a warehouse manager John had discovered enough economic security. But enough to get by on modest means. Working for Comfort Upholstery, it sometimes had felt that he was self-employed as he had given so much time, heart and dedication to the company. He had only struggled with a few issues throughout his seventeen-year history with the company. An unmotivated employee is sometimes equivalent to a blind juggler, useless.

John was a very critical employee of the company, though on two occasions had been very close to losing his job. One time a delivery got mixed up for a very important client and things went pear-shaped. It was only his hardworking reputation that saved him. Then, more recently his feeble attempt at answering back at his supervisor nearly landed him in big trouble. In the end, his supervisor realised what staying power John gave the company and therefore he survived.

Although it wasn't the best job in the world, for a man with limited academic skills it was a sure catch, only possible by taking whatever insults were pelted at him. A sure catch it was, a little like his time with Kate. For a time, she had been a sure catch for him, until he went and messed it up.

The expert and professional training he had received whilst in the army had placed him in good stead to any career he desired where rigidity was required. His time in the army had taught him that whatever he did and wherever he did it, he would apply a portion of pride and effort, always giving his best.

Discipline became key to his life, the ruler of his actions and the master of his ways. He would openly speak of this; that everyone should go through national conscription at some point in their lives. He really thought it would help to banish a castle of indolence. Maybe he believed this because of the coercion he had faced from the strict family he was brought up in, and also the greatness of the past from the British Empire. The nation that led the world in centuries past. John had never freed himself from the nationalistic threads of society, but had realised that society had liberated itself from the prisons of private gain.

Multicultural hype was now on political agendas and it won votes. Governments inviting foreigners into the country seemed the in thing. They liked pizzas, curries and chop suey. Whether they truly loved the people who provided these appetizing meals was another matter. But it sure appeared that way to John. He did feel a mild ire when he saw an Asian man in a suit smiling and tictacking his shiny Loakes as someone higher than he.

Sometimes he had understanding and support for workingman's clubs boasting white only memberships. He had compassion for those, and could not understand why the non-English had any objection. He sometimes found himself shaking his head at the T.V. as he saw the unemployment figures going up, always finding himself looking at only one reason for this; immigrants taking our jobs.

John's ex-wife had been a great calming influence on him though, she brought out the tamer side of him. She had been so light-hearted, bubbly and full of smiles which balanced John out. Her almost childish actions had helped to soothe John's wartime afflictions and tendencies. What had remained though was his dedication to his job. Moreover, it was his determination to do a job properly or not at all. One agreement they did have which turned out for the best given the divorce; never having children. This turned out to be a blessing in disguise and would only have made things that much stickier.

Comfort Upholstery should have been very grateful for John's laborious efforts with the company. His attitude and desire to do whatever it takes for the success of the company whilst having to take the often-regular verbal abuse from his supervisor. Monday to Friday 7:30 am till 5:30 pm plus regular weekend work was normal and he carried out his duties unflinchingly. Yet he was often subject to threats and scurrilous remarks by his callous and uncaring Managing Director, who somehow saw John as an easy target for his perpetual temper.

Comfort Upholstery was one of the leaders in its field nation-wide, selling around seven hundred three-piece suites a day in the UK. John had been there seventeen years having previously worked for a smaller upholstery company. His ten years spent in the army though had been a great learning experience, his education. At the end of the day he now enjoyed his job.

The warehouse was his kingdom. When there were no complaints, he really praised himself because no one else would. No news really meant good news. Comfort Upholstery was the kind of organization that didn't praise much, possible due to its working-class roots. The fact that you were in employment was as close to gratitude that you would get. It wasn't that they expected an exemplary standard of work. Merely that, as a company with hard grafted Lancashire roots, it had been built on sweat and toil.

John was cheerful enough in the role at Comfort Upholstery and also in outside life, but he often antagonised others with his constant mumbling replying and conversing with others. Some people thought he was disinterested but this was just his way.

His ex-wife conveniently (or not, depending on your relationship), worked at the same place. To some, it could have been a burden, but John actually enjoyed his wife working there, even though he always exercised his monotone voice and his colleagues often thought he was disinterested. Kate was just the opposite, garrulous and excitable as compared to his reserved, almost timorous nature. Worlds apart yet glued by a ring. That though, became unstuck when the divorce came through, mainly forced by a change in John himself rather than Kate. She hadn't changed. It was John who had become lazier and seemed to have taken her for granted. He had acted as though nothing could change their being together. But their marriage was not divine; it was made in Britain, where two out of three marriages end in divorce.

Many a time she would ask to go to dinner, but he would always much rather prefer to sit home after work and watch the television, even if nothing good was on. Invariably, he would normally end up asleep. The cherry on top would be when she went to switch off the television, he would inevitably groan that, 'I was watching that!'

It seemed a paradox that when he got home from work to switch himself off, he would switch the television on! The saddest thing was that when it all ended in divorce, he was the destroyed one. Now he had the television all to himself to watch, and often times now simply watched a blank screen of memories detailing the soap opera of his tragedy.

2. TIME

Recovering from one the dreams that plagued his mind, John needed no second guesses as to his site and situation. Uncompromisingly, he was in a hospital bed. He shook himself as if a dog, trying to dissipate his drowsiness as well as his horrible nightmare. He could have easily been a dog, endlessly trying to shake off magnet-like fleas from a normally soothing carpeted body. Fleeting memories of his former dreams dampened his drying brain. Seconds would not pass without his mind referring to his past dreams.

Eventually, perched up and dusting off a pillow, John managed to settle in his cage. It was 2:45 am and he knew he wouldn't sleep again tonight.

John Winters thought long and hard. It was coming to the end of the second week of his nightmares. It seemed to be a regular experience now, and the hours that followed were always depressing and drawn out. He reflected yes, but could never make head or tail of his experiences. Yet still he tried. Tonight, he had awoken rather early, so unfortunately, but inevitably, the hours would be that much longer. Thoughts would be that much more expressive, innovative and uncontrolled. This was something he did not look forward to; something he had never looked forward to. 'One day I'll go mad,' he whispered to himself.

John's immediate interest lay with the other patients all asleep around him like logs on a lake, smooth and motionless. Or maybe they were logs on a fire, waiting to burn out and end there disappearing existence. If they feared their oncoming surgery as he did, they too would be awake right now and unable to relax. Their serene drone-like snoring could only suggest to him that he was somehow different to the other patients. Maybe he was different to the others? Maybe his past life had been too friendly, and now it was his turn to experience the other side? Past adult life for John, like the logs on that lake had been smooth and fairly trouble-free. Now maybe it was his turn? Yin and yang, he thought to himself remorsefully.

Although surrounded by about twenty others, he knew he would be alone for the rest of the night. It was a feeling which he had become customary to the early morning shift. About a week ago during the initial stages of his nightmares one guy was awoken by John's upsetting dreams. Rather than to grumble or carp the man sat up and partook in a whispering interchange with John. The conversation was mainly the normal introductions beyond casual greetings. It gave John a chance to speak about his broken marriage. Without mending John's tarnished emotions, it did provide some temporary relief from his gradual submergence into his sea of emptiness.

John Winters spoke of his marriage to Kate, something he had often dwelled on but never really opened up about. Harry, his neighbour, listened carefully, eyes beaming downward trying to appear sympathetic.

It's strange how people try to feel responsible for something they have no influence over. Harry was just a passing observer. Why did he feel any responsibility and sadness? Maybe the hospital setting? He had never met John or his relatives before, or ever heard of Kate in such detail. So why did he even feel this emotional duty? For John it had been an opportunity to shed some of those leaves of hurt from recent times; a time to perhaps reflect on the good times that had flown by; a warning that now stared him in the face in a hospital bed.

Harry Eastwood, from Manchester, became a patient of Westbury General Hospital two days ago after suffering a mild heart attack. It had shaken him not just physically but also mentally. Although sixty years of age, Harry had not actually inhabited the wrong side of the hospital before for anything major. He had been inside, so to speak, for minor accidents when young. At nineteen he suffered the effects of a car crash he found himself in after driving to a concert with overexuberance. Fortunately, his was a new car so he only had to endure minor cuts and burns. A cut in his arms from splintered glass required butterfly stitches, but that was about the extent of his inpatient visits. Now he was practicing his patience with John. Much of his life was in fact a blur.

Harry could recall very little; that's about how memorable it must have been. Yet, in a dreamed-up trance he occasionally remembered falling of a cycle riding up the scarp of a quarry. It was obviously risk ridden but conversely that made it more challenging. As he got older that set of images would keep coming to him at moments in his life. Some quiet times when he had nothing other than emptiness to consider. At other times, those thoughts interrupted him when he saw kids playing or similar scenery. Each time the clips in his mind would be slightly different yet carry that distinct tinge of him riding up that slope; the memory of when he actually fell always evaded him though, and sometimes that frustrated him. Like trying to reach the impossible, the thoughts never quite reached where he wanted. His childhood was a fuzzy mix of vague memories.

Apart from a few childhood injuries and the car crash Harry had been blessed with a guarded and rather salubrious life. He had never thanked anyone for this, just called it fate. Until now that was. For the past two nights Harry had been having doubts about this. Working as a Senior Finance Officer for Glutton Oil Company, the past thirty-five years had been pretty successful for him. Strangely though, he had never been able to find the right girl to marry, hence lived alone.

At sixty-five Harry retired to travel a lot, flights and cruises, trying to capture his late life crisis. On his return back to Britain, less than six months after his retirement, Harry was greeted with a mild heart attack. It made him appreciate his recent adventures that little bit more, but left him with huge sadness that he had given so much time to Glutton and gave so little to himself. It almost felt ironic that the greed of his former company had stolen so much from him, though it had all been his own choice. Still, Harry couldn't help feeling this bitterness with his company, at how things had worked out. After reaching a certain age it had become too late for any career moves. It had also been Harry's fault partially in his own desire to stay locally based. Hence his last-minute vacationing abroad; a stab at making up for lost time. The hospital though, it was good at erasing memories; left him even more depressed and regretful.

After listening to Harry's stories of regret, adventure and more regret, John got inspired momentarily to follow a similar path to make the most of his time, though he knew his slant towards laziness may well get the better of him. It was similar to listening to a hero's story of success and motivation; for a few seconds so effective at spurring him on. Then John knew the drive would be short lived and life would amble on as is.

It had been an interesting night and his eyes remained dilated until the early hours when as usual, tiredness would grip him but he would find it too hard to sleep. The frustrations of being John Winters. He turned onto his right buttock, his left side at present selling him an aching pain. He also wanted to find out the time. Being in a hospital did make you even more lazy and reluctant to do much, hence turning from side to side in search of the time felt like a chore.

It was 2:25 am and John had only been up for about thirty minutes. 'Time flies when you're having fun,' he whispered to himself. With eyes glued to the nice-looking travel clock, John thought of how old it was; time ages he laughed to himself. It must have been thirteen-years-old he guessed as it was an anniversary gift from his ex-wife. The clock had seen many better days. Holidays away together in the past when clocks used to be used for not only the time but also as alarms. This all became redundant with smart technology and wearables. He thought how efficient the clock had been over the years, and he had hardly ever needed to even replace the battery. It had been more productive and reliable than his marriage, that was for sure. It had ticked along with his life without complaint and was still in great shape. The clock had received the normal bangs and scratches yet had been free of problems, and more importantly, complaints. Oh, if only life was a clock rather than a waste of time!

Replacing his hand back on the bedsheets, John continued his rendezvous with the night. It was to be an interesting, self-informative night, with John's eyes to remain tired and heavy yet active until the early hours of sunrise.

3. HARRY

Sighing deeply and thoughtfully, Harry whispered, 'Well John, how did you end up here?' It was John's turn to explain himself and his admission into Westbury General. Although John ever dreaded the explanation of his married life, it somehow was made less arduous after having heard the turn of events Harry had just exposed about himself. The subtle difference though between he and Harry's demise was clear. John had slowly found his fate down the treacherous road like a tortoise in a race.

He had married and divorced and basically, he was to blame for his demise. He had put these pressures upon himself, in fact making his own plight worse. His build-up of cardiac activity and tension had developed slowly over time, simply because of his own negligence. On the other hand, Harry had committed no crime; had just been unluckily afflicted by situation and circumstance.

The dilemma of John's self-blame prodded him same as a poker does a fire. It added an edge of uncertainty and made him more reluctant to convey his story to Harry. Psychologically, John knew though, knew that he needed to explain his situation; felt obliged as well. He insanely imagined Eamon Andrews belting out 'THIS IS YOUR LIFE!' Then it became clear there were no more secrets or skeletons hidden away.

John took no pleasure in emitting the personal tragedy leading to his present position. In the past three years he had confided in no one about his personal tragedies. His so-called friends were only friends because of his allegiance to Kate. She had always been the sociable one; the one who got on with everyone. He was always the invisible man and it led him to feel a jealousy that led them apart.

He never really had any real friends. He only ever had associates, had an inability to mix comfortably with the majority, suggesting to some an almost pretentious nature to his being, though that was not really the case. In fact, he was simply a reserved, shy character that he tried to mask with an outrageous and confused façade that was emotionless. Whilst with Kate he was happy with this setup. Some importance was better than none. He didn't mind playing second fiddle rather than no fiddle.

In his youth he sometimes made himself sound eccentric, superficial, a class idiot. It often became awkward and he ended up creating little or no school friends. At school he tried to be original, instead of the bland talk that school kids often spouted. In a way he was somewhat precocious, but it was all out of place. The army was the only place for him.

His misplaced childhood had remained with him all his life. He was fine with his own company and the support of his wife whilst he had it. A sheltered existence helped to mould his state of mind; helped to warn him that no one did something for nothing; inserted a reminder inside him that he had no real friends to talk of.

He wasn't particularly greedy or egotistical as such, just a little confused with his own self. From the outside it may have seemed that he was greedy in nature, but it wasn't really the case. He was just very self-conscious and later in life it turned him into a bit of a reluctant withdrawn loner who somehow had attracted an extrovert in Kate. It had been a good run he had been part of which he only realised when it was all over. She had certainly been a big part of his life; now only small bits were left.

Whilst telling his story, John felt a warm, comforting feeling steadily engross him as if he had known Harry for many years. As if they were old friends. They had actually only known each other for about an hour or so yet a bond had already grown between the two. It had taken John only one hour to make a friend he could confide in, or was it simply a door he had opened? He hadn't been able to complete that task effectively in over forty-five years that had passed by so swiftly and remorselessly. Time can become irrelevant if not used wisely; so pointless without an emotional sharpener.

How was it that John had seemed to reach a calmness in terms of his relationship with others? I suppose contemplating the potential of dying. He felt there had been so many inauspicious years dealing with others. Maybe this new home, if you could call it that had released him from his inhibitions, warding away his emotional fears. The other inmates here, maybe they, like he, needed their clocks recharging? All his co-mates here had one thing in common, they were getting closer to death, or at least they felt they were. Maybe that was the reason for John's opening up; the inevitability of death. That depressing expectation of impending death, a throbbing drum rolling down a hill of boulders. To John, he felt the potential of nothing to lose.

It had become a sort of club, or at least an institution. All the members in this ward retained the common denominator of being patients. This common factor relaxed John to a degree, though only a fraction of a degree. Although he hated hospitals, no feared them. The fact that he wasn't alone here made it all a little more manageable. He could at least grade himself in comparison to the others.

Before entering hospital, John's consternation had clutched him like the nefarious hand of Satan. It had been a huge step into the dark. The operation though was essential, and John knew he could evade the issue no longer. The clogging in his arteries had reached such a point that life was becoming more of an existence than an experience. The combination of short-ness of breath and palpations with increased regularity had put him under greater pressure to act. Those palpations really had got the better of him. They seemed to last a lifetime and that too, in slow motion. However much he hated the thought of hospitalisation, it had become an inevitability, like the sun replacing the moon and vice versa.

It had become the biggest acceptance of his life; bigger than deciding on a career moulding job or deciding to have kids or not; it was a matter of life and death. Thus, he was here, prodding on the doors of death. Oddly enough though, since he had been inside, he had found life more relaxing, thought provoking and most of all a much more social experience than he had ever expected. He found friendly and tolerant cohabitants, and in a strange way John Winters had come to hospital and found life! The people were the same people as those he met outside yet the drugs do work, he thought. It was as though the benevolent hand of God had steered him whilst in hospital; the allure of public institutions.

The past ten days had been the biggest, most relevant years of his life. They had showed him, if nothing else, that he did fit in somewhere. He could be more sociable, a new lease of life, or an alcoholic at his AA session. Similarly, this sense of togetherness, integrated with the fact that John was not a million miles from deaths door helped him to accept reality. He may die in the operation and no one would know how he really felt. Bottling things up inside him was one of his hobbies. Well, it was time to take the cork out.

John told Harry that night of his past, his lonesome childhood and quiet upbringing. He told Harry of his family of old and it made him feel better. Talking and thinking out loud about it had let him come to the conclusion that Kate was too self-centred to accept him and his personality. Nobody's perfect. That night John had spoken so frankly with Harry, releasing feeling he never knew he had.

4. NURSE DIANE

John shuffled somewhat. He scratched his head. His greying hair had advanced uncontrollably upward in response to his scratch. John knew this and ironed out his head of hair. Naturally his head had become a little thinner but was still fairly well spoken for. Once the thirties hit, the colour of his hair had started to whiten and he had no desire to bleach that part of himself out.

He had grown to accept this as part of life. John had been fortuitous in that his hair had remained quite strong over his fifty-three years, just that the colour had slowly faded away. But hey, you can't have everything. He had seen adverts for hair growing formulas hidden away at the back of newspapers and magazines. They offered a few moments thought and contemplation, though he always conceded to the idea that to maintain the new look would require lots of time, effort and of course money. He always thought that whilst it would be a nice solution, the headache that went with it would have been head-scratchingly bad. Still, these adverts always prodded at

John's mind in a curious way, but he had convinced himself to 'look don't touch'.

John remembered he used to say to Kate, 'What's the point in getting older if you're not going to let yourself get older?' She would always look at him nonplussed and sometimes resigned, at his lack of personal ambition. To himself, it was perhaps his way of justifying his greying scalp to himself. To Kate, it was like accepting defeat. Unfortunately, the only defeat she was willing to acquiesce to was in her relationship with him. A fact was a fact, and she was, in fact, fed up with him.

He shuffled again, this time a pack of cards. The three of hearts fell helplessly to the floor. John didn't know it was the three of hearts until he bent down to retrieve it. The creaking of rusty, outmoded springs resulted but no one winced. They were either half dead or half drugged. But why would they wince? It was a common sound from an underfunded NHS system asset; an NHS asset weighed down by an NHS liability. Also, other patients often managed the same sound in their sleep, tossing and turning. It took him about five frustrated attempts to recapture the card, each miss topping up his temper. After placing it back he continued mixing the cards then thought for a minute.

It was the three of hearts!

So what? Careful, buddy. Jingle, jingle.

'The three of hearts,' he spoke out aloud concisely. It was very relevant to him as he was in hospital for a heart bypass, a triple heart bypass. 'The three of hearts,' he repeated, more quietly this time. Was it uncanny or just a coincidence? He stopped his unconscious shuffling and looked at the deck, amazed and afraid. Moving the closed deck to the side lamp he gazed the top card. It was a subconscious response to the previous incident, as if he disbelieved the existence of the cards. His imagination arose as he stared down and thought he saw a tarot card depicting Lucifer holding a long fork in this left hand smiling up at him.

Hey, buddy, you ready for the knife? You ready for action, man? Let's play a game of chance, buddy. I'll deal, you can trust me, can't you? You wanna play best of three, Johnny? I'll deal if you like? Jingle, jingle.

A jingle of the jester's hat in the distance.

He shook his head instantly, trying to shake the image. It's just my imagination he thought, portraying a man trying to reassure himself. Brushing and rubbing the card he tried to eradicate the indelible details, resembling a magician trying to change the face of the card. He pressed and rubbed the card hard like a magician but with less grace or effect. Unfortunately, he only managed to bend and damage the card. Part of him realised that it would make no difference, the card was physically in his hand! This was no magic trick. It was a nightmare yet real, a summer holiday spoilt by rain.

The dried sweat from his earlier nightmare reappeared on his now glistening face, with each layer forming and leaving its nasty indelible fingerprints. He was tempted to wake someone to show them his ghastly observation. Looking around, all he saw was people slowly dying around him. He could have seen people slowly getting better around him, but he preferred to look at things his way. He saw no value in waking anyone up to show them a piece of his imagination.

It took him a while to regain his senses. When he did, he calmly placed the cards back into it box and into the adjacent drawer to his left, all the time trying to convince himself that what just happened hadn't happened. Returning back to his position, sitting up on the bed, John sighed. It was a pointless sigh, knowing that he would not be sleeping now. So, he looked straight ahead, a bored empty look... time flies when you're having fun.

His vacant mind was interrupted by the familiar sound of soft shoes approaching. His heartbeat jumped a touch as a well-oiled trolley entered ward 4B. The drowsy, humid room was about to welcome Nurse Diane, who had come to refill the pangs of hope for each and every patient. An assortment of vitamins, sedatives and life savers usually accompanied her like leaves on a tree. The long, or longer stay patients had grown affectional to her, turning her into part of the family. 'Nurse Diane's Late-Night Drug Store' they called it, 'Open all Hours.' She didn't mind, it kept them happy, regardless of the fact that she had some control to their destinies. The fake, soporific qualities of the trolley at least kept her in employment. It didn't bother her that she was flooding their bodies with superfluous drugs and additives. She never even gave it a second thought. It was her job to keep them alive and happy for some time longer; well alive at least. That's how she convinced herself she was in the right job doing the right thing.

The problem Nurse Diane, is that you are drugging them silly! Drugging their reflexes, responses and even their minds. All you want to do is keep as many alive as long as possible, as if your life depended on it! You, with your doctors, consumed by knowledge and ultimate wisdom, baffled by science, only drawn to success through elongating the lives of the old like an elastic band. Doctors and scientists overindulging themselves in the pursuit of everlasting life, only ending up with everlasting insomnolence, which, in turn, is then cured by trolleys of hope. The doctor's signature at the bottom of a piece of paper only actually amounted to placebo senselessness. Who cared, as long as the no one complained, and their minds at least, felt better, or number.

Nurse Diane was not alone in her role as hospital 'drug dealer'. It went around in shifts in rotation, although she was the most commonly seen with her trolley. Not only that, she enforced this by being the most sociable, comforting and jovial with the patients. As she neared John, he barely realised that her stall was low on supplies; not sold out but hibernating for the lunchtime when the table top would rattle with eagerness. But why would John notice a reduced supply of medicine, it was just another early morning.

'Morning John,' she said subdued, so as not to wake the others. It was the same tone that one may consider patronizing if you didn't know any better. She was not attractive in any way but her genial exterior always overshadowed this. The semidarkness of the hospital ward somehow intensified her good features though. John could just discern that broad smile and her shapely figure. John found himself wanting her to stay a while for a little company. It would be a change from the rigmarole of the night that perpetually clutched at his throat. Maybe it was the imminence of his operation that added to his insecurity. He sometimes felt alone in a room full of others.

'All right Nurse Diane,' he responded coolly, trying to mask his appreciation for her visit.

'Awake again John? You never want to give me a rest, do you? I hope the other nurses don't get the same attention I get,' she finished in a more upbeat mood. It did also sound a little patronizing but John wasn't in the mood to notice, at least he was getting human interaction. 'Do you need a sleeping pill, eh John?' she continued trying to sound concerned. But sleeping pills didn't alleviate the fear, didn't ease the nerves.

John nodded his head the wrong way. He always had a reluctance to take medicine, or anything like that, another reason not to be in hospital. It was a tired, noiseless gesture, slow and a little worn out. Nurse Diane understood his apprehension so moved a little closer, sitting at the side of his bed.

They talked more than usual. Why? Because Nurse Diane felt sympathy for John. The worst thing was his effort to hide it. He generally had the natural tendency to mask his feelings and express little behind that bland exterior. Nurse Diane had often stopped to chat with John but never had she succumbed to sitting on his bed. She was taking on the role of social worker. It was not exactly a new experience for her but it was a role she reluctantly exposed.

She had her own problems so why should she want to spend her time fixing others? It was like she wasn't meant to have her own problems, just solve others. Sometimes it felt as if the other patients never realised that she too, had her own mind and the complexities that went with it. She had headaches, got tired, and even occasionally took medicine herself! But this didn't ever cross their minds. Maybe it was just her imagination but it did sometimes appear that she wasn't meant to be human. Worse still, working with all these coffin rattling moodies was enough to make anyone ill and she was no exception.

The depression sometimes hit Nurse Diane. Working with these, these moaning grumpies sometimes was too much for her, but she had tremendous patience. And she was meant to call these people clients. All sometimes a bit too much to take. Those jabs which Nurse Diane carried around with her in boxes could well have been used, round after round, as she sparred with opponents that lay on their canvasses. Often, she wanted to just knock them out and be done with it.

She occasionally thought of the sadistic satisfaction she could have with a night of overindulgence. A prick here and prick there, stab all those 'MOANING PRICKS'! 'Time for your jab Mr. Smith,' she said nonchalantly.

'What jab Diane?' Some of the clients were on a first name basis with her, they had decided.

'This one, you thoughtless git!' She regularly had these moments of imaginary revenge. It gave her much pleasure just to think out loud to herself if not even actually out loud. The thought of breaking out of these regulations that the uniform induced and turn vigilante. Just for herself to break free from this drug-consuming dependency she called her job. Ironically, over the years she had been the one who had grown addicted to her job, perhaps chained in. These occasional thoughts though, were her placebo, just to sometimes sanitise her time in the ring.

'How's your mother, Nurse Diane?' John asked awkwardly, breaking her daydream fest. He didn't know how the start the conversation and his question with cautious spontaneity. He knew it was a touchy issue but at least gave him a foothold to gain her confidence. With a look tinged with surprise she suggested that he mother, although aged, was as well as could be expected. Her mother was bordering senility. She was ninety-two and resigned almost permanently to her wheelchair. She required lengthy care; therefore, Nurse Diane was reluctant to stay out of her mother's house despite her mother's cantankerous requirements. So, night shifts in the hospital were not ideal.

The time passed quietly and serenely. It breathed a kind of relaxation and was one of Nurse Diane's positive attributes. She had a knack for making patients more relaxed and mentally massaged, even though she did find it tiresome at times. In a way it was a part of her job, to be compassionate and understanding. Of course, it did also give her some intrinsic satisfaction to improve the lives of others, that's why she was in this job.

'I hope you don't think I'm being nosy or anything,' John said defensively. It suggested a break in the steady flow of words between the two. Of course, Nurse Diane replied that she did not mind (thinking to herself that 'lied' comes in the word 'replied'), selling her feelings down the road.

In a way, Nurse Diane felt some kind of relief herself in disclosing her personal whereabouts, her problems. It was not exactly a role reversal to the start of the conversation but was as close to that as it was going to get. Her mother's terminally encroaching difficulties always met Nurse Diane when she home. Her disdain for this was clear as the conversation passed. Although she was relieved at being able to express her problems out loud, it did spark emotions inside her and sent angered thoughts around her head. The conversation went on for about twenty minutes. It was a twenty minutes in which John cared not about his operation, or even thought about it. He realised that other people had problems of their own, even nurses. She found herself raising, then forcing herself to lower her voice as frustration simmered.

'I've been a nurse in this hospital for fifteen years, and been a nurse at home for longer,' she said remorsefully. 'What kind of life is that? I've lived in the same damn house for as long as I can remember and I'm too old to change now. I don't know why the hell it had to be me!' It built up into a crescendo 'I don't know why the hell it had to be me!' A little louder this time, but still not fully forgetting her surroundings and professionalism. She felt like vomiting out her feelings but had to hold it in. She was clearly getting more tense, more animated and gesticulating much more.

By now John was losing his sense of sadness for Nurse Diane. He, himself was getting more nervous with her change in mood. Some of the other patients had awoken and were looking around. Some of the other patients were too old to care or too doped to comprehend. The nurse had become emotional, hysterical and it seemed a little imbalanced about her own circumstance. Worse still, her hands clenched a pair of surgical scissors. John's blood pressure was taking no chances; it had soared to 195 over 100 which was high as he generally had this normally under control.

He was frantically looking around for straws to clutch to. When helpless or trapped like a cornered tiger you have to fight your way out or look for help. It was a mixture of fear and helplessness as the person who had been looking after him for the past ten days was in front of him arms flailing aimlessly, with a weapon her in her hands. It was a lifetime to him, though it must only have been seconds. His scarpering glances rested on the two bladed instrument in her right hand; it had grown moist in her hand. She was brandishing it around as if advertising metal wear for Betterware. Occasionally it slipped slightly between her sweaty fingers.

John's eyes became paralyzed and hypnotised by the moving scissors in the insane nurse's hand. His mind was not thinking, simply having a nap. His muscles, bones and flesh were useless and his eyes transfixed. He felt like a puppet who didn't know his puppeteer.

The woman's fingers slid back into place, gripping the round handles firmly. She cried and pleaded loudly now as her frustration rose. The frustration created by her mother's senility. She could just see the image of her mother in the distance, gesturing for attention like a perennial piece of string stuck to a thorny tree. Meanwhile, John waited anxiously for the other nurses to perhaps come barging in. Not to be. He realised that he and the other already unwell patients where slowly getting more unwell.

Her left hand shivered as oncoming tears combined with her sweat matted hairline, partially impairing her vision. It was almost humorous at that point. The scissors had found themselves move into her left hand, the same hand she used to move the hair from her eyes. As she moved her fingers to stroke her hair back her fingers closed sharply on the scissor handles, chopping a clump of her own blonde, slightly greying hair right off.

Did you see that? You just cut a clump of your own hair right off, Nurse Diane! Do you even realise? You are a crazy old fool you know that? You've lost all your senses, most importantly the sense coming from your brain. If you need a haircut go to the salon.

The funny thing was that she didn't even notice that her fringe was now much shorter, or maybe and more likely, she didn't even care. Or maybe she just as well noticed but was too embarrassed and angry to bring attention to it. And you can bet your life John wasn't keen on bringing it to her attention either.

As if trying to bring the topic of her fringe to an end, Nurse Diane switched the blade from her left to her right hand, gaining greater control and confidence as she was right-handed. John comically thought maybe she wanted to chop a clump from that side also to even things up. Maybe that was her way of accepting that she had just given herself a shave closer than the best a man can get, or woman. Or maybe her fingers were becoming increasingly sweaty. For some reason John thought of those talented plate spinners as she kept changing hands to keep better control of the scissors. Circus music drummed into his mind.

The scissors, sharp and pointed, snipped randomly, impulsively. The blades whooshed as they met then separated like strangers. John's craven image had submerged himself as far as possible under the covers, but even then, he continued to try to peek glances from the edges. He was too confused to get out of bed and make a run for it.

Suddenly the scissors jarred onto the stagnant medicine cabinet trolley. The insane nurse had thrown them off her hands; broken the chains. She was quiet now; her contemptuous reiterations had given way to a tranquil but sombre fraction of a second. After bouncing, and sliding, the metal blades found the cold floor below. Echoing and clanging, the silence which followed lasted only a moment, though it seemed like an age.

Heartbeats still bounced as temperatures settled, cardiographs slowed. Eyes rested on an awkward looking Nurse Diane. She was confused and regretful already. She found herself speed out of the ward, head down. Sobs and embarrassed smiles followed Nurse Diane to the ladies, and passers-by could only look sideways in equal embarrassment. Others looked at the stationary scissors strewn on the floor, marking already ugly memories of a splintered life, surrounded by others who life was soon to be cut short. Numerous strands of slightly greying hair lay lifeless on the floor, evidence of the morning's adventures.

A male nurse followed a female one in the morbid act of restoring the ward to its former state. When John awoke after a short snooze the same morning it was as if nothing had happened a few hours earlier.

5. FLY

A warmth filled the spacious hospital ward which John had just left. Rays of light bled through sun facing windows. Funnels of daylight pillars lined up like soldiers optimistic for the battle ahead. Dust fragments flew randomly, imitating shrapnel in the aftermath of war. Generous heat multiplied with each curtain that was opened, glowing up the room with hope and prosperity. The suns limited yet graceful prowess exploited east facing openings, providing an anticipation of victory.

For early spring the heat was extremely generous. The early signs of greenness escaped from the upcoming verdure, merging tremendously with the blueness of an empty sky; full of hope. The blossom bathed bloom had come out a little early as leaves diversified the environment; a myriad of colours, theatrical, auditioning for the leading role. Cinematic windows for patients who cared to watch. A calming breeze, a cooling breeze, a perfect breeze, but slightly disconcerting in a spring which had not as yet had much to say. Still, auspicious to say the least. The developing canopy of trees directed morning flies and insects onto the grounds of the hospital. Greenfly peppered benches beneath trees, camouflaged, hoping to live another day. Wasps and bluebottles buzzed around unconcerned taking to their new role wonderfully as their new lifestyles gripped them. Precocious leaves, young and vibrant performed on branches, masking twigs from waves of heat.

John concerned himself with a larger than normal bluebottle, stagnant on the branch of a tree. Perhaps it's sunbathing he mused momentarily. Spring had always signified a rebirth to John over the years, a time of optimism. It also saddened him being in his present state. He was sat here moribund, whilst other creatures were just entering the world fit and enthusiastic. The sigh which escaped him was interrupted by the pattering of feet.

'Mr. Winters, your moving house' she said. It took him a few seconds to realise what she meant, and then it hit. He had not looked forward to this moment. It meant that his surgery was just around the corner. He knew it meant the end his preoperational rest. He knew it was near anyway because just yesterday he had gone through the anaesthesia test, which must have been given the go-ahead. He now realised that in a day or two he may be dead. Whether it be blunt or not, that's what he thought. In all honesty, it was blunt.

Days of preparation, physical and mental, did not prepare John for the events to follow. You, out of choice, come to hospital in need of rejuvenation, but with such reluctance. John was no different. He wasn't sure whether he would see tomorrow. There had been complications, otherwise John would not have had to spend so many days in hospital prior to the main operation. Diabetes and kidney issues did not help. He had been monitored to ensure stability which the doctors now felt had been a success. So, his time had come to go into battle. He was back in the army.

Drugged and distressed, John reluctantly creaked out of his foam filled chair. It let out a slow oozing sound as the air escaped. The extra-large bluebottle twitched and then took off into the sunny sky as if it had been waiting for John to leave before it did. As he glanced back, he thought he had read somewhere that bluebottles only live a few days or weeks. Poor thing he thought, but maybe it would be alive longer than me. The thought alone put butterflies in his stomach.

Unbeknown to John was the progression of the fly. He saw it disappear into the surroundings. A matter of minutes later the fly steadied and entered a house (being a housefly), about a mile away. It buzzed its way into a bedroom window where momentary surprise clutched the woman resting on, as opposed to in, the bed. Attempting to waft away the fly became a relentless game until the fly took a breather on the window from which it had entered. The woman scampered out of the door, pulling it behind her aggressively. The fly buzzed upwards almost simultaneously with the vibration caused by the woman. Very soon it settled again on an adjacent part of the window. It seemed quite lethargic; maybe it was many days old? It clearly didn't want to move unless it really had to. Well, for a second time, it was forced to, but not quite yet. Contrastingly, the door time creaked open to display to the fly, a glimpse of a woman whose brow was wet with sweat, and it wasn't just due to the warm weather.

Spotting the enemy early evaded most of the panic which

had been welling up inside the woman. She held the spray can like she would her baby, with two hands. The woman reinforced her already formidable position. With index finger approaching the spray the fly must have sensed the brevity of the situation. As the woman creaked forward the fly took off. Panic intervened and was somehow reciprocal. The woman sprayed convulsively everywhere, anywhere, somewhere. The buzzing seemed to grow louder. She then leapt outside, smacking the door shut behind her, making sure the fly could not follow her. Then a victorious smile was on display with a little relief as well. She relaxed and got on with her life knowing the fly would not have survived the onslaught.

The fly struggled helplessly, reflexing with the pain seeming inexorable. Lying on its wings, the fly continued buzzing, round and round as if impersonating a spinning wheel. Its ferocity though, only lasted a few minutes, after which time scant flutters escaped the dying inspect. The last movements finished with a laborious push of the hind legs, then a sudden stiffness and stillness.

The woman meanwhile had ventured back into the bathroom to see that last few movements of the insect, starting to feel a little remorseful. She could have squashed it to put it out of its misery. Instead she just watched with curiosity. She did a final prod with a tissue to make sure it was dead. She had the bravery of a coward and the finesse of a frog, pretty disappointed in a strange way that after prodding a few times, finding that it moved no more. It was a bit of an anti-climax, though what else was she expecting?

It was the end of her little adventure for the morning, which she realised with a mixture of sadness and boredom. The woman went back to eating her lunch in front of the television.

Unknown to John, he had outlived the fly.

6. SPRING

'Now you're sure you're comfortable, Mr. Winters?' told, rather than asked the impassive nurse. Of course, he wasn't comfortable. He was getting ready for major surgery, how could be comfortable? He wanted to say no, but knew he couldn't.

'I'm okay I suppose,' he replied mechanically, with very little emotion. His answer could have sparked a greater response if it had not been delivered with such lethargy. The nurse just laughed it off as it was the type of response the nurse had heard a thousand times in her lifetime, or death time as the case may be.

A quarrelsome relationship with his ex-wife had initiated a spiral of bad luck for John, and this was just the start. As he thought, his conscience wanted to shed tears, but couldn't. It was little akin to internal bleeding. He felt the sadness, the ever-present melancholy, but it had grown so common that he couldn't expose his sorrow anymore. Inside though, tears would well up, stinging and cutting up his insides.

John had been settled into a new room, quieter and more private. The bed he lay in seemed somewhat less comfortable. His penultimate bed, he thought. He had already renamed this bed, 'The Disconcerting Bed'; the bed he knew that possessed nothing but nightmares. Soon he would be in his death bed, he pessimistically professed.

It was sometime in the afternoon and John had just settled into his new home. Being the start of spring, some rose bushes were brimming with colour and redolence. Other less precocious bushes had just grown their buds. Weather conditions often overlapped like this in Lancashire. The bitterness of winter had passed and given birth to this ever-waiting season, a turning point in every year, or was it a pause? Not simply a turning point because of the start of a new season, but mainly because it signified a warming up; a rebirth.

Annuals arose in their splendour, minute and beginning to grow with light and heat. Crocuses sprouted early, purple and proud, stalky and straight. Yet winter leaves its mark. Grasses grew, damp and soggy from leaves left over, decomposing beneath. Early spring with naked trees, their clothes scattered on grass bedding below from the previous night's frolics. Bare patches of trampled ground displaying blotches of mud, some solidified, some still setting. From the winter just passing no rejuvenation could take place; a lost cause, a time for hiding, waiting to seek out the amble of the oncoming sun and heat.

The arrival of spring, welcomed by all. Bright colours, redolent odours beginning with the progression of spring. Cars driven with more confidence; even they seemed to put out an attempt to smile. Their response to the freezing engines and failing batteries, choking them up inside. Things were looking up. People talk in the street that little bit more, ironically, about the weather. Yet despite this their number one complaint, the weather! They mix their negativity with a shower of positivity, boasting the oncoming sun's march. Days start to seem longer despite being the same length. Blue skies increase yet still only remain a shade. Demands on the sun persuade rays above. Increased glances welcome the sky, praying for dry days.

ITCH

7. SIMON

A knock at the door preceded the entrance of an old friend, Simon, whom John had known since his youth. The fact that Simon had to knock before entering the room gave some clues as to John's situation. Firstly, it showed John was quickly approaching his operation; he had been given a private room for him to collect his thoughts and emotions. Secondly, he would not have been given these privileges had the operation not been such a major one.

A sudden mood switch occurred in a matter of seconds as John's old friend entered his cell. A natural smile (something foreign to John as of late) found its way onto John's face.

Finally, the Great Man smiles, after such a long time. Such a timely event just as the last shreds of life were being eroded mercilessly away. Disquietude giving way to delayed satisfaction.

Simon Wayburn was John's best man at his wedding, a friend since school. He was one of those people you could always call on. Someone you could always rely on for support. Despite never getting married himself he had provided welcome words during the breakup, at least to help John through his complications.

Simon was one of the people who'd agree with the tone of the conversation, just to keep the peace and avoid controversy. That was one thing he hated, conflict for trivial reasons. At school he found himself resisting conflict and backing down to avoid confrontation. As an adult he had not grown out of it; not matured enough to break these childhood chains. He was the kind of guy who would, if possible, sit on the proverbial fence. If he was walking in a field and noticed a wooden fence, he would always go and sit on it.

There was of course, a logical reason behind Simon's personality traits. Simon had a difficult medical condition that had been his old friend, or more appropriately, his foe, since he could remember. It was called pruritus, but Simon called it hell. Continuous itching, dry skin, blotches all helping to make him more and more twitchy. It was always so tempting the itch rather than leave alone, though he knew later he would suffer. It was his forbidden fruit that he had taken a bite out of too many times. Various creams and ointments had glittered his bathroom like fairy lights all his life, leaving him dreaming and wishing for some pixie dust. Forty years later he was still dreaming, still hoping, still wishing, still looking for Tinkerbell, each day becoming more and more of an uphill challenge.

It had begun to cloud over. Still a partially blue skyline, but the blue definitely simmering into the distance. John hardly noticed it, and further still, didn't notice his shadow elongating along the bed and beginning to mix into the surroundings. He had also almost forgot about the big event taking place in the next few days.

What? Oh yes, the operation, a life-threatening operation in the form of cardiovascular surgery. Don't forget to put your alarm on, Johnny! Don't tell me you had forgotten, buddy. Don't wake up late for that appointment, buddy.

The wind quickened a knot or two, resulting in John almost unflinchingly moving over to close the window. Conversation was slightly stultified. Simon, not a great talker, relied on John to trigger a conversation himself. It was a strange contradictory role John found himself playing. John, himself a reluctant talker, had to often become the lead whenever he was with Simon.

'How's it going John?' asked Simon. The two hadn't met for about a week, and even though it was only a week Simon felt that his friend had aged greatly in that period.

'Wonderful' responded Winters, trying to be funny and ironic at the same time. 'I just love heart operations' he continued sarcastically, but not in any way offensive. Smiling and accentuating the 'love' portion of his reply was evidence enough for Simon.

'What's it been like in here?' said Simon, 'I hope they are keeping you well fed?'

'In answer to your first question, it is really not as bad as I expected. They look after you and you really have to appreciate that. As for the food, not great, but its free' he said positively. He had always preferred meat rather than cabbage, wanted something to bite into. Often in the past he had found himself overindulging in food. Perhaps one of the reasons why John was the position he was today. It had not helped his health, that's for sure. His inability to show self-restraint at the dinner table was one of his downfalls, but his fast metabolism had come to the rescue often during his early years. Sometimes he felt as though he was one of Pavlov's dogs during his married life, waiting on cue for his food.

He had been quite fortunate that his appetite for what are called 'fatty foods' hadn't made him fat. In fact, to look at him, you could think he was very healthy. It was not the picture his arteries told. Contrary to this then, the food he was being given here was like wartime rationing, never mind NHS expenditure cuts. Everybody trying to present this health friendly façade in an institution plagued with patients outstripping its resources when clearly there was not enough resources to support it. Yet the steam train rolled on, using power for power, antiquated and beleaguered yet unperturbed. The face of British society, the NHS.

'Ah the food, John, I'm not surprised you don't like the food. The famous hospital food. Not everyone's cup of tea.' It wasn't the lack of variety, because there was plenty of that. Just that the of food type was not his type, sometimes too bland and dry for him. The conversation had moved into a more natural form, less congested and stuttering.

'What's on the menu today?' said Simon rhetorically as he picked up a single sheet of paper the size of a cinema slip. It seemed to be a photocopy of a photocopy, so faded and grainy that it could have been created by a ten-year-old for a school project. The paper was on John's rolling table top above his bed. The table, primarily for dinner time use, was here holding the menu sheet. John had already ticked off his choices unhappily. His appetite was inversely proportional to the size of the menu sheet. Simon stared at the menu sheet and muttered some of the items to himself and partly to John in high and low tones.

'Vegetable quiche... hmm.' Simon was wondering what it would look like. 'chicken tikka,' he continued in a whisper. 'Can I join you?' he mused. As he had spent some time inside himself for his itching condition, Simon knew a little about hospital food, but was no expert. The way Simon was joking about the menu led John to think Simon had never seen a hospital menu before. John was beginning to think that Simon thought people didn't eat in hospitals! Then John had another thought. It was nearly three in the afternoon and the nurse had still not been to collect the dinner slip. Based on his previous days in the hospital that seemed late. He decided he would give it another half hour before saying something.

'Polish soup?' Simon questioned. 'What is that when it's at home? Polish as in shoe polish?' It did get them both to chuckle for a few seconds.

'That would in fact be Polish soup, Simon. It is not that bad actually, I've had it before. I think they just put anything they can find in but tastes okay considering, and it is filling. I'm just surprised they are doing it here. But I suppose with all the Polish that have come to our country I shouldn't be surprised. There's so many of them now, they're polishing the floor with us.' John always had that nationalistic tint or shine to his personality. It angered him at times with so many other nationalities coming to Britain and overpopulating the place. He generally kept these feelings to himself, though they often quarrelled with his mind. Patronisingly like an itch just waiting to be irritated. Any trigger could spark his anger... like Polish soup.

'Exactly' agreed Simon, a little embarrassed that he had never heard of Polish soup before. Simon again looked at the menu, noticing, to no one's surprise that Polish Soup had a tick next to its check box. 'Save some for me won't you,' he joked rather than asked. He noticed that John had not ticked any of the dessert options.

He felt it a little wrong to feel the way he did, but he couldn't help thinking that John should have a dessert, it could be his last meal! You've got to have dessert he thought, you just must. He just felt that John should really at least take dessert so close to his final call. Simon played with the idea of bringing up the topic then thought better of it. Not the right timing he thought to himself.

As he was thinking, one of those familiar itch attacks was brimming now and it was an all too familiar feeling. Initially a tingle on his left arm that just would get more and more aggressive without forcing him to actually itch. Mind over matter he thought as he softly stroked his itch, so softly that he was hardly making contact. It seemed like he was tickling it, and to an outsider it would appear he was only making it worse, making the temptation even greater. But Simon had his own logic, a lifetime of experience had gone into it.

As if noticing a strangeness in Simon's reaction to the menu John broke in. 'If you were in my position you wouldn't feel hungry either.' That hit, and made perfect sense. Simon felt a little more guilt as to not understanding until now why John had not chosen many items from the menu. Not only may the food have been bad, his emotional state and closeness to his operation was naturally having its impact.

'You don't need to worry, John, it will all be over before you know it. I've got a good feeling about it. They can do almost anything these days. They can clone animals, make robots better looking than humans, repair hearts with holes. No doubt they'll do you proud. They cloned a pig you know, John, can you believe it? Maybe soon pigs will fly, cloned ones at that? I expect you'll lose weight?' asked Simon.

'Gain frustration you mean.' He quickly responded as if expecting the question. John spoke nonchalantly as if pacified by the time inside. To outsiders he was just another client, another number to be ticked off. There were certainly times when he was a little ticked off himself, in here at least. He had become a little bit resigned to the fate that lay ahead.

The afternoon passed by much quicker as Simon's company had passed the time. Despite the discussions being of no real importance John really enjoyed the visit, especially as he had very few visitors.

John Winters pulled back the bedsheets and headed to the toilet, bladder full despite not really drinking that much. It was now dark outside, with the sun setting about an hour ago. This made it about seven o'clock. It was too hot in the hospital for John but this could not be helped because of the need to keep all the other patients happy, or at least less unhappy. The high, but uniform temperature in the hospital contrasted with the freshness outside. Springtime, with its relatively large diurnal range in temperature, no different today.

A fly buzzed up to the window, crashing into it as if blind and helpless. Its already short existence looked sure to be cut even shorter. John couldn't help feel a sense of helplessness. He had seen so many flies today, as if they had just woken up from hibernation. Maybe it was a portent to make him feel more assured? Well, it didn't work. In fact, quite the opposite.

He only had negative thoughts regarding what lay ahead.

There could be a power cut during the operation, or the surgeon could not have had a good night's sleep prior to the operation, or anything. He was really feeling negative. It was a little ironic that in his trepidation John never stopped to consider a more obvious risk; how would he and his body react to the treatment. How would he mentally and physically react and how would he recover? Maybe John just wasn't thinking that far ahead.

The fly continued to buzz as John continued to stare, mortality visible in front of his eyes in the form of a tiny helpless insect. It was in a hospital after all! The fly was lethargic but not necessary dying. At first John did think it looked jaded and waiting to end its short existence. But now it looked more awake and flying all around the window as it trying to blast its way through the glass. John realised this and without thought went up to open the window. As he was in a private room his freedom to do this was clear and would have no impact on the other guests. Using his hand as a fan John wafted upwards, attempting to usher the housefly to its exit which was in fact its entrance back to the world. John felt he had somehow helped to nurse the insect back into full fitness, that he had strangely provided a bandage of hope and prosperity.

The fly flew up then fell down then up again, then of course down again. Eventually, the open window did manage to eat the fly out of its hospital and out into a spring night clearly optimistic. It seemed the fly was just here to visit. Lucky, you don't want to spend too long in here. Stars were already visible as John closed the window. He walked back to his bed feeling a strange sense of success and embarrassment. Success, as he had just helped the insect. Embarrassment, as some nurse had witnessed him show a strange happiness after watching his endeavours.

John Winters, 'Superfly Guy'.

8. RAIN

A huge field of brilliance; a picture causing goose pimples of the past or a nerve tingling photo of the future. This was a snowfield as large, no, larger than the eye could see. Not only was it snow, but it was fresh and untouched, angelic and virginal. No flakes were falling but it was deep, about four feet or so. The flakes had gelled together harmoniously, interlocking, reinforcing. The blend of white upon white was marred somewhat by a solitary tree in the distance, its branches crispy, looking brown and bony. No signs of snow appeared on this tree as untouched and unaffected by recent snowfall. It stood strong and tall, yes leafless but not lifeless. It was stung by the perpetual frost, but in no way appeared overcome.

The tree reached outwards with naked arms. The sky was white, as if mirroring that below, or was it the other way around? A thick blanket to keep the above warm, or to keep what lay below cold? Whether the world was flat or round, it mattered not; this was simply a great expanse of unmarked ice. Beyond the imagination of a great painting this was simple but spectacular; a portrait of isolation.

A gentle slapping noise awoke John from his sleep. Shivering slightly, he reached down under his bed to pick up a magazine he had been reading before inadvertently losing himself to sleep. The cover of the New Scientist boasted the heading 'US Scientist says No to Global Warming'. I don't know, thought John, it's pretty warm in here he thought. A soft tapping at the window behind him sent him naturally around, swivelling his body as well as his head. With increasing appearance, the fine tapping became a harder beating sound, close to cracking. John's concern eased as he saw miniature streams of water appear on the glass now opposite his face. He watched as water began to race down the glass, changing from pencilled strokes to a messy page of ink blots.

Rollup, rollup everybody, and place your bets. Which raindrop string is gonna cross the finishing pane first? The favourite on your right, buddy, thick and ready to rage; waiting for a lucky drop to pierce its nucleus. That's all it takes, one drop!

John was well awake once again, as he stared right through the window into nothing, wondering about the dream which was becoming more and more cloudy. Meanwhile outside the weather was becoming more and more inclement.

We have a winner, ladies and gentlemen. The favourite on your right made it look easy, what fluidity. No lap of honour? Ah well, never mind.

Streams continued to flow with new blotches being formed all the while. John's concentration continued to stare through the droplets racing downwards, meandering due to dust or grime build-up. Their race against time made him consider his. His stare, through the window created a kind of hypnotic almost soporific feel, yet he hadn't closed his eyes for at least a minute. An uncharacteristic chill or coolness enveloped itself around him. It forced John to almost click out of this self-hypnotic state as he convulsively twitched. Within seconds he had buried himself under the covers, as if programmed to seek this salvation. Yet this strange drop in temperature was internal. The temperature in the room had been constant throughout. It didn't take John long to warm up. His eyes now tired and well used, opening now reluctantly. He was half conscious, and he could care less about the night's recent events and the racing of the raindrops.

Below, the page, half creased, half open, lay scruffily on the sheet tiled flooring of the hospital displaying the headline 'US Scientist says No to Global Warming'.

9. T KUPP

Outside the sun shone with exuberance and potency. It was a dry heat. The nurse bent down to pick up the magazine left on the floor under John's bed. She gave no attention to the story from the magazine. Her movements woke him, reminding him instantaneously of the night's events, shaking away any excess fatigue. Although vague, his memories instilled a fear for some reason. She made no comment, as if it was a common occurrence that patients misplaced their belongings. What a vague dream it was that lacked clarity he thought. 'US Scientist says No to Greenhouse Effect' he thought, misquoting the article. She put the magazine back on the table in the room and muttered some pleasantry.

It was the eve of his operation. Tomorrow was his curtain call, the time for his theatrical performance. The butterflies fluttered frequently now in a soon-to-be tampered with stomach where he hoped the butterflies would be let free. Today was to be a portentous day, but John knew nothing of this yet. It was 8:30 in the morning and he had managed to sleep much deeper since his obscure dream last night. He often felt occasional aches and tightness in the cardio vascular region but strangely not this morning. Today he felt fighting fit. Maybe he could tell his doctor and beg for them to change their mind. I'm ok now doc, so need for any surgery. You believe me, don't you? All crazy thoughts that he explored no further. In the end he knew it was all for the better.

Waiting for his breakfast he reminisced about his past, when his health troubles began. It was more like a poignant daydream, a prologue for the future. He had often felt stronger palpitations but just got used to it. It had just become part of his daily life and he ignored it. People often do stretch out their problems as far as they can, procrastinating until the final hour. I suppose he just hoped it would go away by itself. The palpitations then progressed into tiredness for no real reason and getting slightly out of breath. He just put it down to getting older. Stomach pains then came around more often yet John resisted the urge to seek treatment. He finally went to discuss with the doctor who agreed to do the necessary tests which confirmed what John himself knew; didn't need a doctor to tell him.

'You don't smoke or drink, Mr. Winters, and you're not overweight, so you are a strange case. Do you get stressed a lot?'

John knew is diet was not ideal, too much fatty foods that must be the culprit or at least a big part of the issue. 'I do occasionally feel stressed, especially now that I am living alone and trying to adapt to things. But I hope to get used to things soon.' It had not been long since his divorce at that time, and probably the stress of divorce had played a large part in his deteriorating health. 'I expect that soon I'll get better and I don't feel more stressed than most. At least I think so.'

'You say these palpations come every day then?' asked the doctor.

'Yes, I'd say so. It's been like this for about two months now and they seem to be getting more frequent. That's why I thought to come and see you. I get them about seven or eight times a day.'

'You were more than right to come, John. Heart problems are the most serious health issues there are.'

John acted as though he wasn't aware. Of course, he knew that, that about twenty percent of deaths are cardiovascular related. 'So, we'll take these angina tablets for now and see how it goes. Take whenever you feel this light-headedness or out of breath.' The doctor spoke as if he too was going to take the tablets. It was just his style. 'Just place under your tongue when you feel the symptoms. They should dissolve and give relief.' How do I know when the time is right, thought John? The instructions passed on by the doctor were so carefully delivered that John knew this was no passing thing. It was serious and they both now knew it. John digested the news with unease like there was a nut in his gut. But at least now he realised, better late than never. He knew that this was a new phase in his life and that things would probably not be the same after this. It was a new stab in his back after the divorce. Just when stress was the last thing, he wanted it was sure not to disperse now.

John walked out of the doctor's office, clutching a bag containing his salvation. It seemed the bag itself was breathing and beating like a heart. As he stepped out, he took a long deep breath of fresh air. Fresh air, he questioned to himself. Inevitably this fresh air had been tampered with the invisible glow of pollution, making it not so fresh after all, as if angina and its baggage wasn't enough. In some parts of the world the pollution was in fact so bad it was in fact even visible. At least Lancashire had not quite reached that dangerous point yet. He consoled himself with that. Still, the way he felt was not unlike he had been smacked over the head with a brick, hard. Or maybe it was the feeling when you've just banged your head very, very hard. The feeling went right through his body like a lightning strike.

Then he found himself at his flat. His mind had been so side-tracked that getting back from the doctor to his home seemed to have slipped his mind. The flat where he now lived stared unwelcomingly back at him. Not the gleam or sheen of a home. It was like it didn't even want him to come in. Sombre, even on a summer's day, his door banged shut behind him. Whether the curtains were open or closed it was still a dark, cold place.

He'd been alone now for over two years but still not grown accustomed to it. What a painful crack on the head, painful for the whole body; a huge thump on the head lasting two years. He had realised that being lonely was a very personal thing. Although he was quite introverted anyway, he did in fact, strangely enjoy others company. Since his divorce he hadn't really had even that pleasure.

In a sadistic, cowardly way though, his solitude had got the better of him. To ameliorate his loneliness, he had removed himself even more from his old friends, hardly ever keeping in touch. He had grown used to his own company, so much so that he actually wanted it to stay that way and did not look forward to visitors popping by. That was the way it would stay anyway, whether he liked it or not.

'Eat up, Mr. Winters, you need your strength, it's your big day soon,' interrupted Nurse Diane from his daydreaming. The comments actually made John feel worse, giving him a reminder of what he knew. He could still see Nurse Diane's hairline where she had cut her own hair by mistake. He laughed about it to himself but of course was far from amused at the time. She hadn't even tried to fix her hairline.

John's hand went slowly up towards his own head trying to ease a mild pain which resided there. But the pain stayed, with John only succeeding to locate the pain itself. It made no difference. He didn't even stop to think how and why the pain had occurred.

Breakfast came and went on another splendid spring morning, early blossom and singing sparrows added to the occasion. Picturesque blueness bloomed above; a vast sea of emptiness, as far as even telescopic eyes could see. It was pretty wonderful outside looking from the inside. It looked like a painting, exhibiting radiance and energy. Although not a ninety-degree angle, the sun was very penetrating, shining effortlessly on rooftops, making them appear as solar panels. The transfer of hydrogen to helium ninety-three million miles away being felt.

He did always try to keep himself to himself but that was not always easy in hospital. It wasn't him being especially impolite or unfriendly, it was just his nature.

Tony Kupp, a former house builder, electrician, and jack of all trades, lived adjacent to John, in fact in the room next door. He also remembered seeing him around in the open ward. To this day, Tony had not lived down the jokes about his name. Since school he had been a T. Kupp, the brunt of all jokes, and for him at least, not too refreshingly so! On more than one occasion his friends used to say to him 'What are you going to be when you grow up, Tony, a Kettle?' Even if it had been funny, he had heard these jokes so many times that he never found them funny anymore, simply expected.

He used to curse his parents for giving this ailment of a name; couldn't believe how they had not realised the implication of calling him Anthony. Sometimes he did try to stress that he was actually called Anthony, not Tony, but most people never listened, or half ignored. Registration at school used to be a killer for him. Paradoxically it was the highlight of the day for the others at school.

'Wait for it,' they would whisper in anticipation, as the morning excitement simmered.

'Howard?'

'Yes Sir.'

'Howarth?'

'Yes sir.'

'Jacobs?'

'Yes sir.' Jacobs got his fair share of cracking jokes to endure as well.

'Jones? Jones? Jones?' No reply. Jones had been a bad influence, also a bad pupil. He was late more often than a British train. Today was no exception. Coming from an all too common broken home didn't help. Then, 'King?'

'Yes sir.'

And finally, 'Kupp?'

Sporadic laughter as always followed. 'Yes sir,' he reluctantly replied. It was almost a resigned voice as he half expected some sarcastic comment to follow. And as the teacher was so used to it, he himself would not even try to suppress the jibes. Some days it was worse than others, some days you could hardly hear his 'Yes sir,' amongst the smothered heckles and laughter. Obviously, it wasn't very nice, but sometimes school days are not meant to be.

He had never actually explored the background to his name Kupp, but did know that he had a German grandparent coming from a farming background. He then would add that his parents rebelled against Hitler during the Second World War. This was his own little addition to his background story. It was his polite way of stealing revenge from short-sighted jokers. It gave him a satisfaction, in fact even more satisfaction especially as he had made up part of the story.

Tony Kupp had struggled his way through school, comprehending it was not for him. His name had not helped. He ended up hanging around with the wrong people and ended up having to do favours just to get through school and to be accepted in his hangout group. Hanging around with the wrong group of people meant learning the wrong habits. By fifteen he was smoking regularly.

Over the years he made no effort to try to curb this addiction and being a builder, felt that it was part of the job. He also saw no great problem with his habit, smoking two packets daily and for many years. He would exhibit that typical smokers cough and deep tone to his voice that came with it. It had just become part of his character, and he never really questioned his own health issues. That was until more recently when throat problems and smoking side effects had resulted in breathing difficulties and the inevitable heart related complications.

Tony Kupp coughed huskily, like a man twice his age. John looked over at him thinking just that, he did in fact look a lot older than he was. The clipboard at the foot of Kupp's bed said 'Anthony Kupp,' and John thought… that's a strange name. Then he thought that if you shortened his name, he would be called T. Kupp, if you used Tony. It only momentarily amused John, who had been staring at Tony's personalised clipboard all throughout. Then he saw Tony had been gazing at him all along. John even noticed one of the nurses had drawn a drinking mug next to his name with a smiley on, and that made his grin a little.

He quickly hid his thoughts with 'Hello.' Tony croaked a nonchalant reply, knowing what John had been thinking about whilst staring at his name. John had been in the hospital a while now but couldn't help wondering why a lung patient was in the same ward as him. He thought it may be a result of cutbacks, putting patients together. He was not aware though, of Tony's complications that had caused him heart related issues.

Neither was in the mood to talk to each other too much, not from malice or disrespect, but more because it had been a long day. To be honest it was always a long day in this place.

10. JESTER

The sun had set, and so had John, on his recliner adjacent to his bed. He felt tense and time was going extremely slow for him. He could hear each tick of the second hand of the clock to his left reverberating in his ears. This echoing made it seem as though one second was two, and two was four; not a pleasant feeling when you want time to go faster. It was not fun, but it was not meant to be. His conscience barked out for the key to these chains. Something to release these shackles; this painful disquietude that dogged and paralyzed him. And the encroaching darkness only enforced this trepidation, adding to the closeness of his operation.

John never showed his anxiety overtly. His screams would reside inside him. He was too well mannered for that. His introverted traits dictated his actions. A graphologist may see signs in his handwriting, strokes slopping at an angle. John would never even want to ask a nurse 'Why me?' Part of it was pride and part of it was habit. He now enjoyed his minds company, and his mind enjoyed his; they were best friends, though sometimes the fires of frustration raged inside.

It was just getting dark when John cast a customary glance out through the window behind his bed. Outside he noticed a man passing by, lighting and inhaling a cigarette. The orange glow expanded as the puff motion was compressed.

The man's tension eased as he let out a long breath. With each of the initial puffs the man felt better and better, then his normality resumed. It was clear that the man had just finished work, not just because he had a navy-blue suit on, but also the calmness that was now being released from him with the smoke. His own personal sauna? Not quite. Clouds from heaven, to him at least. Then he set off urgently as if fearing he may miss his bus. Short term gain for long term pain, as he inhaled the poison once again. At least if he got ill, he wouldn't have to go far, thought John. John wished he could have introduced him to Tony Kupp to scare his future away. Perhaps the man's urgency in his smoking had something to do with the no smoking policy at work.

Forget the fact that governments all over the world, milking billions of tax payers money from selling cigarettes. Then as if in contradiction, ending up paying back in the form of lung cancer and health related complexities. Sucking the last drops of hope from the weak. The way he had been dragging on the tiny weed would suggest it had been a tough day at work. The smoke would help to relax him, his salvation.

A smoke. In a way that was just what John needed. No, no, John would of course refuse to do that. Not only because of his present situation, but also due to his abhorrence to this diseased drug. John had not smoked for decades, in fact from when he was a kid. It had been a disconcerting experience for him as a kid. A fairly normal child in abnormal circumstances.

He spent many years with his aunt, from his mother's side, who was bestowed with the unfortunate responsibility of tending to a young John Winters after his parents had died in a car crash. The parents did have their seatbelts on, but not properly, and they suffered a head-on crash.

The mother was triggered straight into the windscreen, cracking open her skull to die instantaneously. Father suffered a similar fate, though they tried to rescue him at the hospital for a few hopeless minutes. The horrific image of his one and only mother shooting like a javelin into the window was too much for anyone to take. This double blow left him, a child practically homeless, without even the embarrassment of boasting a single parent family lifestyle to his friends. John ended up living with his aunt.

Aunty Sheila was fifty-two at the time she took responsibility of John but she looked more like a seventy-two-year-old, and she had developed the walk of a ninety-two-year-old. She was a small woman with back problems. Her hair was short, curly and grey with grease. Being small with lumbago, Aunty Sheila appeared even shorter due to her ailment. Thus, we have an aunt looking after John, a young boy, in the role of mother. Her appearance was more a grandma than a mother figure. But that was only the start of it.

Aunty Sheila had black teeth; well somewhat yellow and black with the effects of smoking. Her diseased gums and teeth made it a chore even to observe when a wide smile coaxed itself onto her face. Her grins were painful, not to mention when a broad smile reached those hilly parts. Watching her was like putting your head inside of a tiger's mouth, scary.

John sat there in the chair as he thought of his old Aunty Sheila's smile, no, her wide smile. Although it was a gruesome sight you always found yourself peeping and sneaking glances. The scene in a film when you hear a noise in a dark house and the actress always looks up to where the noise was coming from. Everyone in the cinema is telling her not to go into THAT ROOM! But everyone knows she will. This air of irresistible inevitability, gripping you like a force. It was the same kind of thing with Aunty Sheila's teeth. Disconcerting just to look yet in the end you know you would, caring little if she realised or not, or even that she may take offence.

In truth, Aunty Sheila never realised about others fascination with her teeth. Even if she had have done so, it would not have made any difference to her life. Clearly if it was to make a difference, she would have done something about it by now. Such a discernible feature cannot really go unnoticed. It was not unlike black tar from a joke shop to scare people with. John shivered as he pictured those teeth.

He was so innocent in his youth, his growth stunted by the subtraction of two. As such, he had become such a quiet and reserved kid, with very few friends. Yes, he spent some time out playing with friends nearby but he was always the quiet one. This, with the addition of Aunty Sheila as stand-in mother and father sometimes had multiplied his problems. His frustrations at times though did cause divisions between the two, as John mentally questioned why his parents had been taken away; his Aunty Sheila was no equal.

In her own way, Aunty Sheila had been enrolled into ensuring John received an adequate upbringing, even though sometimes it was a burden, but where else could he go. She had set up rules and procedures and chores for John, like washing the dishes at weekends, and cleaning the yard weekly. She refrained from having him iron his clothes out of fear for his damaging the clothes or himself.

His aunt smoked too much. Undoubtedly this contributed to her gruesome set of teeth, nicotine smeared. Yet John had never felt any desire to smoke, I suppose after seeing those teeth. He had never been tempted, even when a packet of Marlboro lay inviting on the table in front of him. His few friends did occasionally smoke, but he had some kind of abhorrence to this practice. It had become a kind of mental allergy where others had a mental addiction. He also strangely associated it with the loss of his parents, in that if they had still been here, he would not have to have been exposed to that filth. It had now become symbolic for him.

Aside from Aunty Sheila, the heath aspects of smoking also jarred with him. He saw the inhaling that his aunt did and realised that although a lot of smoke was coming out, a lot must also be staying in, inside that body, and that too jarred with him. It didn't seem rocket science to him, just common science and it turned John right off. Yet he had to go through the routine every day, many times, watching and smelling, smelling and watching.

He never said anything to her out of his more reserved side and knowing that she was the one looking after him. But inside he tried not to breathe when she smoked. He tried to hold his breath for longer periods. Her filthy habit was another reason he would try to spend as much time as possible outside when allowed.

One summer afternoon John, as usual, had gone around to

some of his friends to play football. Aunty Sheila had not yet come back from work. How she still retained her position as shop assistant with a that smile was beyond John. She worked in a local grocery store and had been there five years. John intentionally never went in there, especially if it was her shift. He was so often out when she came back from work that he never even cared to leave messages as to his whereabouts.

The afternoon hours passed by, but it was not yet dark, even as the evening had set in. Even more surprising, and in fact alarming, was that John had not yet come home. John was usually home hours ago and it was very unlike him. Aunty Sheila was not only worried; she was also angry as she lit up another cigarette. It must have been the Irish blood inside her from long but still evident distant relations. She was a woman of cynicism and ire if provoked, and had a low boiling point. She would always say what she felt.

As if John's lack of punctuality wasn't enough, Aunty Sheila had blown her way through ten cigarettes in the last half hour. Instead of using her time constructively phoning around to his local friends' houses, or going out to look for him, she sat there smoking and fretting on her own. Her mind was occupied, occupied not with heavy concern, but instead with weighty plans of retribution. Her obligation to keep a roof over his shoulders kept her going, not real love.

As the story went, John was actually with his friends, who got bored with the football, so decided to travel to the local railway line in Helmshore. It was a local line that had fallen into disuse. The encroaching twilight just allowed vision of the outstretched line although, as every minute passed, the light was getting weaker and weaker. The ground was stony under foot, causing the boys to occasionally trip up, but it did not worry them like perhaps, as a portent, it should have. The twilight only made it that much worse, but at the same time that much more exciting and inviting. Sunset had passed and John, in his mild excitement, had not only lost track of time, but had found himself getting more and more engrossed in the experience. John did get moments when he realised he should be back home, but found himself unable to go back.

Sunset had passed long ago. John was enjoying the thrill. Unfortunately though, he would have to pay later.

It was the first time he had gone along this rocky track, although his friends had been before. They knew the route having been so many times. As they travelled along the line and looked forward, they saw nothing, only darkness now, with the silhouette of the track lacking clarity. The previously enveloping twilight had given way to common darkness. Yet it did not strike John in any way with alarm; he was lost in the moment. Wasn't he supposed to be home three hours ago? Wasn't he breaking fundamental rules of the house? Wasn't he in trouble?

John took a nonchalant glance over his shoulder, then a more concerned one. There was as much visual identity behind him as there was in front of him. He felt in the middle of a gorge surrounded by slopes and cliffs. He felt surrounded by a spacious and evil world, yet looked along this passage like the train itself. Even so, he still felt the need to carry on, not only feeling obliged to do so, but also because of the adrenalin pumping through his body.

John felt a chill transcend over him. This had just followed the news that he was somewhere on a railway track and he could see neither forward or back. Even summer evenings in Lancashire were often cold at night. This was no exception. The sky was clear but the moon seemingly non-existent, Cassiopeia coming into prominence, soon to walk in the wonder of a watcher's world.

John's mind was now floating around as if incongruous. His thought waves seemed to be cracking up, lost on the world of the evening out with friends. Every few minutes though, his mind prophesised on the events to follow at Aunty Sheila's house. He could see her blackened teeth chattering angrily at him. John's head was not in a clear place. He thought he could see shapes, human shapes around him. Yes, he was with his friends so it was partly true, but he thought he could see more. It added to his confusion, convulsing his thoughts and feelings. These sights, merged with noises of his friends and the wind around the trees, he was utterly unsure of himself.

His mind and his eyes were playing psychological tricks on him, the darkness playing hide and seek with him. His eyes now shifted, alert to the most sensitive of movements; rabbit-like reactions he now possessed. Each step he travelled, each breath he took, it weighed more and more on his pressurised mind. And yes, the chill, it tingled into his bones similar to an ice massage. He knew he couldn't go back now, had gone too far, wishing though, that he could.

The track was long and narrow; maybe it meandered. Walking slowly and seemingly straight you never even noticed this deviation on the track. Only on looking back would it become clear if it was not so dark now. This perspiration began to appear now on his forehead even though it was far from hot out there. He realised this after brushing his hand through his ruffled hair. He wiped his semi moist palm down his black shadowed jeans.

He was being tortured now by his own mind. Tortured by his home town, this part of which he never really knew existed. He was all alone now, or at least that was how he felt. Splintered images and jerking shapes caused panic and alertness. Even the sounds under his feet seemed to crunch animal bones. It was yet another vision his pulsating mind had concocted. Oops, there goes a skull.

A tap on his shoulder, his left shoulder. It was like an icy iron finger. Yes, it was on his shirt and not on his skin but it prodded him as if he was an amusement piece; a stick-like prod. He felt its coldness maybe insulated by the combined layers of his shirt and skin. He pivoted around, nearly losing balance, significant degrees of uncertainty the only thing that was certain. His horror seemed to be devouring him further, as the face was there, a breaths distance away from his own.

Suddenly alarm bells hit him, a huge pendulum smacking his ears, each time getting stronger and stronger. It was not Satan in front of him, maybe John wished it was. It was Aunty Sheila. Instinctively, the first thing he noticed was her teeth, although they were hardly recognizable in such darkness. Her smile was cynical and inhuman, tortuous. Why was she smiling? Why was she here? How was she here?

Then it was Jeff, one of his friends in front of him, not Aunty Sheila. It was Aunty Sheila; he was sure it was. Blinking repeatedly in such a way that he had an eyelash stuck in his eye, all he saw now was Jeff roaring with laughter at John's dreamy confusion and aloofness. His other friends were also giggling nearby. The panic eventually dissipated.

Embarrassed and awkward, John found a pseudo smile just when he needed it. Join in and maybe they won't notice he thought. Then a kind of sweeping relief passed over him as he realised that it wasn't his aunty after all. She hadn't tracked him down, and also that it was no serial killer or assailant that had prodded his shoulder with such terror.

'Is there anybody out there?' laughed Jeff looking through and over John. 'Where are you going you idiot?'

John's smile became a catalogue of umms and ahhs. What could he say after being sidetracked and confused so much?

'Err, I don't, I err, was waiting for you lot to catch up,' he finished quickly. 'How far does this track go?' he asked trying to change the subject. It would have been more appropriate to find out how far they would be travelling, and when they would get back. Instead, he babbled on with a question more nervous than anything else. Also, at that moment he realised that he had better go back as it was very late now, after ten. His friends had already decided to go back, so John's wish had coincidentally come true. Not only was it getting late, but also, they had travelled further than they normally do this time. Luckily, there was no chance of getting lost, just follow the tracks back.

'We'd better get back if we want to be in one piece tomorrow,' one of them said. He too, had just realised the time. John remained quiet, not wanting to sound too fearful. They agreed to head back. Once they got back to the start of the track they headed in their own directions. This was fine with John as it would let him get home quicker. So, he ran home, all the way home, ignoring the feeling of fatigue which he was really feeling. This tiredness didn't stop him as the adrenaline got him home in ten minutes. He didn't stop once, not even to tie an untidy looking shoe lace.

Panting like a rabid dog he headed towards his awaiting house. The house had been waiting for him. He visualised his aunty in her angry chair, smoke bellowing out of her ears, and not from her excessive use of cigarettes. He could see those foul, fetid features behind that grin. All he could imagine were those rickety, cadaverous and foul formations presented in front of him on a daily basis. The punishment, well he dared not think about it. He knew she didn't like him being there to start with. It was as if he was a burden. He didn't like it himself but realised there was nothing either could do about it. When he got to the house, she would avenge the miserable responsibility she had been made to endure.

Those lovely teeth, SAY CHEESE! Don't be rude now, Johnny. Give the lady a big smile.

He eased down to a canter and was virtually at his destination. He would be able to see the house in about thirty seconds as he half ran and half walked the last few steps. He had never been this late before, never even LATE!

Why had you said YES to the question, 'Do you want to go out to the railway track Johnny?' Why hadn't you made up some excuse?

John had reached the top of his street and could see his aunt's house.

Why didn't you just say 'NO.' It's shorter than 'YES' you know. Why you always make the wrong choice, Johnny? Stick with me, buddy.

He needed friends, especially after losing his parents and even more so being cooked up in this madhouse with his aunty for life. Trails of sweat had begun running a race down his head and the sides of his face. He could not hide his trepidation, not from himself let alone others. He glistened now under the street lamps like frost forming on a cold winter night.

Oh, you've found time to give yourself a sauna, Johnny. Cause you're gonna be roasted alive tonight young man.

A drip tickled and trickled his eyebrow, forcing him to finger his forehead. He was shocked by the amount of sweat that had formed. It only added fuel, liquid fuel, to an already apprehensive mind. His head felt like a pressure cooker coming to boil, but he couldn't find the off switch.

The house sat there, a spider's web, waiting for him.

Come into my parlour, buddy. We have thousands of wonderful surprises for you!

It may sound a little farfetched; John had only been a few hours late, and to get chain sawed for that seemed a bit much. You could say his mind had gone a little over the top in anticipation. The personal agony he was putting himself under could seem a little much. You could argue that if there was an inch of compassion in his aunt that she would not be too punitive. But there are two things of inescapable note. This was the first time John had really gone beyond the limit. He had never been even an hour late in the past, let alone four or five. John had always thought to himself that anyone who disobeyed the rules went straight to the gas chamber.

Well, you were right, weren't you, buddy?

Yes, John was naive and fearing, but he was only thirteen and was a young thirteen despite the turmoil he had been through. What had scared him a lot was not knowing what would come next in life. He feared in life and more immediately in his present predicament exactly how his aunty would deal with him.

Until you've been in detention you only know the anticipation and potential worst of it; teachers grinning with sadistic satisfaction at the thought of you shivering with terror.

His fear always took a nastier twist due to his relationship with Aunty Sheila. It had always been a little formal and forced. He had no urge to stay with her and more importantly, she had no desire to keep him. The situation had forced things, and both were in this suffering state. It was not simply John's naivety or emotional overreaction to things. She bordered eccentricity. There is a saying a dog without a bark. Well, she was a dog with a bark, a loud one. And sometimes to John she was like a lighthouse in a power cut, useless. Furthermore, she seemed to care about nothing other than herself. Thus, it does seem that John had some justification for his lack of confidence in this evening's outcome.

The last leg of his journey to his house was all downhill as Peel Street was a street of high gradient. Luckily, he was returning so was going downhill and leaving the uphill part behind him. As a result, he was able to use economy of energy in his final sprint. Flying down the slope like Franz Klammer, John found himself needing to put the brakes on like Michael Schumacher.

A noise. It was a dog strolling around the street. It started barking with vengeance as if John had murdered his pup. It caused John to make a heavy thudded crack on the floor to stop himself and alleviate himself from the minor quandary he found himself in. Easing up he then nonchalantly carried on his way, his heart slowly reverting back to normality. He kept an eye on the dog with the corner of his eye, fearing its control of the street. The dog in reply gave a controlled look back as if to offer a final warning. His heart was returning back to a normal beat. Well, it wasn't really normality. More like the level at which it was at before this minor hiccup. Still above normal, but not freakishly high on the cardiograph as the past few minutes had been.

Then John thought. Maybe the dog was trying to tell him something? As if telling him to stay away or at least prepare for more than names; sticks and stones resided inside her. It was as if John's mind expected the worst, putting everything into a bad light. Maybe (as was in the back of John's mind, latent yet somehow unclothed), the dog was just doing what dogs do. Maybe it was simply acting with a mixture of fear and caution to anything unprepared for, like dogs do?

Get a grip of yourself little, Johnny, the evening is still young.

The dog, once a cauldron of anger, was now hardly a simmer as John felt for his key. Inside his stress levels were still bubbling away. He'd only been given the honour a few months back, his aunty vesting her limited trust in him. He now expected that to be the last time he would ever be afforded that privilege of using the key with independence. Such a small piece of metal with such large physical and psychological capabilities. It seemed he had flouted that hand of faith tonight. After playing his part in the plot, the dog cantered off to another street on the lookout for other unsuspecting customers. Maybe he would find a drunk or someone putting the bins out to bark at.

He looked at his watch. 11:20 pm was displayed on his cheap digital Chinese watch. At least it worked, even though this time he wished it didn't. He couldn't believe it was 11:20 pm. He could have sworn it was about nine.

The newish lock on an antiquated door opened with ease.

That was one thing, he thought, at least it didn't creak. It did though, have a problem when closing. This being that the new lock clicked shut very loudly, especially when all else was deathly quiet. There was no way around it. The knob for the lock did not turn fully so forcing the door to click shut with volume audible enough to create unease into already disquieted wounds. Breathing heavily when trying not to breathe at all, he made his way through the hall and past the stairs. He cast a glance upstairs naturally, as he always did. Nothing to report. The odd thing was that no lights were on upstairs or downstairs. The deathly silence coupled with hellish darkness threatened John's cool. He didn't know what to expect next. It seemed clear to him that either no one was in or, or, maybe she was asleep. It would be perfect he thought, if she was asleep. The evening though, had become less and less predictable.

He opened the door to the living room. Black shapes littered the space around his eyes. So many shapes looked human. So many shapes seemed to look at him, motionless. His mind was playing tricks that only the mind can do. It was an army in the room, so many potential hurdles requiring John to rub his eyes incessantly. Was that a dagger in his hand? Is he smiling or snarling at me?

Thankfully nothing moved. One image though, looked like a jester with his cap on, hanging to one side. He tried to stare it out for clues and for the concealed identity. Squinting his eyes, he dared not move much further until the appetite of his conscience had been fed. Threads of light from a streetlight tried to creep through the stitches of the velour curtains. It only helped to create further distortions, shades and shapes; strings and drapes. Minutes seem to pass and he could still see the jester.

It seemed to be smiling at him. Was that saliva running down his lips?

You look tasty... You want to start running now, buddy?

Insane thoughts were rummaging their way to the surface of John's mind. He was sure he could see a smile. He squinted and moved his head around to search for a better view in the darkness. Surely those were not teeth, yellow and black, he could see? Eyes getting wider and wider with every grin as he was sure the thing was moving. It seemed clearly the case.

It had become vital now to John to try to calm himself down. He took two steps back but did not blink or avert his gaze in the slightest. His eyes were triggered on the jester, waiting to fire.

I'm gonna eat you!

The jester licked his lips. It had to be a reflection of light or something. It could even be a towel hanging from the cupboard, he hoped. John's right hand rose and groped for the light switch nearby. It was almost as if he had forgot about Aunty Sheila now and the jester took centre stage. There were three light switches together, one for the hallway, one for upstairs and one for this living room; that was the key one, the jackpot. That was the switch John urgently needed lighting RIGHT NOW! There were three switches and John knew which to press; the one on the far left. Eyes focused directly ahead and concentrating on the jester, John pushed the switch. The hallway light clicked on. Damn! Why did the hallway light come on?

Because you put it on, you fool!

It seemed like the jester was speaking to him now. The jester was only stating the obvious. It all happened in a couple of seconds. John seemed to notice that the jester's eyes had lit up.

'It's the light from the hallway,' he whispered to himself. It was not the most sagacious of assertions but it sufficed in his self-inflicted predicament. As he spoke, he switched the main room light on. A click revealed...

11. STOREROOM

Let there be light... and there was light.
A sigh of relief began to transcend through John. A marvellous glow inside, casting aside the jester's long floppy hat, with the bell to end the round. He took a few quick sharp glances around the room as his brown hair moved in similar, but slightly delayed motions.

John's so-called jester's hat was a head scarf of Aunty Sheila. The equally so-called face of the jester was one of her sweaters, a thick one, unscrupulously disregarded onto the recliner. His brain then started to function. It was clear his aunty had gone off to sleep. But she never or rarely went before midnight. She must have been tired, that's all. All very logical, nothing strange at all. A lot of people go to sleep early, especially old folk. Nothing sinister about it. Somehow, he just didn't trust his conscience though, especially as the nasty man whispering in his head was muttering strands of negativity. I was right about the jester wasn't I, he said to the friend inside his head.

Hey Johnny, I was only kidding. I just wanted to see if you believed me or not. Jingle, jingle.

Although his brain had regained working consciousness, he had become confused. Confused about the situation he found himself in.

They had a storeroom where they got changed, not a bathroom or bedroom; a storeroom. It was not used as much to store things as a storeroom usually is, that was the odd thing about the storeroom. Small with no windows, the storeroom was pitch black when the light was off. Sometimes John had gone inside to play, turning the light off and seeing if could ever make out any shapes. He never managed to. Yes, they always changed in the storeroom. Might sound odd, but when you saw the bathroom that was annexed outside with no heating it would all make sense. To say the bathroom was cold was like saying the storeroom was dark; an understatement.

What's common about storerooms? Not only are they surprisingly used to store food, but they are also very small rooms. In John's case this storeroom was no exception. One uncalculated stretch could be fatal. You could end up crashing into the surrounding wall, or worse still, into some pans or tins of food. And thankfully he and his aunt were not claustrophobic. The storeroom would then have been a punishment.

His mind was still unsure, reluctant to accept that he was in the clear. His aunty would obviously ask him where he was last night and when he got in. I went with some friends up to the reservoir and got back by 9:30 pm. That could be his story, but that was a little risky, he thought. He may opt for 10:00 pm or 10:15 pm. Whatever he decided, some well-constructed punitive measure would surely await him.

He still couldn't believe the fact that she was asleep so soon. His memory could trace no time when she had ever gone up to bed so early before. He knew he had to do one thing then to put his mind at ease. He knew he hated to have to do it, but knew he had to. Like watching a video when you know a scare is coming at the end, you just had to follow it through to the end. For his psychological benefit he just had to do it. Furtively, he began his ascent upstairs to bed. Thank God I've got a separate room, he thought.

The house was about ninety years old and was in fact built by her father. He had seen a photo of him but that was about all. The fact that the house was so old meant that the old engine often needed an oil change; the arteries had begun to clog up. Thus, for as long as John had lived in the house things had started to get older and older. The stairs leading to upstairs always creaked, some days more than others. He knew that it would creak again tonight and that the creaky stairs were near the top. If he tried to sneak up three stairs in one go maybe it would result in no creak at all? On the other hand, putting extra pressure on the last step near the top could mean increased pressure and that could mean a louder creak? At this stage it was all a bit of a gamble he now thought to himself. The intense pressure being placed on the third step would undoubtedly create a high, more pronounced reaction. Eventually he decided on one step at a time, but any sign of a groan from the stairs and he would have to revert to plan B and attempt a two stepped approach, to alleviate the risk.

It was the equivalent of trying to cross a minefield. Danger signs strewn everywhere, skull and bones adding to the fear. He could be the hero tonight, just as long as he travelled with care across the tinderbox of creaks. Then, he even had the audacity to smile broadly to himself as if acknowledging the tricky task which lay ahead.

Low moans liberated themselves from the first few steps. He was feeling quietly confident after all the mental planning. That confidence though, soon humbled as a cracking sound emanated from the stairs like a very squeaky door; a release of tension as if the steps had been waiting for their chance. It was too late to step back as too much pressure had been applied not only on the ground but also on John's confidence. Maybe the initial overconfidence had caused this unexpected downfall. His mouth screwed up into a face of extreme pain reminiscent of Steve Vai pulling a high pitch guitar string. To accentuate the pain would be a more revealing and accurate portrayal of John's immediate response. He then stood there for about a minute, waiting for that inevitable response. It did not come. He couldn't believe his luck. Getting to the top then became a doddle. It's not often that the hero gets to stand up like Rocky at the top of his steps; a soldier who reached his home without touching a mine.

He just had to take a look into her room to make sure she was really in there; to make sure the celebrations were not premature. Her door was just slightly ajar, it always was. By now he could see well in the darkness and was glad he had taken his share of carrots. The strength and appearance of the external streetlamps helped to shade the interior of the house. He was very much thankful of that too. He couldn't risk putting a light on yet; couldn't quite see enough of an image in the darkness through her door. I may see the glow of her yellow teeth he thought.

They will eat you one day you know Johnny…

'Shut up,' he whispered to himself. The darkness was trying to play tricks on him again as nebulous shades triggered false illusions at the head of her bed. He was in her room and had taken a couple of steps forward.

You go back now, Johnny, while you can! You go back.

This time it was the jester who was shouting at him.

Would you please listen to me? Would you just? If you don't there will repercussions.

After satisfying his appetite with the delicious tones of her gentle groans and snoring he exited and felt his way to his bedroom, again thankful to have been granted a room of his own.

What he didn't notice was that as he exited her room to enter his own, Aunty Sheila turned around in her bed, now her face was in the direction of the door that had just been gently closed by John. Her gentle groan was no more; her snoring was gone; she now made no sounds, only a smile. It was John who had made the sound. One sound too many.

A bead of light from the streetlights outside shone perfectly into the smiling teeth of his aunty as the smile broadened into one of insatiable victory.

12. POLICEMAN

In bed and light off, John lay on his side as he looked across the cupboard door that was open. Why was it always open? Ever since he had been here that door had been open. Was there too much stuff in the cupboard? It seemed not. Maybe someone wanted to get out from behind the bed sheets in the cupboard and linen but never could? Maybe someone was sleeping in there? Well they had bedsheets at least. The brown antiquated but well sculptured door and brass handle just lay in its regular position but not correct one. All the years he had been there he had never tried to close that door. All the time he had been there he had never mustered up the courage to close it, until today. He had been perturbed by the unclosed cupboard door before, but never felt strongly enough to want to shut it. The thing was that he was he a little scared of the damn door, especially at night with all the shadows that it produced. Tonight, his night needed capping off.

He rushed out of bed with sudden but not so convincing actions and pushed the cupboard door shut. Seconds later it casually and slowly returned back to its open state, comfortable state, squeaking slightly as it did. It was as if it was at some kind of downward angle. Edgily pushing some of the linen further in he gave the door a more solid and heavier push. It shut with a seemingly magnetic pull. Equally quickly John shoved himself back into his bed.

Fatigue was rising when a tiny squeal escaped from somewhere above John's drifting head. His tiredness had left him as he lifted his head to see the possessed cupboard door ajar once again. Bouncing his head back onto the pillow John found sleep about twenty minutes later.

***

2:00 am the same night, the eventful night was not yet complete. A few creaks from the other room.

John was at Blackpool, The Pleasure Beach, and it was scorching hot. He had been on a lot of the rides, at least the ones he got allowed to go on, and was desperate to go on again. It must have been three hours he had spent on the rides but he wasn't tired at all. He had never been able to go on the very fast rides. The Big One was one such example, but his parents would never allow it. Somehow though, he found himself riding the Big One; he went on three times and wanted more.

On his way out he noticed the Laughing Policeman. Surprise, surprise it was laughing and doing so at a degree beyond human capabilities. He stared into the policeman's eyes somehow fascinated by this eccentric madman, mild rather than the savage amusements of the rollercoasters and its brethren. Yet in a hypnotic way it held John's attention. As his parents watched him, he too was expressing a gentle grin. He wasn't thinking about what the policeman was laughing at, he just stood mesmerised. It was more enigmatic than the Mona Lisa, at least to John. Its puppet-like features and perpetual expression bored his parents but to him it was hypnotizing and genius. The most impressive thing though was that the intense laughter had created spurious tears to roll down the cheeks of the man. They gave even more fuel to a conflagration of interest burning deep onto John's bubbling excitement. John was not just smiling now; he was laughing with an equally addictive quality.

It was also a bittersweet moment for John. A moment he always loved in his dreams. Whenever he saw his parents in his dreams. It always gave him a warmth he could never remember in real life. Dreams of this nature he lived for, and they made his existence so much more worthwhile.

The Laughing Policeman had a truncheon in one hand which bobbed up and down mechanically as if wafting at air. The next time he sees a policeman, his father thought, he's going to roar with laughter.

13. AUNTY SHEILA

Laughing out loud, John heard a sound, louder and clearer than the others. He could also feel warm smelling air on his face. His own laughter reversed itself into the gentle grin he had before, but he felt he was still staring at the amusement, the hilarious policeman in front of him.

He opened his eyes and all was quiet. All he could see about half a foot away from his face was the ugliest policeman – no, it was a woman. He was not at Blackpool Pleasure Beach and not enjoying himself anymore. The amusement had transmogrified into his one and only Aunty Sheila and the wails and cheers had become a deafening silence.

He blinked a few times before realising for keeps that he was not at The Pleasure Beach. Anyway, in real life he would never have been brave enough to go on the diversity of thrills and spills that he thought he had been on. His previous excitement had quickly given way to a kind of incongruous perturbation. Fragments of his earlier moments kept easing his discomfort. But, as the real world's reality started to hit him it hurt him more and more, wave after wave. Memories of peace kept trying to block out images of war. Stark realisation pounded him hard when he looked concertedly at her broadening grin. It was compounded when she spoke.

'Come out of bed now, Jonathan,' her soft vocal cords harped. In truth it was coarse and comparable to a wheezing sound, simultaneously creating a buzzing sound. Her soft voice was far from soothing, especially when she began chauffeuring him out of bed, and even more so at two in the morning. He was so contented a few seconds ago, in a different world, enjoying life. His mind was elsewhere and physically or emotionally was in no position to complain. He felt helpless, his head was not where his body was.

By the time he had been escorted downstairs his head had got much clearer. His alcohol-free hangover had ceased but he was still heavily inebriated with confusion.

'What time did you arrive last night?' she said in true sandpaper fashion. It was all coming back to him now. But what to say? He had planned all this hours ago, what to say when asked, but his mind was a blur and all his plans had gone up in the air like laughing gas. Lie, and she was probably awake when he came back last night. Tell the truth and you're in deep trouble.

When you went into her room last night, she was asleep, remember, Johnny? The jester's smile turned to him.

Where was his decisive confidence now? 'Speak to me,' he shouted to his mind.

'I was, err…' That's all that came out.

'What time?' Much louder this time, as she started to find her form.

'Abbbout half past ten I think,' he lied. *Bad move Johnny.*

'Half past ten hey. And you think I'm gonna believe that, especially as I was up then.'

See, bad move, buddy. The Eleventh Commandment – Thou shalt not deceive Aunty Sheila.

She was starting to cough a little and breath a bit heavier. 'There's only one thing worse than a bad kid, and that's a bad kid who lies. Now you do realise you're gonna have to pay for your wrongdoings, don't you, Jonathan?' She was now starting to enjoy herself a little.

'I promise I won't be late again' he pleaded. But now somehow controlling his stammer. He had a horrible feeling inside, nausea.

'You bet you won't be late again. Your mother and father would have been disgusted if they were alive today. It's not allowed at your age to do whatever you want. There are rules. You're gonna have to pay. You play by the rules or pay my dues.'

John considered rummaging in his pockets for money. After all, he had to pay, didn't he? Thankfully he didn't entertain that stupid idea. He couldn't grasp what she meant, what she wanted off him. He had said sorry hadn't he, what more did she want.

Yes, but that's not enough, we want your blood.

Aunty Sheila was now traipsing up and down the room as if thinking of a punishment. John meanwhile sat silent, head down and quizzical. His head was asking too many questions for his brain. His silent exterior shadowed a frantic plexus if ideas and thoughts. Without looking at his aunty he remembered how she looked when she woke him. It was a delayed reaction. She didn't have any hair curler clips now, and that was rare. Normally pink ones as well. She always had those terrible clips in at night as far as he could remember. She still looked ugly, oh yes, no doubt about that but it was odd.

Glancing half upwards in silence, John again noticed the thick sweater on her recliner, aka The Jester. He did not even realise until then that he was downstairs. How did he get downstairs? A few seconds ago, he thought he was in his bed, wiping the tiredness from his eyes. Now he was left wiping the disbelief from his mind.

About two minutes of silence took place. During this time John was trying to digest the anomalies about his aunty, whilst at the same time she was trying to concoct a punishment worthy of his crime. Dressing gown tied and long bright blue slippers donned, Aunty Sheila carried on lolling around the room. Her impaired back caused a bend in her walk. Years of factory life had caused this and she knew it. Her orangey brown dressing gown was all John had ever seen her wear at night, she must never have bought anything new for years.

'I wasn't in all night you know, Jonathan?' she said with delicacy. 'Did you know that?' He didn't know that or what she was hitting at. Didn't even want to think about where she was going in her mind. Then it struck him; her sweater, no hair clips, and now he had just noticed her muddy shoes on the carpet which were about two sizes too big, and always had been.

She had been out looking for him! Obviously, she hadn't found him but this only fuelled her suspicions and John had to try to put out that fire. He had to be more tactful than a bent screw in a prison.

'No, I didn't' he replied.

'So where do you think I was then?' She smiled as she said this and John looked away from that aged, cynical grin. His confusion still showed on his face though. He had a pretty good idea where she had been. Probably to the area in and around the garages where he generally played. To get there you had to cross a grassy stretch, hence the muddy shoes. It was also a cool night and his aunty very rarely went out at night at all, so she must have worn the sweater. And maybe in her urgency she just left the sweater out and due to lateness must not have put her hair curling clips in. But he refrained from any assertions or clever responses because he was already deep in the brown stuff. So, he had a pretty good idea where she had been last night but thought against vocalizing any ideas.

'I don't know where you went, Aunty.' He was so concerned with making sure he sounded veracious that he did not completely answer the question. To be honest he had forgotten the question, and had memorised an answer to keep some kind of peace. She did think the answer was a little strange but relayed nothing, not yet. She was building up her points against him mentally inside her head.

'Well I'll tell you where I went. I went looking for you because I was worried about you. You weren't on Grange Road or at the park.' Grange Road was where he often played nearby although he had not played there for a few weeks. He had already guessed that she had been to the park based on the condition of her shoes. 'And you were nowhere in sight. Do you mind telling me where you did go last night?' It was sterner now. She was clearly getting to her point now; her reason for staying up late last night and for waking him up this night.

He resigned himself to the truth. 'I was at the railway line down Helmshore with some friends.' Yes, he was being truthful but also a little reluctant hence vague. It was as if his concession, his admission of guilt had reduced him into a begrudging admission. 'I didn't realise it was so late until I got home. It was the first time I had ever been there and just seemed to pass so quickly.' He couldn't bring himself to a grovelling apology but his explanation was clear coming from the lips of a youngster. Whist being truthful he had decided to throw in an unasked truth, that it was the first time he had been there. It did add to his case a little. He could have also gone on to talk of the enjoyable time he had there but that would not have gone down well. He decided to retain a degree of brevity to his story.

Although the story did in fact wash with his aunty, it did not pardon him of any disobedience.

'Right, now we are starting to get somewhere.' She sat down on her recliner. The 'V' in her pyjama top extended just slightly, but was bisected by her vest, worn underneath. The chair creaked slightly under the bulk of Aunty Sheila. The seat of the recliner already had the shape of her bottom naturally etched into it, obviously through age. Her tension seemed to ease somewhat with her words so that when she said '... somewhere' it took on long relaxing tones. But, and there's always a but, the way she spoke told John that she was demanding more in the kind of way, but not exactly like the way Columbo would squeeze out that last confession. As he observed her relax, he found himself stiffening inside further.

'Now you do realise your gonna have to pay, don't you?'

He was sure he'd heard that sentence before, and also the way it was delivered. He didn't answer it, all the same. He couldn't because he felt a vagueness to it, almost a rhetorical question. Why should he have to pay? It was only the first time he had been late. He felt like saying *'Why should I have to pay? You*

are not my mum!! It's like the first time I've stayed out past eight.'
Thankfully he didn't let his emotions out on this occasion.

She got up from the seat she had occupied for only thirty seconds and went into the kitchen. Seconds later she reappeared with a lighter and cigarettes. Phew, he thought. It could have been a kitchen knife or scissors, but it was a bit late at night for her to be smoking. Must be the nerves, he thought. 'You did know you'd have to pay, didn't you?' He couldn't believe she had said it again.

She took a cigarette out and threw it on his lap. 'Put it in your mouth.' It was delivered in monotone and monosyllabically. No smiles, no teeth, no grin. John just stared at her. It was odd. He was so used to her smiling those yellow teeth at him that now, when she didn't, it just seemed odd, perturbing.

He even felt like saying 'Smile Aunty for the camera. Why won't you smile?' Desperate thoughts. He strangely didn't recognise the woman who was speaking to him now; the woman who had been looking after him for years now. This was not the Aunty Sheila he had grown up to… to hate at times. It was a different, unpredictable, almost schizophrenic distant relative that you had not met before. The kind of relative you had heard of in the neighbourhood but never visited because of the rumours of notoriety and infamy that surrounded them. The kind that would reluctantly visit with butterflies all around, not just in your stomach.

'Put it in your mouth!' This time with a crazed madness mixed with a cough. Like a scream but very short. Nothing else. All the times his friends had asked him to have a try and he had always turned down the offer because it was disgusting to him. It was just breathing in smoke and he just couldn't see any point in it. Even the thought nearly made him sick, mainly due to the smell which he hated. And now he was being asked to pay for coming in a few hours late, something so trivial (to him) with something in such a bloated way (again, to him). Ironically, her coughing demands for him to smoke were delivered in such a way that it was probably the worst advert for smoking you could imagine. Being asked to smoke by a spluttering, wheezing host; not great.

She had taken the look of an assassin now to John. The foreplay had been terrific but this had become her forte; somehow her purpose, her profession it seemed. No glamour, smiles or talk now, just business.

Uncontrollably, John began to pick up the little long object like a robot, pulling it towards his own mouth. It was as if it was not his own hand, maybe a prosthetic arm? She stood there in front of him, and he could smell her, that smell of old people. She stood there, hands slightly shaking with a lighter quivering in her hand, mainly yellow with a little blue making up the fluttering flame. He didn't really know what to do despite having seen what needs to be done a hundred times before. Still, he didn't know how to do it; how to smoke. But he tried all the same. The quick way to learn how to smoke; get up at two in the morning and have an old woman force you to suck a tube of paper filled with chemicals.

He wanted to scream but knew he couldn't as he was being handled via remote control now. It was his punishment and he had to see it through. He didn't even dare to ask how he should do it although he wanted to. He was paralyzed. In television he had seen dimples on people's faces as they dragged on the cigarette, but he was a little afraid of the poison and smoke that would enter his stomach; the puffs of poison to pervade his privacy. He put the cigarette to his mouth in his own time as the old woman nodded continuously to help him on. She drew the flame close to his mouth and he felt he could hear the roar of the tiny flame escaping from the liquid below, burning it; or was it the roar of the crowd? He instinctively blew on the cigarette like an amateur. The crowd booed and jeered as nothing happened.

'Suck you fool, suck. You don't do it like that. You're not supposed to blow. Suck the thing.' He could also hear the crowd screaming at him to suck. 'SUCK DON'T BLOW, SUCK DON'T BLOW, SUCK DON'T BLOW' the crowd screamed in unison. It was as if a rush of blood had overtaken her, or puff of smoke, like she was smoking herself for the first time. Sweat all of a sudden appeared on her now forced through an injection of adrenalin. If nothing else, the tension incited John to drag on the cigarette. It was puffing in poison, breathing in pain.

SUCK, SUCK, SUCK...

He thought he had passed out but he hadn't. He felt as though his whole body was smoke filled. No blood or bones; no water or flesh, just smoke. At that moment (possibly because of this feeling) he coughed and spat very suddenly, half retching as he ran and stumbled to the toilet where he was physically sick, extending his facial muscles beyond where he thought it was possible. His aunty did not stand in his way. His mandible felt like it was cracking at its joint.

He was fitful with convulsions but nothing was coming out, not even smoke it seemed, as uncontrollable spams jolted from him. It was the sheer horror and contemplation of his activities earlier; the thought of omnipresent smoke engulfing him. Meanwhile, his aunty smiled in victory, knowing this was only partial pain but a permanent solution. In the periphery of John's coughing and creasing his aunty had already began making her way back upstairs.

It was the middle of the night. It had all only taken about twenty minutes but there was a sense of satisfaction. The same wooden stairs creaked as she ascended this time with more consistency. A few minutes later John re-emerged into an empty room, lonely, bar the street lights that glowed inside his room. The intense retching had reaped hardly a few drops of spittle. Not only were stretch marks starting to form, but also a nerve rash as a follow-on from the mad convulsions.

Pink dots of blood beneath the surface of the skin had sprung up on his cheeks. He looked like a moving dot-to-dot puzzle. How would he explain these painful shreds to his friends? The puzzling looks on their faces, and ironically on his too. Moreover, how would he live with his aunty and her retribution tactics?

14. SHEEP

That was all about forty years ago but he still remembered it in the vague way you remember a special birthday or the day when you broke your leg that one time. Whenever he felt the smell of cigarette smoke, he thought of his late Aunty Sheila now in a peaceful way. Cognitive memory in action. It had been a lesson he had really learned in his youth. It was also depressing when he thought deeper. Living most of your teenage years in a way you wouldn't choose to if you had a choice. Existing in a home that not only stank of cigarettes, but also wickedness, reluctance and cynicism. But in the end, she had at least looked after him when there was no one else there.

His phobia towards this unhealthy habit had been reinforced that day by an aunt either inadvertently being cruel or wisely being kind. An aunt reinforcing a strangely punitive measure marked with sadism. Some nights, when he closed his eyes and couldn't sleep, he ended up seeing that smile of hers, counting her teeth as opposed to sheep.

15. PAULA

Nurse 'Open all Hours' Diane was saying her goodbyes to her work mates as she was leaving after her shift. It was only her mentally trained mind that brought a degree of happiness onto her exterior. Going home from work in a hospital to work on your worsening mother was not easy.

It was 6:00 pm and she was leaving for the day. A shift on its own was surely enough to take that smile off your face, but 'Open all Hours' Diane was well experienced, and the only thing that was changing was the deteriorating state of her mother. In the past few months, she had become incontinent. Diane, being a nurse, would be (or would be chosen to be) the one to clean up the pieces. She often thought that when an old person reaches the incontinent stage that they should be put out of their misery. It was the point one step closer to senility. Almost like humanity going full circle, back to the limitations of life as a helpless baby.

Nurse Diane and her young compatriot Paula went on their way to the bus stop. Paula had learned to drive but couldn't afford a car yet. Oddly enough, Nurse Diane had never learned to drive and sometimes did feel it had been a missed opportunity, though she did drive her medicine trolley with the upmost confidence. They both lived in Rawtenstall but about two miles from each other. No doubt there was potential in buying a car and it was on Paula's to-do list.

Paula was a young attractive girl in her mid-twenties with ginger hair that was more natural that the safaris of Kenya; and she prided herself in that. If anyone even asked her as to the authenticity of her hair colour they would never do so again. It was the richness of her orangey red locks that made people look and question, not in a nasty way but in amazement as the colour was so strong; too rich to be true to some. People's stark disbelief and admiration reached Paula in the form of a comical jibe or attempt to undermine her ginger locks as if dye induced. Over the years she had embraced quite a complex surrounding her hair and unfortunately had never seemed to overcome that hurdle.

The bus would normally take them both to the same town and they would make their separate ways home. On the bus they sat like anti-twins; different in so many ways. What Paula would give for that nursing knowledge and control of the patients and confidence? And oh, what Nurse Diane would give for a second bite at youth and that indefatigable desire for life. The most striking thing was that they both wanted each other's traits and both couldn't attain them.

The bus squeaked to a halt and Paula got off. She appeared timorous in front of her elder's physique, even though her own was nothing less than average. They exchanged departing pleasantries and Nurse Diane was left to smile away her young protégé. Her, and two others were left to accompany the bus home.

Paula still lived with her parents but respected them enough to do so without any complaints or reluctance. They appreciated her company, that she at least was still around to help from the impending distraction of old age.

Rawtenstall was a very respectable part of Lancashire, hilly and full of panoramic views. Being the only child, the semi-detached house she lived in would one day be hers, though she never really pondered over that as she was more interested in saving up enough to buy and run a car. Tonight, was a squash night for Paula, something she really looked forward to as the week progressed. The excitement sometimes put butterflies in her stomach, she loved it so much.

The central heating sprung out at her as she keyed her way into her home. Spring evenings did get chilly regardless of how hot the day may have been. She exchanged greetings with her parents who knew from her impetuous nature that it was only a brief sojourn before one of her common disappearances.

Upstairs she kept a list of the things to remember, her memory was that bad. But it wasn't always bad. It was just the routine things like remembering when the milk was low or when needing to put special alarm timings on. But if she planned to buy her mother flowers or have her hair done, she would never forget (you sure your hair is not dyed?).

Living in a small town meant traveling to the local sports centre was not a real problem. It was just a good job travelling wasn't a problem because of course she didn't have a car. She was also very reluctant to use the buses late at night and she wouldn't get back till after nine so always had that niggling concern with the squash timing. She often complained to her parents about the low frequency of buses after nine.

'Paula, we'll help you get a car love. You can't keep using the bus, especially at night,' her father would say. She always hated that because she was sure she wanted to get her first car on her own from her own pocket.

Not being the kind to make a scene Paula often kept her thoughts to herself but had clear issues with the state of Lancashire's buses. It was plain to see, like stripes on a zebra. The buses were not well maintained, often dirty and not always kept well. Unlike the stripes on a zebra, the dirt on the buses was not natural nor beautiful.

'How was work?' Usually a question you ask when someone has just got back from work, but Paula got back over half an hour ago. Anyway, she answered unperturbed. The reason for the late question was that she had come home, rushed upstairs and not even shown herself to her parents until then.

'Oh, just the same. No one died today,' she said morbidly. Yesterday Allan Walmersley gave into death. A third heart attack bore down too heavily on his heart, especially as he was seventy-five. It was all too risky for him to go through more surgery, mainly considering his diabetes adding to the complication. He did last seven years after the second heart attack so there was something of a success to boast about.

Paula had not been a nurse all that long, only two years. In that time though she had grown accustomed to death quite quickly. Death, that is, of others. The blessings of the NHS. Regardless of how close she had become to the patients it was totally different to lose one of your family.

She had been a nanny and a shop assistant in the past, only

acquiring her nursing position because of her references from her role as nanny. Small stepping stones leading onto bigger things. She had a caring nature to her, and often considered roles in caring homes as well. Despite the often depressing nature of the role, her compassionate nature had brought her so far into her present role. At times though, she felt burned by her profession, emotionally tired out.

People become harder over time, starting off with clean hands and a clear conscience. The palms get dirtier and dirtier until their conscience becomes blurred. Compassion loses fashion until rogue becomes the vogue. The practice of morality conceding to the procession of ignominy.

Within only a year into her new role Paula had become herself. It had been a real challenge at times and a hardening of the heart at times. In her role as nanny she focused more on handling and playing with babies. Here it was the opposite. She found herself duelling with death, some racing to it faster than others and was getting used to the finality of it all. It had become clear this was the role for her, christened into this world of swirling emotions. It had found her as much as she had found it, a child crying for its mother.

That job application would change her life forever and help to grind out emotions of stone. That invitation to work turned out to provide the most concrete response. It was a career opportunity she was going to wait around for; a nugget of hope she was not going to shun. She was not going to miss that train. Whether she knew where she was going was the real question. Going to be the next Nurse Diane? Yes, she admired the confidence of her elder and control she showed, just at times wondered about the emotional implications to her life.

Could she handle a lifetime of uncompassionate dissolution? Or, maybe it was simply controlled compassion? Whether she could cry those crocodile tears for a lifetime? But who would turn down such an opportunity?

Her dye had been cast, the gown had been donned and the smile had been placed. She was working on her diploma in nursing, so far so good with only one year left to complete. It had at least been a choice she had made, because prior to this there was little direction in her life. Nursing had become her art; dead bodies unfortunately her portfolio; live ones becoming masterpieces. Quite often your career falls in your lap rather than due to a sophisticated plan. In Paula's case the former was the likely deciding factor.

She did enjoy her work as nanny but working as a nanny didn't involve looking after dying patients. It didn't involve being prepared for the unexpected and most traumatic. As with any career it had its vicissitudes. She had collided into the disturbing side of human activity, but twinned with that, also to experience the pleasure of the easing of human pain, customers reborn passing through the checkout with hearts still beating.

Scoffing some prepared tuna sandwiches and orange juice (matching her hair colour), Paula asked how their day was. Father, a computer programmer, had been working on his new accounting package designed to make estimation and analysis that much easier. In actuality all the new version actually offered was the same tools as the previous one he used to use, just in a different colour and font; more appealing to the eye and arguably slightly more fashionable. One could argue the latest version made things a little less confusing.

By now Paula's father had realised that computer packages and applications changed more often than passengers at an airport. The idea of this package update was to allow for only one keystroke or at least minimise keyboard interaction so that the Accounting Department could more efficiently pass sales and purchase ledger information around the company. It wasn't an inspirational idea or particularly jaw dropping, but was needed in his company, reactive rather than proactive. He had been working on it for a few months now and was close to completion so found himself quite busy and involved.

The door closed quietly as Paula left. UPVC double glazed doors and windows have their benefits. Not least that the windows and seals didn't chatter like old clunky basement doors. They had been expensive but her father had really wanted the added security and wanted to save heat and soundproof for some time. As she left, she didn't think twice about having just eaten before going out to play squash. Not advised and not good for digestion. She just looked forward to that game of squash with an uncontrollable buzz; an effervescence.

Then she sweated, then she won, then she left.

***

The sports centre was not far away from their house. About ten minutes by car or twenty by foot when you took the park route using the short cut. Going via the park turned the journey into a diagonal walk, shaving time from an alternative walking trip via roads and streets only. The negative side of this was obviously that travelling through an isolated park at night was not without its problems.

Her parents repeatedly pleaded for her not to go the short

way. But she was stubborn. She had also barred her father from coming to pick her up or drop her off, explaining that she was no longer a child. The banning of her father actually went back a year when he came to pick her up from an evening of squash after she had promised she would be fine to return herself. The scene that followed did so in front of her friends and was not a pretty sight. She actually sent her father home empty handed and she trekked her way through the park in solitude.

That scene, and the motive behind that episode made any future journey home slightly disquieting, not only for her but more so for her father who sat home chewing his nails. Maybe it was more worrying because of a prophetic plea from her father, maybe to scare her into submission? If something did happen, she would never forgive herself (let alone her father forgive her). Thankfully nothing untoward had happened until now; nothing encroached or whispered its way towards her. The only murmurings were of her own conscience.

'It's quicker and safer to come with me... well I'm here now aren't I, Paula. It looked like it was going to rain so I thought it was better I should come... I can also drop your friends off if they need?' It was just a barrage of polite suggestions from a caring parent. Well Paula was having none of it. Sometimes she really wished she had a car just to avoid this kind of interaction with her parents who had offered to help out to lend her the money for a car. But she would have none of it. Wanted to live her own way, do her own things.

'Just go, dad,' pulling him to one side like a misbehaving school boy.

As she trudged her way down the path that day, she cried her way through the park muttering and snivelling to herself. 'It's quicker and safe going through the park. Don't see what his problem is.' Why then, did she speak to herself when she was in the clear, on the parks path, surrounded by street lamps? And why was she still sweating as she strode home. The rustles from the nearby bushes took on an amplification that evening as any passer-by was treated with increased alertness and second then third glances. Her mind did fight with her on that particular trip home; that short journey home that seemed to last hours where she had the hearing of a dog.

That was then, and this was now. Mother and father sat fidgety on the sofa. Paula 2 – 0 Parents. The television was on but no one was watching. That was because they knew she would be taking the park route again.

Warm enough and zipped up, Paula left homeward after declining an offer for company on her way home. The sky could not make up its mind whether to cloud over or remain clear; typical for Lancashire. When she had set off it was cold and clear. Now, in the distance clouds were forming above. And the wind had picked up as well so Paula was not particularly looking forward to her journey home.

After the incident with her father her friends still held a feeling of responsibility to look out for her even though it was a long time ago. Paula knew this and it gnawed away at her even more, made her even more reluctant to take any mental or psychological support. What's this fixation about the park everyone has she would repeatedly think to herself? She couldn't even remember how many times she had gone this way with never even a hint of a problem.

The heart of winter had invited a breeze into the conversation; a strong breeze, symptomatic of the time of year, chilled as ever. Branches, not leaves, wavered in the gusts, winter howls repeating. The general climate was cold, especially when that wind arose. Isobars clung closely together like opposite poles of a magnet, best of friends. Nebulous clouds had formed above and were only slightly illuminated by the invisible sun's rays on the opposite side of the horizon reflecting onto the clouds above. It was not dissimilar to the way the sun's hidden light reflects off the moon when high in the sky.

The chill was expanding with the advent of time in the darkening evening. Crossing the motorway bridge brought forth the raw wind, a constant and unhindered tempestuous flow of cold air blowing like great guns. It was the kind of wind that deafened you. No way could you hear anyone, even if they were within touching distance. It rattled on your eardrums; reverberations amplified. Yet ironically you would hear the sounds of wind thrashing into tree branches. And if you didn't, your imagination would force you to imagine it, just to ensure your mind as well as your bones were chilled.

This long walk across the bridge was so similar to walking through a wind tunnel. Paula knew the wind would greet her there like an old uninvited friend. It always did, yet she was never quite ready. Like when you have a tooth extracted. You know it is coming but you are never quite ready. Some things you just can't anticipate, and this thing she couldn't; the uninvited guest.

It must have been the openness of the area she thought as she wrapped herself up a little more. It frustrated her as always, as if it was her first time.

Well, you should have accepted your father's offer of a lift, shouldn't you?

Maybe it makes my journey home and my squash evening more rewarding she thought. The sturdy railings at the sides of the motorway bridge were now most necessary she realised, not least to ease the chances of anyone being blown over.

As she made it across, a significant drop in knots was experienced. It must have only been a minute, but it seemed longer, as cars passed at high speeds, unaffected by the high winds. The many faces of winter shown in a short spell.

Sighs (of relief?) to get her breath back as she approached the park without a second thought; the bruising weather was normal and expected. Her face was now rosy red with the chilled air pressing forcefully against her skin. Now hair and face were almost matching. The Nike sports bag hung happily over her shoulder not at all impacted by the weather. Just Do It; just get home as quick as possible. Hands in pockets, she marched on, to wade through a park very much easier to navigate in terms of nature's hurdles.

Surrounded by the natural and unnatural, she plodded on, the wind still trying to howl but with less venom as her side was protected by trees. To her right, wild vegetation, parkland and trees; oaks fighting for domineering positions but pretty much mostly bare. To her left, the screech of tires on tarmac; the revving of engines and pollution of light. Not only was the motorway and its cars to her left, but they also travelled in opposing directions. The natural and the unnatural blurted out messages of alarm and caution to those able to hear.

Venus was visible above, soon approaching superior conjunction. She looked back, unable to see the wind at the bridge, but had experienced enough to be able to imagine its severity. It looked so calm, natural and normal which it was, but then the street lights disturbing with noise and the cars screaming with rage.

The path meandered like a stream as she walked adjacent to a spotlight mainly for pedestrians. It was her moment under the spotlight as her shadow gave her even more importance and fame in front of the cheering crowds. Or was it the spotlight stare from a prison guard soon to be followed by blaring sirens? The motorway too, meandered; the homely abode of passing vehicles.

It was much quieter now. The silence was louder. The Dead Sea was calm. This only helped though, to illuminate the chords of cars and lorries, orchestrating their vibrations. The perpetual drone of nearby factory life never faulted. Lancashire industrial life hadn't really recovered from the olden days, leaving it beleaguered and stagnant from the decades of slow-moving manufacturing lines. Shreds from cottonized lives lay tattered to a large degree, laying a blanket over the areas technological decline.

Microscopic sounds of shuffles in vegetation and scuttles of miniature creatures filled her head, further accentuated by the contrast to what had been the violence only a matter of minutes past when traversing the bridge. The telescopic murmurs of engines burping and farting energy further afield, expounded by the raw clarity and drop in nebulosity of outside sounds; a fight of the natural verses that which is not.

The first sounds of this type began; taps on the ground and on her bag and coat. Soft thuds all too familiar for her and neighbours alike. It had started raining. She hardly noticed the cloud growth above that had turned in her direction. It only seemed seconds ago when the sky was clear; when Venus was still in view; now it had gone without even a kiss goodbye. As she looked up, Paula got a drop right in her eye. She jerked back and grunted something in frustration. She quickened her pace.

The waters thickened as the she entered the darker more covered (protected?) surroundings of the park (muddy waters on the horizon?). Forked skeletons pronounced themselves, announced themselves above and to the side, twigs twisting and twitching in the gusts. The dark skyline provided the only light against a darkened x-ray like a plexus of nerves; not too dissimilar to an ordinance survey map, contour lines or crooked signs? The forces of Satan jabbed their horns further as the now distant safety of motorway cars broke the silence.

The protection of the Milky Way above (way, way above) was not so milky, the town's light pollution ensuring that. Yet still it was there, somewhere, if only guided eyes knew. Not tonight though, as the rainclouds above had decided otherwise. To those who tried, the Milky Way provided that clear, unsweetened outlook. Our own galaxy imperceptible amongst other fancies.

She could taste the air, the oxygen stronger here as the rain combined with whatever vegetation was left and of course the increasingly muddying ground. She was, after all, not only surrounded by the limited verdure, but also by the ever enthusiastic winter time, surviving weeds and wild growing plantation. The dampness within the surviving vegetation was a mixture of the past few hours of dryness and the wetness of the winter months, inertia-like qualities lengthening their efforts.

Further arthritic fingers felt upwards for miracle cures, branches bleeding for their bareness to be beaten. Vessels of smoke curled from overactive chimneys, inhuman yet at a twist these veins of cloud could so easily exemplify the ugly paradoxical reality of human affliction to weed. The resilient grasses, wildflower and other weed grew quietly below. It was a chilly night, especially once the wind had played its part.

A bowling green to the left now. An old aged residential parlour 'No Children Allowed'; only those over the age of sixty, or is that even being generous? Far right labels brandished randomly on the walls of the antiquated entrance to the bowling green 'Mozzer woz ere' also modelled on the old brickwork, half depleted, half eroded. Not only was there far right graffiti on the entrance to the bowling green, but also the park entrance itself, warning immigrants to KEEP OUT.

A swastika showed its age alongside more colourful Rastafarian illustrations, proving the arrival of other nationalities. A cosmopolitan bookend of dialog on this literary absurd exercise of artistry. Uncleaned toilets sat deprived of action, brandishing their own eau de toilette. Locks denied entry now but when the day arrived human conscience and limited personal hygiene would make those gates of heaven open.

Occasionally refracted light from distant engines intruded this solo venture along the meandering path. It helped to temporality illuminate the way home (a beacon in the night?). The thought of spontaneous unnatural light greeting her from her side should be met with a degree of caution. To the contrary, though, it broke the creepy sound of fighting vegetation and the crawling whisper of animation. It eased the mild tension incited by the encroaching night, the irrevocable sensation of wanting to look over your shoulder, sensing someone was watching, begging for no one to be there waiting or to follow her on her voyage home.

Navigating the path was not difficult, it was just getting dark now and making images out in the distance proved a challenge. The bigger issue was the developing rain and muddy path she had to traverse. She knew her parents would now be watching the clock, minute by minute, second by second; like the rain, drop by drop.

She occasionally stood on raised flags, badly positioned over time and decay, but at least not mud-covered. It was 1912 when The Titanic hit an iceberg. She occasionally hit soil to the side where the flags ended, frustrating her as her trainers got dirty going off route, scattering damp soil to the sides. The bowling green looked rather vacant with its very own spotlight focusing on nothing. Twinkling streetlight echoed contrastingly with the adjacent darkness now.

Old seating frames now more wooden and dilapidated than the woods used by the bowlers stood regimented, protecting the green further. It wasn't the most professional of habits but it provided a safe haven for those in the slow lane, those whose life had entered the final lap. Taking pride in their costumes, they would dress impeccably, as if going for a job interview, only to find they were only going for a game of crown green bowling. Rising early, never after eight, part of their religious duties. As if they had realised at the tender age of eighty that life is in fact a precious commodity. It took bowling for them to realise?

The grass, carefully combed, stood upwards shining as if well-conditioned hair in the occasional light. A small swarm of moths circled around the spotlight, itself small, as if prohibited to fly far from the circle of light. Their paths so restrained yet frantic, appearing like sparklers on the fifth of November.

Massing moths, winter weeds, spinning spiders.

Paula could see the old, opened iron gate at the entrance to the park. For her it was the exit. The branches and trees blocking the light had passed, the harbour was in sight. With a scant look upwards, she noticed the night sky still cloudy, rain still falling but not too heavy. A more concerted look up would have noticed Megrez and Merak making part of the body of the plough. Gaps in the cloud allowed the astronomical display.

Her uneducated eyes turned towards the rest of her journey home, carefully looking all around her for killers and highwaymen. She was now on the finishing straight of her journey home. The motorway had gone, the car lights and engines with it. In their place was an estate of houses newly built and carefully housed by upwardly mobile families. Houses spawned from cheap foundations and high-rise inflation; homes for the naive or the more unconcerned. An example of the sprouting up of estate housing plastering the pockets of private producers.

To her other side lay the relics of the park. She was out of the park trekking down a part muddy path, parallel to the park, just the sound of her steps and body movements audible. Comparable to a peninsula on a map, she carried on along this thin shielded stretch; the last stretch; a lap of honour? A long gaze upwards finally lowered. In the distance a vague blackened figure grew. Her heart bumped a little more as she had not seen anyone since entering the park.

It was dark in this hoodless tunnel alongside the park but streetlights were lit on the side littered with houses. High rise prices glowing under high tech lighting. This path had just enough room for one person at a time let alone two. Paula began to think of that uncomfortable scenario where there are two people trying to squeeze through. There was hardly enough room to swing a cat. One person would end up treading through the dying dandelions and nettles, wishing for the best.

As she continued home, she got closer to the blackened figure she had once seen in the distance. Despite her slowing down a little the figure was now much closer. She could make out the opening behind his large figure but it seemed so far away. She didn't know whether to speed up or slow down. If she went faster, she would have to confront him that much sooner but if she slowed down her exit would seem that much further away.

The bass drum inside her heart was pounding at thrash metal speed – Why? She didn't really know. All she could make out was a shadow. It was as plain as that, as if he was just an outline. Worse still, the rain had picked up and soon it was pouring with cold droplets, punishing to skin and non-waterproofed clothing. She tried to wrap herself up more and tightened her hood in protection.

A car passed close by, only the sound identifiable and sudden as she had no time to... to call for help? The light was not identifiable because it was hidden by the high fence close to her.

Paula's tension rose as she grew nearer but she had no reason to suspect anything to worry about. The car; was it a sign? Her last hope? But she had no way of knowing or calling for help. The purr of the engine melted away into the splashes of the outside world. Full cloud cover had grown now as a combination of howling winds, splashing rain and water thrashing on distant cars dominated. It seemed to be only a matter of seconds ago when she had beckoned the ethereal stars with her eyes… praying for divine assistance?

An anxiety now swept over her as she noticed he was heavily clothed. Well wrapped and wearing a hood of some kind. It helped to explain his dark heavy appearance. It seemed that all the world was asleep, except for a few cars.

They say 'All the World's a Stage'. Well, this one still had tickets left. She just wanted to appear nonchalant and fright free. The dark would help hide her latent fear, her expected unease at being out at night alone approaching a stranger with a hood. But the mind, it cannot but drift off and think about thoughts of unthinkable possibilities. When in the past, Crimewatch UK used to tell you not to be afraid because serial crime was very rare after showing that exact thing; it only made you feel less secure. One hour of repetitive depictions about real crimes around the country with sobering reconstructions can only make things worse.

She still couldn't make out features but was now not far away from him. It was a Him, she had decided. She had decided from his build but also because he was out at this time alone. She didn't stop a moment to even think that she, herself, was out alone! Was he hiding something?

A spectrum of ideas on what he could be hiding now coloured her head into a chorus of confusion. Thoughts of paranoia also questioned her. Struggling to stay calm but managing to look so, she drifted past his right side, treading unscrupulously into the previously mentioned dying dandelions and nettles.

The nettles were innocuous due to the layering of clothes she had on. With a pounding heart she glanced upwards to a mass of mist and cover. It wasn't much of a look up, the pounding rain ensured that. Her rosy face was now filled with water within seconds, some from above and some from her own body as tension gripped her like only her father could have warned her about.

Taking her mind away from the sky she casually, even forgetfully turned around. Greeted by the unwelcoming surge of a shadow onto another shadow. She panicked. Without thinking she ran, and ran fast. Even after a night of squash she had the energy to run and not look back until temptation got the better of her. In the distance she again could only make out shadows, movement, nothing clear enough to speak about with confidence. But she was sure she saw an attack of some kind, a scuffle, but more than that she could not discern.

The momentarily broken canopy of cloud above like a bare body began to clothe itself again, perhaps trying to protect its nakedness. Within seconds, the blanket reformed itself, warming those beneath and hiding those above.

Below, the unnatural purr of car engines burned petrol on a nearby main road. The more natural flow of thick dark liquid into muddy soil beside the path near the park followed.

16. ECLIPSE

John sat in his own private ward. It was the eve of his operation. It felt like he was in death row awaiting in his own execution cell. His final luxury before his final call. The evening had again drawn in and John had taken care to see the sun set on the horizon. It was as if he was making sure the sun was going to set this evening.

It was a picturesque, almost scripted sun, descending on the horizon. The quietness of the world was noticeable after the rush of wildlife and people from early morning to mid-afternoon. It was close to the time of sunset but the generator of heat above was not only gleaming, it was still releasing good warmth. It was the day after they had predicted the partial eclipse. It seemed that the clouds had misjudged astronomical hearts by one day.

Yesterday, during the evening of the partial eclipse, a towel sheet of cloud had blurred out any fragmented possibilities of a vision. Agony combined with nature's nonconformity, and the years partial solar eclipse had been missed. As if rubbing salt into the wound, looking at the sun now would burn your eyes.

'Look at the eclipse through binoculars or a telescope,' Mr. Moore would have said, 'and you'll burn your eyes irreparably.' Frustrated eyes were bowed to the commands of higher authority. Sweaty hands plagued by unwanted clouds above, maligning the telescopes intentions.

Nature, in its own divine way is master of men. Nature decides when it will rain, triggered by forces above. Men, whether masters of art or supermen of science still could not succeed if nature was not going to allow it. The beating of a heart during cardiac repair can stop at any moment and the swagger of surgeons left to stir quizzically at the cardiograph.

Despite now feeling his doom, John Winters had his own private room and it made him feel more important, but not really in a way he would have liked. The sunset today had been beautiful, even his evening meal (last supper?). It had been divine. The texture of the lean beef had been like velvet and even the vegetables seemed silky and tender. He had begun to appreciate some of the necessities of life.

The quietness with which the evening drew in, even that was enjoyable. The gentle buzz of engines and flutter of the wind acted as a sedative for the appearance of life. The awakening of the night sky was smooth and precise.

Yesterday's canopy of cloud had been correctly predicted as was tonight's weather. The weatherman had not sounded remorseful to astronomical ears for the painful prophecy in missing out on the eclipse, but why should they? When pirates of peace living on their isolated islands hook onto the treasures of revolutionary scientists, their only response to last night's failure was furtive and reluctant congratulations to the hands of nature.

Even if it rained, which it was unlikely to do, it would not have spoiled the atmosphere; the appreciation of earth which John was going through. His emotions were mixed. He felt no assurances for his operation. At the same time, he wanted to enjoy the evening as much as he could.

Eventually that night John slept. It followed the painful thoughts any normal person would undergo with the onset of a life-threatening operation like this. Three hundred sheep and counting. They were all different shapes and sizes but all eventually made it. He dwelled on all his sins, but who hadn't sinned? He spent ages taxing his brain for answers to his questions, finally earning himself some deserved sleep.

He found himself in a huge field of whiteness; it seemed to go on forever. His dream was puzzling and when he realised, he was in and surrounded by snow he was no less puzzled. Stood almost knee high in snow he found himself spinning round trying to find a change in the landscape.

There was nothing but the silhouette of a mountain many miles away. Otherwise the brilliant capacious white place was magnified by daylight. And John found himself shivering in the snow. His teeth were knocking together chattering to themselves in cold and fear, maybe discussing the weather. He wore a chilled closed mouth look, not a grin or a snarl. And he stood there like a fool, not knowing where to put his hands or where to look. He also seemed locked to the spot, or maybe he just didn't see any point in moving. He just felt helpless with no merit in running or calling out for help.

It was the only dream he could remember having that night.

That night to end all nights. It could have been the night Frankenstein was born or when aliens first landed on earth. But it had been a vivid dream, like it was still happening. A picture of such clarity and isolation, where cries or screams would only result in a painful larynx and even more, a loss of hope.

Sat up in his private room, John now felt no security in having his own room. The darkness was now all around him as it was only 4:00 am. He had slept for only a few hours but was not sleepy any more. He was though, tired of life and the situation he was in. Worst of all, he was tired of this hospital and this waiting game he had been asked to play where winning and losing didn't seem to make any difference. He wanted, even now, after waiting months for this operation, to unclasp his shackles and have out of here. He was quite willing to answer 'Yes,' to the question 'Are you prepared to leave now and let the angina eat away at your life?'

John's eyes became heavier and heavier but he knew he would not sleep; knew he would not because of the other even heavier weight at the back of his head called insomnia. The time passed slowly but surely. A new epoch was reached as John, now sat on his armchair, noticed a glimmer of light emerging from the eastern horizon. The sun had begun its ascent into a New World. A world where hope had to be paramount and dreams equally dominant.

17. BLACK CROW

It was in fact still a little dark outside but there were murmurings. There was deathly quiet. Quiet to such a degree that you could have heard a pin dropping on snow or even snow dropping on a pin. A single sparrow then chirped; more followed it in time, their own time. They were just doing the regular thing that they do. Or maybe they were telling the sun to wake up? If so, it was listening.

The sun was rising to an almost cloudless sky. A tiny but bright glowing globe. Venus, the morning star, fought indefatigably against the might of the brightening object but never ever won. A majestic rusty tinge, then orange shades, transforming into friendlier auras. Sometimes regal, it soon became a bright undiscernible glow.

The abstract silhouette of a hilly landscape marked the distance; directed the horizon; allowed the horizon to appear. Straight cloudy formations spoiled the blue sky, air traffic lines occasionally forming. Further disruption and pollution from nearby factory life, now almost a twenty-four-hour event. The proliferation of jet cloud formations slowly developing then more slowly spreading into the sky, comets for the innocent.

Pendle Tower protruded out in the distance, a local tower of historical and cultural significance. Legend has it that a castle stood there a long time ago. Well, long enough ago that there were no remnants there now. In its place a memento to visit that was itself pretty old. More congestion to the morning sky came in the form of small chimney activity from early risers. This though, was few and far between and only from wood burning houses. The nakedness of the sun was now hidden by one of the highest hills in the district. In other areas the divine brightness was starting to cause eyes to squint.

On a roof near to the sun's ascent a black crow with a tremendous beak perched itself. Scratching its innards, it settled onto the corner of the roof right on the guttering. The silhouette was again picturesque. It only lasted a few seconds though as the crow flew off in search of a better spot. Some of the debris from the jets had now become misty and nebulous, strands of cloud well-formed for artistic use. The eastern horizon was still much brighter than the rest of the world.

John yawned as if waking up with the sun. Well, they had almost awoken together. It was his first yawn of the morning.

The yawns continued throughout the morning as John began to feel more and more tired. Simon had popped his head around the door for a quick word of good luck. Most resounding though was it when Kate came in to wish her best. All he had to do now was to give his best. It was a strange restrained relationship they both had now, as if closed off by a door neither of them wanted to open or had the key for. Both were happy not to meet each other nor look for that key. It wasn't the kind of amorous rendezvous of forgiving and tearful eyes, more an awkward awakening of thoughts not verbose or elaborate. It was reserved and short, not dissimilar to a Mike Tyson fight. Unsurprisingly though, the visit would stick in John's mind, more so because it was Kate rather than his last visitor before the big day.

'Your operation today, John,' she had said.

'Thanks for reminding me, Kate, I nearly forgot,' John tried to muse. None of them laughed, though they did grin to each other; a victory. John very rarely called her by her name but today he did. The stifled grins partly due to them both being in a hospital setting and also due to the fact that they were former friends and not really present ones.

She left after about two minutes in a dress John had never seen before, still with some of the attractive qualities she still possessed. Just as John was about to step into the emotional past he stamped on his conscience, determined to at least give himself a chance in the theatre of pain where he could be the hero for a change.

The world's roulette wheel ticked on, carried on spinning as John's numbers were called.

18. OPERATION

The heart bypass operation seemed to go well... at first.

The hospital operating theatre was as dramatic as one would expect. Objects and fluids were well marked as normal. In the middle of the room was John, helpless but the main man all the same. There was a mask to one side which would come onto play a little later in the show. He lay naturally perturbed and very alert waiting on any sudden movements like a scared rabbit. The spotlight was on him as the main starring role. There was a plethora of implements all around him, but especially to his left a little distance away. So much silver all around him, for his role on the silver screen.

Generally, he hated needles but had grown a little accustomed to them as age progressed, even when light shone fiercely down on the needle, piercing the eye as well as the skin. The theatre had more tubes than a Smarties factory and more drips than a restaurant kitchen sink. It was busy in terms of the amount and placement of medical implements; the equivalent of an accountant with a desk bathed with pile after pile of paper, disorganised in an organised way. In a similar way, the surgeon, Dr. Ward (who seemingly named himself after the hospital rather than the other way around) knew what each utensil was and where it should be. You never did know when an emergency would strike. You could call it organised chaos, but in time you would just call it organised.

The two nurses, one junior doctor and surgeon each wore their green face masks, all well-costumed for their role. It was quite a relief for John that it was not the junior doctor himself who was playing the leading part in the operation (or maybe the villain?). With all the NHS cutbacks John felt lucky that at least the main man was going to perform the stunts. The lighting was also immaculate. Not too bright but still strong and clear. Too bright would have meant a lack of clarity for Dr. Ward's observations and actions; too dark would obviously have created its own issues. But the main light, the spotlight, well that was just so strong and sharp but thankfully only occasionally used. As lead for this scene, perhaps it was right to be focused on John.

There was a hiccup or two during the operation, when the surgeon seemed to get one of his lines wrong. It was often possible to transfer a vein from one leg to the heart. On this occasion at the last minute it was decided best to use the radial artery from the arm as it often provided better long-term results.

Eventually, take two had declared the arm was the best option for the grafting between heart and vein to ensure the most suitable blood flow. Dr. Ward therefore cut along the inside of the arm to obtain the relevant artery to act as John's new supply route of blood to his heart via the graft. For some reason the doctor had decided to change his plans and use the arms artery rather than his leg but only took this decision very late on. It was a tactic he had used many times before.

Having two arteries blocked pushed John up the waiting list queue, but still a six month wait for the operation had not been the most welcoming. After such a time you had almost grown accustomed to your condition, the insecurity and having adapted to life with the blockages. But, after the six months John had become lucky still to be one of the privileged few to have finally received his care.

The junior doctor looked on, not in the least bit queasy to be witness to John's internal juicy parts. He was a human biologist and hoped soon to be a master of his trade as he was keen and had to be to competent. The nurses, they were nonchalant, had been there so many times before yet had accrued no signs of boredom; showing equal compassion like it was the first time with benevolent fervour. This was the caring profession, not voyeuristic junior doctors looking to voyage over the gore or capitalistic surgeons waiting to capitalise. These were the 'Backroom Boys', the producers, directors, make-up artists, all rolled up into one. The ones who obtained little credit or reward, remaining on the undercard, with mention only in the small print at the end of the film.

One further incident during the operation, albeit minor was that John awoke unexpectedly. It was at the moment the surgeon was switching scalpels. Of course, John hardly knew where he was for the first few seconds, and was extremely groggy. The gas somehow had worn off as John moved more with his eyes than anything else. 'Help me' he eyes screamed like a helpless child calling upwards; upwards in search of hope and salvation like a worshipper begging for guidance or a beaten boxer looking for inspiration.

With all the drowsiness, John could also have been a drunk waking up in the morning in search of the black coffee. Despite his drowsiness he did realise he had awoken in the operation. Minor unease hit the medical staff almost as much as John, though his paralysis fortunately had not been contagious. A plethora of eyes searched for partners in search of a solution. Finally, the surgeon called for the unemployed gas mask, sat sleeping at his side, ready and willing to play a part. Instantaneously, it smothered John's mouth in relief like a diver's mouthpiece. This time though it provided unconsciousness rather than a diver's welcome perception of his surroundings.

It had been a short scene of complication in this story of many jigsaw pieces. Soon after this, John settled into familiar territory as dreamland overtook him. This time his dream possessed a sinister reality and familiarity, in its odd way reassuring. It was familiar to John like his old Aunty Sheila who was there to rear him as a child (or stunt his growth?), or the way Kate used to pick at the end of her long nails when under stress.

His dream world had that familiarity that he knew so well, but didn't necessarily want to visit that often. Like that uninvited guest that you know you'll find knocking at your door at some point of the evening. The uncontrollable truth knocking at your door.

During his operation John again encountered the familiar dream, surrounded by snow in a huge spacious world. It felt so real even though it was a dream. And he felt so helpless, unable to move, paralyzed and lacking lucidity. Stood there, knee deep in a bath of ice and snow, John knew he had to run but did not know where to go. More importantly, even if he did know where to go, he would not be able to move, he was stuck in this ice and snow; a paralyzed patient. So, he ended up glued to the spot fretting internally.

On his couch John shivered, the bed shaking and implements responded in turn. The surgeon noticed this and was clearly a little surprised. He glanced over at his heart rate monitor. The green lines looked normal and as should be expected. They resembled palpations when looking at John, but nothing showed up on the machine. The intuition and experience of the doctor correctly conjectured that it may be a dream of some kind causing this. Ward had realised that operations of this magnitude would have or could have a variety of reactions on human activity, sometimes different, sometimes strange.

But the heartbeat kept quickening as the green lines got closer together as if themselves in a race. Ward himself began to sweat as if he was in the race himself. A flash in John's head now. He saw a sun, huge and bright and hot, and not before time. It settled John into a serene tranquillity, now ready for the rest of his ordeal. The past images though, hung in the back of John's mind like a bad egg. And even in his unconsciousness the images sent shivers down his spine; a chill emanating from somewhere in the back of his mind. The theatre of dreams was delivering a taste of a nightmare beyond his control. John was again surrounded by snow and not too far away, a tree, naked, bare and old. Its fork branches grasped upwards.

And there was nothing John could do as the doctor saw John's personal television screen graph turn more and more jerky; it was turning into a soap opera. The screen started to look like the NASDAQ on a more turbulent day, with a mixture of V's and W's bombarding the screen. From being a picture of calm John was now shivering with almost panic? It was now more like a crash with day traders frantically looking up for inspiration as lines jolted in all directions and no sanity was identifiable amongst the ups and downs. Were the curtains about to close?

Dr. Ward called repeatedly for heart beat readings, blood pressure levels, he was clearly concerned. If his haste was not enough then his perspiration was. John too, was sweating, or maybe it was cold sweat? Inside he was cool, his bones felt like ice, and despite being under anesthetic he had some awareness of what was going on. He found himself stuck again in this sea of snow, paralyzed, yet strangely knowing he must move.

The puzzled looks on the medical staff faces was odd because everything looked to be going to plan as they could not figure out what the anomaly was. John seemed under control for most of the operation, just started suddenly shaking for no apparent or identifiable reason. He would just start shaking. Now and then the chaotic circus would kick in and John would start to shiver. Ward had performed many operations over the years but never seen a response like this before. Over time, he just put it down to John's own way of dealing with the anaesthesia.

Shaking, shivering…
Shaking, shivering…
Shaking, shivering…
STOP!

19. VISITS

And then it was yesterday and John was still alive. The operation had become just another statistic; part of another graph despite the drama; another tick in the NHS box of ticks.

It was early April and spring was starting up but starting up, auspiciously. Vernal signs had begun earlier but true blue skies had failed to penetrate until today. It was a great day; a day of change, change for the better, not a change from summer to autumn or autumn to winter. This was a change to better climes as always, the case when spring approached. The days had started to get longer. Finally, leaves had started to shine early green from the sun's rays; a façade of wetness amongst a truism of dryness. Cloudless skies approaching; reflections thus all a glitter; petals sometimes all a flutter. Rusty, almost dusty car door handles greeted their owners; windows creaked as owners opened them, early spring heat welcoming drivers. It was a splendid day and time of year. Window cleaners lived for days like this; gardeners awoke for welcomes like this. The preamble of summer was now in scope.

Market stalls in full bloom, displaying auras of occasional grace. Fruit and veg designs, designed to dream up desires. Chatter from folk much more concerted and cheerier. Eyes pleased with the thankless role performed by meteorologists, messengers delivering words of prophecy (or doom) to homes of hope.

Tree branches were now a little stronger, gaining strength and life. Although not leaved in abundance they were comprehensively thicker buds and twigs from the season anew. Branched arms stretched higher. The birth, the growth, the bright side of life marked by the hands ruled by nature, reaching up and grasping high for life and energy.

Today, the calls for warmth had finally been answered and the previous disappointments now a distant memory. Nature was displaying the tell-tale signs of seasonal norms. Newspaper reports would have read fine and sunny, with temperatures warm for this time of year. That it was and it was also a wonderful start to John Winters new lease of life.

John knew little or nothing about his past operation. He just felt very fatigued, as if he hadn't slept for three nights. It was that strange kind of tiredness that coerced you to shut your eyes for a little comfort, due to the soporific designs of drugs, then the restlessness evoked by this capitulation causing eyelids to close. It was, of course, very frustrating but obviously a desired effect of the drugs to invoke rest.

Intertwined within these bouts of tiredness and restlessness was John's ex-wife, who had found it in her heart to pay a visit. He recalled her asking him if there was any chest pain now. There was, but John had been told this was to be expected.

She at least tried to be compassionate without looking him in the eye. It was as if there was some great barrier between them now. There was, and it was called 'Not Enjoying Each Other's Company'. Due to the effects of the drugs and in a merciful way John did not even recall too much of her visit. To prove it wasn't his imagination she had left a get well soon card.

It was the way she had spoken in muffled tones. 'How was the operation?' she had asked him, 'Are you okay?' It was the standard question showing her lack of genuine interest. It wasn't the most sympathetic act of concern from his estranged wife. As if she was concerting the already well moulded knowledge that there was no possibility of them ever returning to each other. John had become a desperate man, and would probably have greeted her back if he saw a ray of light through the door or hope.

Some of his other friends, more like acquaintances, had also been to see him with the conclusion of his operation. Although not bequeathed with a wealth of friends, John did have a share of those who brought themselves out of the woodwork to see how he was. It was as much for old time's sake than anything else. As if an obligation. Simon of course, paid a visit. Neil and Sarah did, as did a recent friend Steve, from the block of flats where he was staying.

Simon, his only real friend, had been to see him before and after his operation. He was genuinely concerned and relieved to find out it all seemed to go well. Well, at least, all's well that ends well. Throughout John's separation Simon had been there to sympathise and listen to John, viewing him as the culprit in the whole affair (or lack of).

Simon had relived the thick and thin of the marital collapse and was relieved he had not had to become a part of the meta-phorical conflagration. Even with his inexperience of marriage problems Simon proved to be commendably sympathetic and concerned. He had been the one who had supported John throughout. Perhaps he understood more having gone through so many hospital visits himself.

Neil and Sarah had known John for years, soon after they got married meeting him and his ex-wife at the local cricket club. Neil and John also knew each other from work. They always got on well together, especially when they were a foursome. The tide had turned somewhat since the divorce though, but the couple still clung onto the vague sympathy and understanding of being fellow colleagues.

As time had passed, they naturally met less and this had been the first time they as a couple had met outside work for over a year. He noticed quite clearly Sarah had put on weight but he was reluctant to mention it. It was almost as if she knew the way they looked at each other and the shifty way she shuffled uncomfortably in the small NHS sofa.

Yes, I know I put weight on, John, her mind spoke to John. She was clearly uncomfortable with the little visit and had always been Kate's contact. John never uttered a word to her as he feared he may end up mentioning something about her weight. Was she trying to hold her stomach in, John had thought on more than one occasion during their short visit? It was obvious she was. He knew it and she did. It was conversational telepathy. John let her know about her weight problem through his and her body language. They both knew it but both wanted to hide it.

Neil, long-legged and fair, had visited occasionally to keep up appearances but John, emotionally scarred by the divorce had not been to visit him as he felt a little embarrassed. There were clear awkward moments that accompanied having not met someone for a long time. It had been a long time since John had also not been to the cricket club, probably five seasons now. Being a social place John of course had not been that social, thus had not been best of friends recently. Neil and Sarah stayed a while and were interrupted by the arrival of Steve.

Steve was a short hypochondriac from the same block of flats as John. It was little awkward as they had never been introduced before, so naturally Neil wondered who this was. Steve had been a good acquaintance over the past year or two. Even being in his forties he always carried around his Ventolin inhaler, as since birth he had suffered from asthma. What kept the friendship going was not only the fact that John had very few options but also that Steve also had a good sense of humour, being able to give or take a joke. Neil and Sarah soon left, clearly feeling out of place and not part of the crowd anymore. Well, they had at least ticked their box, their visit box.

John enjoyed the sense of humour Steve brought to a conversation, even though he could hit below the belt. Call it insensitive or call it down to earth. He at least cheered John up after the operation. 'Any pain John?' Steve questioned after a while, feeling more comfortable since Neil and Sarah had left.

'Never felt a thing' said John, 'Quite amazing what they can do nowadays. Feel some minor pains now but doctor said that is normal because the body got so used to it. I almost feel like saying I feel like a new man but that is being a little premature, I think. Where the stitching is it does feel a little itchy though. Again, I think that's normal. The wonders of modern technology. They take a vein or an artery from the arm and link it to your chest. Can you believe that?' John almost couldn't believe it himself. It made it all that much more amazing to Steve, who had become genuinely attentive. 'And they say the new bypass with a riveted tube allows for ventilation and easer movement of blood through the new passage. It should mean that this vein is less likely to get clogged up again. In short, I might live forever!'

Steve was genuinely impressed and surprised. 'So, the Big Macs are on you then, John?'

'Ah… not for a while yet,' said John excusing himself. 'Bit chilly for spring isn't it Steve?'

'Cold, it's five degrees higher than last week, where've you been, in a coma or something?'

John actually felt quite cold, but thought of it as some kind of aftereffect or body change. At least his heart was now clear and pumping happily now he thought.

20. STEVE

'So, how are you, Steve? I haven't seen you for a while? Are you still seeing that Helen?'

'Oh her, no, we parted ways ages ago, a mutual understanding, or misunderstanding as the case may be. I'm going solo at the moment. Much easier to agree on something when you're solo.' Steve was always like a breath of fresh air; always came and left with a smile that was quite contagious. Even though he was in his late forties, Steve often still behaved like he was in his twenties.

The truth was that Steve was very rarely going out with someone. Time, and his own manufactured wisdom, had led him to the conclusion that he eventually always preferred his own company, a sole trader. He didn't like the baggage of life and responsibilities and whilst still able to live independent, he generally chose that route.

The first thing that struck you about Steve was his height, as if stunted, though not quite a dwarf. He put his vertical challenge down to the fact that since he could remember he had been an asthma sufferer. His had read somewhere that being a weezer could stunt growth though it was not a must and, well, he just got unlucky. But he never let it get him down. His carefree attitude to life kind of suited his challenges as he had successfully made his way into his mid-forties.

John was clearly feeling chilly. He kept shivering and trying to cover himself with blankets. He kept looking towards the window as if trying to find out where the draft was coming from, or maybe trying to use powers of telekinesis to make the air warmer. Trying to ignore the obvious shivers of John, Steve tried to break the silence. 'So, when did they say you could go home?' asked Steve.

'Hopefully, in three days I was told. Let's see. The flats are still there aren't they?' It was a rhetorical question.

'They're missing you mate, or should I say, flat mate.' It was one of Steve's common attempts at being funny and clever at the same time. Steve had been one of his closer friends since moving into the Warner Street block of flats a couple of years ago. They were reasonable and not too dilapidated like most of the rest of the town. But still, after life with Kate, this living was a real depressing way of looking at life. The bottom line was, they were not homely.

Steve stopped on his way out to speak to the nurse to go check on John and the heating in his room, though he knew the temperature was just fine in there. Maybe he has a fever from the operation he comforted himself with. The nurse did reassure Steve, confirming that erratic body responses were common after major surgery. It's just a case of waiting for your body to adjust, to accept the new way of life; adjusting to artificial engineering; allowing for one to accept a new norm after sometimes decades of ugly living.

The days and weeks passed as John continued his rehabilitation. Springtime was passing but John's cold spells and shivers continued.

21. CUPBOARD

It was a many weeks after his release from hospital and John was just getting accustomed to his lonesome home again. Spring was coming towards its end; the approaching long awaited smile of summer was nearby. Although John had lived on his own for a few years now it still left not only a morose feeling, but also an acrid revengeful one. It was like starting all over again every day in this place of emptiness.

Early morning, and he found himself shuffle out of bed. He just took it for granted that he wanted to go to the toilet even though he didn't want to leave the nice, warm comforting bed now. How he hated entering back into a ruffled cool bed. The cold appearing darkness seemed to be everywhere, as it does when one leaves their beds. Scatterings of thin light filtered through the dark coloured curtains providing what limited guidance there was available. The synodic month was just past its midpoint. The moon, with its mares becoming increasingly visible to binocular eyes and more so to telescoped vision. The dominant Copernicus and Tycho showing their skin unashamedly; gigantic craters and mountain features for watchers to drool, overzealous and excited. Light was not only emanating from the moon; streetlamps also presented their form of artificial light through slits and into John's bedroom window.

Without even bothering to turn on the light John, figuring out it was the middle of the night, stumbled out of bed and made his way to the bathroom. What was to follow was not dissimilar to receiving a stab in the back.

John had become very carefree and negligent, especially over the last year. He would use household goods and leave them to put themselves away. They never would, of course, and often remained there for weeks like undisciplined children. Screwdrivers, milk cartons, old newspapers, all left untampered around the house to pick up dust. It was all rather subliminal to John who had not realised that his grip on reality was getting looser and looser. Dustbins collected more and more rubbish, a symbol of John's reluctance to try and move on in life. Even after the operation his encounter with divorce still haunted him.

Surprise, surprise though, about six months ago John went out, as if on impulse, to purchase some self-assembly cabinets and a cupboard and drawers for his bedroom. It must have been one of his more optimistic days; had to have been. When he got around to it John finally managed to create a bedside cabinet and set of drawers for his bedroom. It was a smallish room in the flat he had as he had lost a lot in the marriage breakup. He felt a lack of justice, though Kate did also work with him at Comfort Upholstery. Maybe he should have fought harder to get more financial justice for himself from the divorce? Problem was that he still had affection for her and part of him didn't want to hurt her feelings so allowed her to take financial advantage during the divorce. Now though, he was having belated thoughts; feeling himself robbed of his own home and wealth, an internal exile. And now a lonely man in an impassive flat.

A moment of glory accompanied the construction of his furniture, even though in the past it would have been no big deal. His background in the upholstery world had given him enough knowledge to assemble this kind of furniture. Now though, due to his emotional disturbances the simplest of tasks for him had become a challenge.

He sat there are a while and stared into space, a blend of serenity and success. Putting the new furniture in place meant replacing the old furniture, hence John, now tired, just put the old cabinet and drawers in a small aisle section in his bedroom. He gleamed at the additions to his bedroom, picturing further improvements; perhaps a little too far into the future. For a moment John's cognitive mind thought back to his childhood days. It was a very vague and cloudy memory of the bedroom cupboard at Aunty Sheila's. Over the years the memory had become more and more sinister as the image of that cupboard never, ever being closed and the squeak that accompanied trying to close it. It just never closed, but if you ever closed it, at least temporarily, it would squeak its way open within seconds. He always thought there was someone inside pushing that door open.

He's looking at you. You see the saliva running down his mouth? He looks hungry... You look tasty... You wanna start running now???

The image of the Jester flashed in his mind; an image spawned from his torrid youth spent with her. Maybe it had been the jester after all that lived in that cupboard. Maybe it made those noises; noises that at night would be too much for anyone, given the situation. As a child, things took on a different meaning for him. Things that could be reasonably defined taking on the realms of the impossible. John was sure at times he saw eyes gleaming through the hinges of the cupboard, continually just staring at him; insatiable eyes, waiting for the right moment. And there were times when Aunty Sheila would ask him to bring a sheet from that cupboard. That moment he would always dread a fear with inevitability, so much so that most of the time he would conveniently forget to make up some random excuse. And if ever he did end up going into the cupboard it would be with the utmost caution, ensuring numerous glances all around the room before going anywhere near to the cupboard. Sometimes he could swear he heard a sound from in there; breathing or even hissing coming from inside. It was all as real as reality.

John's surprise, as mentioned earlier, hit him again as part of him shook himself to wipe away the distant memories of the bad old days with Aunty Sheila. He was back in the real world, him and his new heart stumbling his way to the bathroom. Automatic movements gained him some distance, but a great bony and loud thud welcomed his progression. The old bedside cupboard, still in the aisle, met John's carefree foot heavily in line with his stride forward.

Doesn't the bedroom look lovely, new cabinets and all…

For a split second the pain didn't hit him, as if suspended and gathering up momentum to send a crashing warhead right through his brain.

What a pretty bedroom...

The pain nearly obliterated John; had never felt anything like it. It was as if a blunt knife was cracking into your leg, no... the bone. More like a thumping, thudding pain than a sharp concise connection. The pain seemed to spread in a matter of milliseconds, initially attacking the biting point then over to his toes. It was awesome, but not to John.

Wow, new cabinets!

Due to the immediacy of his injury John was able to stagger over to the bathroom, now not even feeling any urgency to vacate his bowels. Yet John sat on the toilet all the same, not wanting to accept a wasted journey. Cool air glided across his head. Alarm then studded John; urgency plied at him; even more, shock shouted at him. It took him a while to even realise what was going on. A new feeling... no, a new old feeling. Thirty years, more maybe, since the last time. It was migraine attack, but not a normal one. In his teenage years they bred like leaves on a tree. Then, snap, like a winter tree, the migraines, similar to leaves, just disappeared.

It was a migraine on drugs. Déjà vu clutched at him as his right eye and above became a hive of pulsating stars too nebulous to discern. It all happened in seconds. Blindly raising his pyjama bottoms John floundered for the door. A feeling of nausea then emerged. He had never experienced a migraine with nausea before though had heard it was a common symptom of a migraine.

Sweating, John's emotions seemed to be in overdrive. He was confused and that didn't help matters. Amidst the confusion he even thought that he was having a brain haemorrhage, the pain was so bad. He hobbled back to his bed, dreaming of somewhere to relax his mind and thoughts. He punched the door open, this time being more aware of the cupboard so as not to bang into it again.

It was dark in his room, yet comforting. Half dangling off the bed, John drowned himself in the warmth of his sheets. His migraine was easing, though he was unable to relax for a while as he eventually shivered himself to sleep. His foot was still throbbing with heat and natures electricity. An envelope of sweat, cold sweat, formed itself around John's body as he curled himself up more and more.

The next morning newer buds were clearly visible in the local park, that is if you were willing to go and take a look.

22. SUMMER

Snow-like particles dotted the verdure, thickening with each day. The more appropriate weeds, buttercups and dandelions had begun sprouting simultaneously. Uglier weeds, the nettles and dock leaves also had sprung up in time, evening up the balance of nature. It was an unscripted plethora of green shades and bloom scattered all around, yet probably the most naturally well written piece of art nonetheless.

In areas blossom had begun carpeting parks and gardens, a choice of colours at your disposal. As a preface it had been windy, displacing the newly flowered trees and plants of their flowers, as nature's own planting formula cycle took place. Squinty eyes as shades of May approached. In a week, temperatures had doubled, the funeral march of winter now a distant memory as it had now fully fallen into hands of the precursor of summer. Azure above, a shine below. A turn of fate in the weather, for the better.

As the days went by, a greater abundance of miscellaneous growth had developed, with the ground hardening slowly until the inevitable rains would fall and change the tide. What appeared like wedding blossom coagulated at certain points, puddles in places yet dry and fresh. In other areas the blossom had massed itself into corner steps or other welcoming confetti abodes.

Insect population multiplied, that is bar the cantankerous spiders who often preferred the dampness of autumn. Yet bees, wasps and other mites had already migrated enough to encroach upon the usual suspects. A time when fly spray sales soar to keep the aggressors at bay.

Summer was coming.

23. BOGEY

He felt hard mucus in his nose, sometimes slightly painful. Something had to be done. It was pretty normal in many ways but was on both sides of his nose. So, he ambled over to the bathroom to get the bogey out. Turning the sink tap, the gush of the water spat on the sink base.

For so long he had been meaning to buy a filter for the tap to slow down the speed of the flow, but had never got around to it. It would also have meant wasting less water, lower bills and better for the environment. To be honest despite having so many reasons for getting the filter, he had one reason why it had not been done, indolence. It had become his nature, to procrastinate. His laziness was directly opposed to his upbringing, especially spending many years in the army, but that was a different life. So, the water continued to burst forward as if escaping to a better place; as if relieved to rush to a draining death.

He slapped some of the escaping water on his face and nose without hesitation. So much so, that half of the water slapped onto the floor. What a relief for that water, escaping the lair of the drain, hence avoiding a painful death. Droplets of water sprayed onto his trousers, making it look like he had peed his pants. He instantly thought to himself how embarrassing it was, even though no one was likely to ever see him with water stains on his zipper. Instinctively, he tried to wipe the water droplets away from his trousers, only making it worse. Now it really looked like he had peed his pants, as if he was auditioning for the role of 'The Man Who Drank Too Much.'

He wiped his nose few times, normally it helped clearing out the dirt from his nose. But this time it only really worked after he had flushed out his nose with water like a pipe. This time he had to really snort with vigour. The bogeys would not succumb. They were fighters of the resistance. It was war and both sides knew it.

John blew hard, almost turning his face into a purple balloon. It made him look and feel like a clown, but John was in no mood to play games. Finally, the bogeyman was exhumed and swimming in the basin like a desperately drowning swimmer.

It had been a titanic battle, whirling around the room uncontrollably battling against the force of the water. But there could be only one winner. The more he willed the bogey down the drain, the more it seemed to swoosh around the sink; the orchestra still played on. The water was certainly going down in a clockwise direction John thought to himself. He had read somewhere that in the northern hemisphere water goes down a sink in a clockwise direction and in an anticlockwise direction in the southern hemisphere. John believed anything so accepted it, even though he was more focused on the bogey evading extinction in his sink.

That's typical thought John, as the bogey got a lifeline and stuck on the side of the sink. He opened the taps again, splashing water inevitably all over the place. The last thing he was going to do was use his hands to push the bogey down, that would be disgusting. So, he cupped his hands full of water and threw it harshly at the aggressor. Water again flew all over the place, even onto the mirror opposite him. He tried two or three times. Eventually he sunk the ship and his sink was clean.

John wiped his face and especially his nose, checking to make sure he was clear of any remnants from his little problem to rid himself of aliens. He could breathe nice and easy once again, and felt satisfaction. He headed back into his room to get on with his life. Well at least he tried to.

He casually wiped away the damp remnants again from his face as he walked back. It was a promising, almost optimistic morning now, as spring was coming to a close. Optimism was something John had not been too familiar with of late so he took all he could. The springs of hope amidst a past cauldron of sadness and bad news. Since his divorce and subsequent operation, he had not had much to cheer about. Nothing to sprinkle a little tinsel about. It had been a season of discontent and today it felt like hope finally had sprung eternal. And, having very few friends to get him through his hurt it had not been a bed of roses.

As he walked back, his face now pretty much dry, he took a nonchalant wipe of his face and nose; just a normal check to make sure his face was still there. Then a drop slapped onto the bathroom floor. It was tiled carpet, now old and due for change. Because it was this type of surface the droplet made a small slap on the floor; more of a high pitch sound yet audible as a small crack on the floor. John wondered why his nose was even dripping especially as he had just cleaned and dried it well enough. Well, he thought he had, but obviously hadn't.

Instinctively he turned back to dry his face again, the light still a little low for the early morning. It had only been a casual wipe with his index finger like he had done a hundred times before. Then he glanced down at his finger; blood. It didn't register at first because it felt just like water until he looked at it. Then, knowing it was blood made it feel different on his finger. A bit like eating a rodent. It tastes similar to chicken until someone tells you it is a bloody rat! It was the same for John until he saw the crimson liquid drip down his finger. A more concerted look down told him that the drop on the floor was also the same. It was a little shocking and surprising.

Yes, buddy, it's real blood. Not messing around now. Not child's play now. This is for real.

He had never had a nose bleed before in all his life.

Welcome to the club, Mr. Winters.

It was strange because it felt so much like a drop of water, nothing different. It didn't feel in any way thicker. That is, until he knew it really was blood.

In any case, it was strange to him, unusual and John instinctively turned to the sink, opening the tap once again. The water swooshed around and splashed once again, and this time he was not too concerned about the water splashing around all over the place. It fired over his trousers again, making it look like fresh pee. But this time he could care less. He was more concerned about the red droplets now dripping down the sink. Each drop added a fraction more alarm to his state. He was also feeling colder but the blood loss was somehow returning heat back to his body. Each red drop though, getting diluted amongst the clear water, oddly spreading so quickly and effectively that it looked like paint, water colour paint. Mini droplets dissipated from the main drop were also spat on the walls now.

At least the escaping blood from his nose was making him feel a little warmer, and somehow strangely he welcomed this. Almost paradoxically, the loss of this fluid was making him feel better. A few seconds ago, he was starting to shake and he felt a migraine coming. Maybe the shock of the nose bleed from the effort to release the dirt from his nose had scared away those feared emotions and feelings. The sense of normality though, however bizarre, was a welcome guest.

Casually, the blood drops leaked from his nose, like it was a simple nasal discharge that happened whenever you got a runny nose. Within a few seconds though, it was over. The blood had stopped and there were sighs of relief.

For a while John just kept on brushing his nose, more of a self-conscious reaction. To an onlooker it would look like he was checking that his nose was still there. Each time he touched his nose to check it was dry, reassuringly so, it was. But it sure was a strange episode, especially as he had never even had a nose bleed before.

John sat on the edge of the bed, relieved yet a little confused. After a few minutes he got on with his life.

24. BUS

At the weekend John went window shopping, though he didn't come back with any windows. It was predominantly to get him out of the flat. Although he did feel a new man in many ways (or an old man in new clothes), he was still wounded by his own self-inflicted loneliness.

His actions were very cautious and very self-conscious. He didn't want to overstretch or push himself too much especially based on medical advice. He was still under instruction from the medics but could not believe how at ease his body felt. He'd felt no pain since gaining consciousness, not even many shadow pains the doctor said he may well feel.

A little tired, John decided to bus it back. He had walked it to the nearby town of Ramsbottom but wasn't used to it and how he felt it; how he felt it now. Cramp had caused him to almost hobble and curl his toes to ease the creasing pain.

Ramsbottom was only a small town with only a couple of main streets and a few thousand residents, but with scenic views of the nearby hills. There were a few big retailers there and an industrial estate with some factories as well as some office staff, but other than that it was a far cry from city life. John knew the area well, having spent all of his life in the region. It was great for the locals, though the youth now could not live without weekend trips to Manchester or Liverpool for amusement.

Sweat had formed on John's forehead as he sat, tired and waiting for the bus. It was only a half hour walk through splendidly forested roads, old roads. You could paint a picture of immense attraction for city folk; green scenery, inspiring summer walks and even nature trails. Yet even though the sweat had formed on John's head he didn't feel the warmth. His feet were sweaty and hot but his body as a whole felt cool as if the wind was somehow chilly. It wasn't though, not chilly at all. It was a beautiful day. The air was warming, mild and not at all chilly.

So, there were two main reasons why John had decided to return by bus. Firstly, he was now not used to such a tiring walk especially since his operation. Secondly, he was also feeling cold, even though the sounds of summer were echoing through the trees. He just couldn't figure it out. Why the hell was he feeling cold on such a lovely summer's day? He dismissed it and just agreed that it all seemed too trivial to confront. There was no pain or distress, no ache or even fever. It was just strange for want of a better word, as if he was in the grip of autumns encroaching temperatures.

Waiting at the bus stop was a few degrees cooler. John felt this and made it apparent by huddling up inside his jacket. Some of the others waiting at the bus stop looked in surprise as it clearly was not the weather John was responding to. Others carried on unperturbed. Some just gave themselves a little distance as he did look a little weird.

The 464 from Rochdale came to a familiar screeching halt. The queue of people rose like a wave at a football match, as the departing passengers left the bus like football fans leaving a match. John joined the queue as people glanced cautiously at him, their interest in his appearance remained untainted.

The bus was already fairly full when John got on. He was near the back of the queue as he entered and found only two spaces available. He was feeling a little self-conscious due the fact that he was so well wrapped whilst all the others were dressed in such a summery way. He chose a space next to a Chinese girl who looked about thirty-years-old to John. Surprisingly, she was almost as wrapped up as he was, in a jacket with her long, dark and straight hair hanging out of the jacket. She didn't flinch when John sat next to her, didn't even notice him. This seemed quite odd to John who had been given so much attention from the other passengers.

Two elderly women sat in gossip at the front of the bus. One sounded undoubtedly insane, whilst the other was bordering insanity and on her way to succeed as she was so intrigued by the insane conversations of her compatriot. They would talk about one thing then switch to another without completing the first one; a definite sign. Or the other would hastily interject with something completely different. 'You know James is getting married again, his third time, but this time we're all sure it's the right girl. Oh, he's such a great boy.' One of the women spoke with such love for her son in his forties like he was still ten years old.

The other woman interjected in high pitch but almost whispered tones. 'Oh, you know Jack from number thirty-two, he was screaming so loud last night, must have been drunk.'

'Did you see they put up the prices again at Finley's, cigarettes gone up again,' bounced back the first woman.

'Oh, you know Jim, he slept so bad last night, all the shouting and screaming from the neighbours. Enough to keep he dogs awake all night.' It was verbal table tennis. They weren't really interested in each other's conversation. All they were interested in was their own comments and getting them across. Cynical, yes, but in a paradoxical way they really loved each other's company; were accustomed to this gossip centred way of life. Each would have their turn with the other agreeing, conforming comfortingly. In truth though it wasn't really that comfortingly in the way they spoke.

The other passengers could just hear a blur of high and low tones, laughs and coughs, wheezes and sighs, all intermingled with laughs and looks of amazement. As one of the women began, the other was researching her mind for her next comment. It was like a competition. Who could talk the most and irritate the other passengers the most? It was about equal; they were both pretty good.

'You know that tuna they recalled last week, Liz, the one they found had fragments of glass in? Well our Roger only had a tin of it in his cupboard.' She spoke in disbelief in a formation of higher and higher tones.

'Oh. I heard about it, Mary, I heard about it. It was in the Free Press I think, wasn't it? Isn't it amazing? I once bought a six pack of mixed fruit yoghurts, and when I got home, they were all off. Can you believe it? It never used to happen. All these chemicals and artificial things they put in nowadays. I remember when they used to cook food. Now look at us. The younger generation using microwaves for everything. You'll never catch me near a microwave. Unnatural it is, it really is. No wonder everyone has cancer these days. Never used to happen.' She was on a roll now. Ironically Liz had been living with breast cancer for a few years now but the doctors had decided to just treat it and keep it in check. She seemed to have forgot that detail in her roast. 'Mobile phones too, I'm sure they also cause cancer. Well they're not gonna catch me. Who needs a mobile phone? Not me, I assure you that.'

Ironically the girl in front of the two old women was madly chatting away to someone on her mobile, seemingly enjoying every minute of it. The two pensioners looked at the girl, then looked at each other, then shook their heads simultaneously. Their mutterings could be heard all around the bus, ironically just as distracting as the girl was continuously talking on her mobile. It was only when the bus driver put his foot on the accelerator that their voices became inaudible.

In another metaphorical attempt at dissing the pensioners, a few seats away another teenager sat, foot tapping whilst listening to music on his phone; further evidence that maybe the pensioners had quite possibly become 'out of date'. This girl was loudly and impolitely listening to what seemed to others to be very tinny music. It wasn't necessarily the case but just sounded like this from a distance. It was her own private party, and the more she turned it up, the better she felt. And the more she turned it up, the worse it became for the others on the bus.

It was a scene of satisfaction for some, distraction and disturbance for others. Peace and quiet it was not, but for one man concentrating on Harry Potter on his third year at Hogwarts it somehow was. Oblivious to exterior distractions he was concentrating happily on his own things.

A woman on the bus shrieked a shriek of what to her was terror. It was so sudden and seemed to come from out of nowhere. It was so high pitched, so unexpected, so sharp and over within a second or two. Even the pensioners shut up and looked around. The woman bolted up simultaneously like the legs of a patient of which the doctor had just tapped the knee to test the reflexes. That shriek, the shriek that you hear, total surprise.

The people on the bus looked at each other, their shock almost as evident as that of the woman herself. One person stood up to find out what was going on, as others looked out of the window as if embarrassed or not wanting to be part of the scene.

When they found out what happened many stared into blank space on the bus in astonishment, still taking it in. Others then stared at the man in anger, shaking disbelieving heads. The man next to the woman had tried to attack her. That much was clear, or at least touch her. Only the woman and the man would know really what happened. He might have been trying to kill her or simply get a more comfortable seating position.

But no one on the bus was prepared to confront the man who looked fairly eccentric himself. No one else wanted to make a scene. Thus, the woman blew past her aggressor who panicked himself, eyes everywhere, letting her pass at the earliest. He was sweating himself, confused and afraid. She ran to somewhere near the front of the bus where a vacant seat lay waiting for her. She quickly sat on the aisle edge of the seat as if her aggressor was still sat next to her on her inside. If she wasn't the nervous kind before she certainly was now.

People continued to look, heads shaking and minds questioning. The woman, the shrieking woman, the attacked woman, was the Chinese woman.

She had been sat next to John.

25. SHIVERS

He was still shaking when he got home, fingers jerking as he stammered to open the door. For a second it sounded like Woody Woodpecker at work as he tried arduously to put the simple metal key into the well-designed keyhole.

Sweat had formed and dried a dozen times and he felt dirty, physically, mentally and emotionally. He was shaking as if he was a leaf, almost tremulous, but it was a mixture of things that made him shake. Obviously, the incident on the bus, but also that he had been feeling cold recently even though outside temperatures did not make sense with this.

Schizophrenic thoughts splintered his mind. He really felt like a man with two halves; two halves that did not match. He certainly could not recognise the man who had done this disdainful act to the Chinese woman on the bus. And he could hardly now even remember much of the details. How could it have been me, he thought? It was strange though, and in a sadistic way it made him feel better, warmer. Yes, he was still shivering with the cold that had gripped his body, but certainly part of him felt comforted after a while following the attack on the girl. It was as if his conscience was moulding some sense out of the whole affair. Something had wanted him to go through with that heinous act, and was willing to reward him for it. Somehow his hidden conscience had forced his will.

It didn't comfort him now though. He had the shakes of an alcoholic inspired. Even the convulsions came with it, free of charge. He was disgusted with himself as much as the thirty or so other passengers were obviously perturbed by the proceedings on the bus.

Retching gave way to another layer of sweat, his eyeballs now red and bloodshot from trying to pop out of his head. The only ray of comfort was that for the first time in a while he did not feel cold, and that was a little odd. The shivers now, were purely a result of this indecent act, and his realisation of it. Thankfully for John, nobody had reported the incident to the police. Probably if it had been a blue eyed white slim lady the repercussions may well have been much more ominous.

Still, John had some thinking to do.

***

He shivered himself to sleep that night, heart beating like an athlete. It had been a trying day for John and especially for him recovering from his major operation. Sometimes he felt like he wasn't improving, and on other occasions he felt that at least the angina pains had ceased. The silver lining was more like a smudged grey world at times, though he knew he had to keep hope.

He was convinced there was something wrong with him. He felt there was some kind of emotional growth trying to live off him like a parasite. And how could he go and see the doctor again? There was really nothing wrong with him. What would he say to the doctor? 'Doc, I've got the chills and I can't help myself from attacking people to ease the condition.' John sensibly accepted that this was not the way to progress. So, he would go on with his strange life full of strange dreams and equally strange feelings, hoping that at some point something even stranger would happen, and the strange person that had entered John's mind would be a stranger no more.

26. GANGLION

The next few weeks saw John trying to live his new life. That's what they say when you've had a heart operation of this nature. You'll feel a new man when you get out. Well, he certainly felt a new man, just not one he could not recognise.

He would wake up at various times during the night with severe headaches for which he took the regular pain killers. Pain killers for head killers. So much killing. He would experience that all too familiar but quizzical dream of himself surrounded by thick, thick snow, whitening everything. The isolated tree at one side of the picture, a picture chilled white with fresh ice and snow. He would feel twitches on his left eye, as if nervous convulsions were erupting from inside. Not to mention the ganglion which had developed on the inside of his mouth.

By now, used to his own company, John very often found himself questioning his own thoughts and sanity. Why was he feeling colder? Why did he try to attack that Chinese girl on the bus? Also, what about the nervous twitches and the ganglion ripening on the inside of his mouth.

Loneliness and post operation trauma, he told himself. But he had not convinced himself very well. Thus, he decided to make an appointment with the doctor. This he did, arranging a visit as soon as he could. The nurse had maintained that the following morning was not possible because of the amount of work and especially the number of operations the doctor was already booked in for in the near future. 'The doctor will only deal with emergencies early in the morning. So, if you urgently require him could you ring back then please?' It was quite austere and obviously well practiced but a fact of a rising aged population.

He thought about ringing in the morning for an emergency appointment but decided it wasn't an urgent requirement so made his appointment for Thursday morning. Today was Monday. Until then he would go on feeling like E.T. on earth. Moulding the ganglion around his teeth and tongue, he went on living his ever-changing life of a human chameleon. As he did so, a joke came to his mind of a man who went to see the doctor.

The doctor said, 'Hello Jim, I've not seen you for a while?'

'No,' the patient replied, 'I've not been very well.'

… It didn't make John laugh.

Then John settled back into reality, his momentary bout of humour quickly being clouded over by an all too common sharp headache striking him. His headaches maybe could be migraines he thought, as they always seemed to trigger in the same place on his forehead. The other thought he had was that they could be a result of sinus or phlegm or maybe even tension headaches. Well, he was not a doctor so this was all conjecture.

Crunch, he heard in his head as he bit down on the nagging ganglion pursuing his attention. The twitch continued to irritate his face, his eye and his mind. There was another strange thing John thought about. The previous Wednesday, one of his brief visits to town, he had just gone to do a little shopping, mostly of the window variety. The odd thing he noticed as he looked down at his wrist was that he had forgotten to put on his watch that morning. It might not sound that strange, but John was a very regimented man who never forgotten his watch before.

From his training in the army he had learned certain habits and steps he always followed. In all his years at Comfort Upholstery John had never once forgotten his watch. It was a part of him. The aphorism that man is not whole until he has his hat was slightly different in John's case. His hat was his watch, and he had just forgotten it for the first time since living memory.

He remembered looking down at his wrist that day and thinking nothing, just staring into dead space in the form of living skin. He tried to convince himself that it was nothing, no big deal, not at all. These things happen. In truth though, it was a little strange and it was another of John's little oddities slipping into his everyday lifestyle. When a man goes decades without even once forgetting to put his watch on, every single day, you could feasibly say it is not normal at all.

Now, thinking back to that Wednesday, as the world passed by, as time had left him behind, John realised, whilst chewing his ganglion, whilst twitching his left eye, that the Western

Front was not that quiet; that peacetime Britain was not that peaceful; that he was not a hundred percent.

Summer was here!

27. PSYCHIATRIST

Summer was, in fact peaking. Birds were chirping, this time out of contentment. It was not a wishful chirp but one of relief. High pitch chirps creating a wondrous audible picture of satisfaction. Hills to the sides of Haslingden's valley turning the scenery into a painting, refreshingly green. Blue skies encouraged flowers to smile. The feel-good factor of summer made the people feel good. The heat was so good it was tasty. In the distance the Halo popped its head above the horizon to welcome the citizens to attend a wonderful day. Flags were cracking as the heat waved towards them, occasional hidden weeds enjoying life in abundance.

Yet John Winters, as he awoke was clearly unsure of himself. He'd been to the doctor on more than one occasion but always came out thinking he hadn't got anywhere, or not explained things the way he had intended. He regularly now chewed on his ganglion like it was gum. This morning he woke and found himself irresistibly crunching away at it. Most people wash their face or read the paper in the morning. Not John, he enjoyed a good munch in the morning to chew on. Yum, Yum.

'Family Fortunes asked a hundred people what they did first thing after waking up in the morning. Top six answers are displayed.'

'Chew on their ganglion, Les?'

'If that's there, I'll give you the money myself,' laughed a bemused Les Dennis, the crowd egging him on. 'I don't believe it. It is!'

John's little entertainment for the day as his mind started playing tricks on him... again. In truth it was the stress and uncertainty about his new body that had created a bit of a wreck out of John. More to the point he was still embarrassed and afraid of himself, especially after the incident on the bus. He had told no one about this, no one had spoken to him about it either, which was good, meaning it had not been reported by anyone. That was a real concern to him that he had attempted to harass and touch a woman. What had possessed him, seeming to have no control over what happened? He didn't just seem not to have control; knew he had no control over himself on that bus and on that day. Oddly, he could just remember feeling free of all worries, all pressures, in a kind of ethereal state of strange relief, and power. Resoundingly also, that chill he regularly felt causing a sense of alarm inside him had eased that day. Some sort of a pill taken by an addict, it made him feel great, though he would not confront that emotion, could not. So much so, that he chose not to even think about it. Truth was that John was not a bad person.

He had always been sensible, and lawful, so why would he do something like that. His years of military life gave him valued training in that regard. The incident; that incident; would fit nicely underneath John's metaphorical carpet. Should he have mentioned that incident to the doctor? Should he go one step further and even see a psychiatrist and open his mind up even more? Up until now John had answered an emphatic 'NO' to these questions, continuing almost nonchalantly to mould shapes out of his ganglion.

Gotta Chew, Johnny, Gotta Chew…

Chew to be free Johnny. Chew to let the juices flow. Chew for you Johnny. Chew to ease the pain and warm your soul Johnny… Jingle, jingle.

This was the voice he often heard, eating away at his mind, helping him regain his sanity, or maybe to cement his insanity.

It was a little over-the-top to talk of psychiatrists he thought, comforting himself. After all, one mistake should never make or break a person. This did make him feel better. It was just one of those blips of his life; the vicissitudes of life.

He rose from his heavily layered bed to take surreptitious glances from the sides of the curtains. It was a great morning he thought, noticing the sun well risen. His thoughts though, were not in unison with his feelings as he considered plodding on for another day.

28. ROGER

The phone rang. It was Roger, his manager from Comfort
Upholstery, where he had not worked for a couple of
months now due to the operation. Roger was one of those
bosses you really did not need to have. He was in his late fifties,
married to a lady in her early forties. Roger had a bad temper,
a bad temper which often emerged at work, and often when
John was around.

Comfort Upholstery was not a huge company. It was a
medium size nationwide firm with deliveries all over the UK.
Being a Lancashire business born from the North West it really
had its roots in hard work and toil and the expected working-class origins. Roger had been the Chief Financial Officer for
over twenty years, and to him he treated Comfort Upholstery
like his own family business. As a result, Roger did not take
any weakness, or lethargy lightly. On numerous occasions you
could hear him firing verbal abuse at his underlings, and John,
although Warehouse Manager himself, often felt the brunt of it.

On one occasion, during a busy November, sales were

normally good on the build up to Christmas, and nobody had time for anything. Most of the trucks were out delivering countrywide except for three trucks that still slept in their bays. The warehouse was quite empty which was a good thing because it not only meant deliveries were going out but that also there was plenty of room for tomorrow when a large shipment of sofa sets was coming into the warehouse. John felt quite content with himself, quite intrinsically pleased how work and life was going. Kate was still married to him at this point.

He enjoyed being busy and at the factory he rarely got time to breathe, organizing important shipments in and out and the general planning of warehouse space. It was to some a stressful time at work but at the end of the day it also reaped satisfaction. After all, John was not only interested in seeing his pay check at the end of the month, but also, he wanted to see higher growth, prosperity and success for the business. He didn't want to work for a company that simply paid wages, irrespective of performance. At this time in his life John was forward looking with a conscience and fairly career minded. He was sincere, and it really showed at the factory. Roger appreciated and knew this but had a funny way of showing, or not as usually the case may be. He often treated John as his punching bag.

On this particular day, John had found himself a bit more relaxed, a little bit more in control of his bays in this busy November. He was having coffee in the very basically designed break room, where he seldom took breaks, but when he did, he did so at free will. Despite being of a working class background the company had worked to give as much limited independence as it thought affordable.

The spring hinged wooden door of the break room opened, naturally twinned with the sound of twisting spring coils squeaking painfully. Roger walked in confidently and force-fully, clearly looking for someone. At moment of first sight Roger stopped in his tracks. Two other warehouse staff also turned around, almost to attention, wondering if, for whatever reason one of the big managers of the company wanted to speak to them. It was a natural response as Roger had that air of command. Within less than a second it became apparent. Roger stared straight at John, unflinching. 'There yer are. Yer see, I told Peter yer hadn't left the company,' Roger said sardonically and in a strong Lancashire accent. But he wasn't laughing. In fact, he never laughed whenever he was being sarcastic, even rude. Whenever he did laugh nobody else laughed with him. Director's privilege it seemed. He was overseeing the wages, so wanted to get the most he could for the money.

Almost automatically the two embarrassed staff who were on their break stood up, trying not to make too much of a squeaking noise with their chairs and stepped out. Neither John nor Roger even noticed them leave, it was such a common occurrence. 'Quiet today is it, Winters?' continued Roger.

'I've been snowed under all morning, Roger. I just needed a break.' He wasn't lying, he had been busy.

'Come to my office, Winters.' John knew an argument was coming but was just a little concerned about what it was. When we say argument, you could more realistically use the term verbal battering, as John very rarely actually argued with Roger. These verbal beatings were a familiar theme of working with Roger, but still the butterflies had started in John's stomach as he considered what it was about this time.

It was almost as if Roger felt on foreign soil arguing in the break room, like he couldn't really fire his machine gun abuse at John's war-torn face.

John followed Roger the short distance to his office via the factory floors; this was no cosy office setting. As he followed, John thought of the stern and angry walk that always seemed to accompany Roger; quick, heavy, harsh steps. That same spring coiled break room door flung backwards twisting and turning, squeaking and squirming.

The offices were built in a makeshift almost incomplete looking way, just to suffice the needs of health and safety. Although it was a short trip to Roger's office it was up and down a lot, across the factory floor into very well soundproofed and well protected premises.

As Roger's office door closed so did the sounds of machinery from outside the office. The ending of those sounds also ended John's comfort level. Whilst John had the sounds of the factory as emotional support he felt more at home. Now they had been muted. His home was the factory floor, where he felt the comfort of familiar surroundings.

The closing of the office door was an end to the external distractions and noise; distractions for Roger that is. The same could not be said for John's apprehension, and the caution encroaching John's mind. He was used to bollocking's from his manager but it was never enjoyable. It was a busy part of the year and John did not want to waste more time being abused here.

John had only just noticed that all the time Roger was holding onto some papers, rolled up making it difficult to figure out what they were. 'I suppose yer wondering why I brought yer here, Winters?' John simply shrugged his shoulders in his usual casual way. Of course, he wondered but was not going to give Roger the pleasure of him showing fear.

As far as he was concerned, he had done nothing wrong, and another thing, Roger never ever called John by his first name and that irked him. He never himself dared begin an argument with Roger but inside he argued with himself. What kind of respect is it when your manager does not even call you by your first name? This got John mad, mad sometimes like a bubbling pit of rage.

He shrugged again, thinking back to the fact that he had been summoned here for a reason. It gave sanity back to the situation. 'Well, Winters, are yer not wondering?' Roger asked in a half rhetorical tone, yet somehow questioning at the same time.

He had only done it again, the man inside John's head said. Call me by my first name. 'Yes, I was wondering, boss,' he said almost sycophantically, already seemingly having forgotten the recent words of his boss. What kind of a loser's riposte was that he demanded from himself? Despite his pride being hurt, he knew it was the thing to do to try to weasel out of this hole. Today he did not like the tone coming from his boss.

'How's business, Winters?'

'Sorry?' replied John, in a genuinely unsure way.

'Have yer been busy?' demanded Roger, raising his deep Lancashire strained voice.

'You know we've been busy, Roger. We've had the usual workload you well know for this time of year. But we are managing. The Du Vay order left this morning and the C & C order was delivered yesterday.' These were big orders that

189

should provide good revenue and this was what Roger normally wanted to hear. 'The Cosy Holmes order set off this morning too with Bed Heaven.' As John spoke, he noticed Roger's hands fingering the pieces of paper in his hand. So much so, that he noticed the papers in more detail. He knew it looked familiar, knew exactly what is was now with another movement from the hands of its maker. It was a shipment note, and not just any shipment note.

John realised immediately what is was. It was the Du Vay shipment note that he had just said had set off yesterday! So, what was the shipment note doing in Roger's hand? Surely it had not been cancelled. The driver had not rung in sick or anything so what was going on? How is business, he thought to himself.

Roger realised from John's erratic eye movements that he may well just have figured it out. Discerned that the shipment note, which should have been somewhere in Brighton was actually now somewhere in Roger's hands. Du Vay Plc was one of Comfort Upholstery's largest customers. Offices all over the country but their head office in Brighton.

'Yer know what this is I have in my hand don't yer, Winters?'

'The shipment note,' replied John a little muted.

'Yes, the shipment note indeed. Bravo maestro. The shipment note that should not be in my hands should it, Winters?' it was sarcastic now, extremely. 'Now why would I have a shipment note, Winters?

Don't call me Winters!

Don't let him, buddy. You tell him, Johnny.

'Shouldn't yer driver be the one with this shipment note, Winters?'

I said don't call me Winters!
You tell him.

'Why is it in my hands, Winters?'

That was it for John, at least in his mind. He flipped... in a polite way.

'Why do you always call me that?'

'What?' Roger replied calmly and a little surprised not only by John's audacity but also by the changing of the conversation.

'Why don't you call me John like all the other people?'

'I'll call yer what I want, Winters. Yer've just missed one of the biggest shipments of the year and yer have the audacity to complain about that? What planet are yer living on?' Roger was now shouting. The formerly well soundproofed walls had become like paper, with everything clearly audible to the adjacent rooms. 'Do yer know what yer are, Winters? A gormless idiot. If I want to employ a muppet, I'll go to the joke shop and buy one. In the meantime, I'll expect yer to pass onto yer drivers the correct papers to do their job. The Du Vay papers were still on yer bloody desk. How do yer expect the deliveries to happen when they are sat on yer desk, by telepathy?' Roger was pretty much spraying anger at John now. 'Winters, yer a disaster.'

'Please call me by my first name, Roger.' John seemed more offended by that than anything else. At that point Roger went ape.

'Yer said what!? What are yer on? Yer more interested in yer damn name that yer company and responsibilities! What the hell is yer problem? We missed a vital delivery and all yer can think about is yer bloody name.'

John couldn't get the image of Ali stood on the canvas asking

Terrell 'What's my name?' Just that in his vision he was Ali and Roger was Terrell. It was only a split second but it led him to clinch his fist slightly. But that was all changed as it was Roger who was now completely boiling over. Who was Ali? Who was Terrell? Who cared now? He quickly picked up the nearest coffee mug from his desk containing the residue from the morning's coffee and hurled it at John. Although not expecting it, John had no problem evading the flying cup (not saucer), which smashed into the prefabricated wall, ending up in a few pieces. John also avoided the coffee itself that of course flew with the mug. A string of coffee could be seen dripping down the wall where the impact had occurred and where the evidence was clear.

It did not faze Roger in the slightest. He continued as if nothing had happened. 'If I ever find yer've done a thing like this again yer'll be out do yer hear me? We can't afford to treat customers like that. The customer always comes first, always. Don't forget that.' Of course, John knew that. He had been in the business over fifteen years and had treated all his customers with the highest respect. This was just a mistake and John was now paying for it.

John, not listening, had already begun to turn, and before Roger could begin his next torrent of abuse he was out of the office. On his way out he nearly ran into other office workers, most of whom had heard the punishment he had endured with Roger. Not only was he offended about nearly been hit by a missile, he was also very angry at constantly being referred to as Winters, treated like a piece of rubbish and given zero respect.

The harmless string of coffee continued its patient journey

down the fabricated wall, unaffected by any of Roger's insults or John's emotions.

The next day, Roger got on with John as though nothing had happened. It was Roger being Roger.

29. CALL

Roger's call to John was one of courtesy it seemed. 'How are yer, John? Are yer recovering okay? I was meaning to come around but something came up, yer know?' John was struck by the calmness of Roger, but mainly by the fact that he called him John. This was a real crowd pleaser and it put a grin on John's face. It must have been a real humble moment for Roger, thought John as he listened like he was speaking to someone else. It was probably fake, he thought, but better than the usual way he spoke.

Then, as if intent on spoiling the moment Roger continued. 'Are yer still okay to come back to the office in two weeks?' And for a small collection of seconds John thought Roger was a little bit more human. But then he asked that follow-up question and it became a little clearer to him why Roger had been so polite. Good old Roger. In a resigned way, John acknowledged that he did expect to hopefully be back in the office as planned, though in truth he was far from one hundred percent.

There was the inexplicable incident on the bus and he had

also been feeling a lot colder even though the outside temperatures were great. Also, his ganglion was somehow maturing, and not going away, continually begging him to chew it. Sometimes it was too tempting.

Chew, chew, chew, chew for you.

'I hope to be back in a couple of weeks, Roger,' he lied, especially in his mind. It was a slightly tired response, as if noticing that Roger was not at all interested in his wellbeing, just simply in getting his pound of flesh. A pound of flesh that was seemingly reaching its best before date.

'Great news, Winters, great news. Good to see yer getting better. We've all missed yer at the factory, all of us.' It was not often you heard a patronizing Lancashire accent; it just didn't match. Well this time it was an exception. 'We're all missing yer over here yer know?'

John yawned, 'Okay see you in a few weeks, Roger. Bye till then,' and put the phone down. Tired and cold, John wearing his green sweater, stumbled over to the window from which he had a limited view of the valley's hills.

The valley's hills were greener, fresher now since he last looked. They had been hibernating, sleeping over the cooler times, fighting to gain strength for the days ahead; vitality to boost the exhilarating verdure over the summer months. The occasional dandelion seed glided into view like a snow-flake beckoning after the hidden past. An equally occasional butterfly fluttered by, and then, bye, bye; natures symmetry symmetrically natural.

Poetically, the butterfly's wings waved a gentle au revoir to John from the other side of the window, as if auditioning for the leading role. Two kids skirted by, passing a football between each other on the street, a passing reminder of John's own history. Dressed in t-shirts and shorts, they contradicted John's overdressed appearance. An unintentional, over conscious glance upwards from one noticed John looking at him from his flat. The kid quickly looked away as if embarrassed, though did have a couple more looks of curiosity in John's direction. John felt no embarrassment; his window was his frame, and he was simply admiring his picture. People don't really change he thought, as he remembered he often used to play in his youth not too dissimilarly.

John stretched his arms long and wide and then yawned a big one. He shivered in an uncontrollable way for a second, not from cold but from the yawn taking control of his body. His bones creaked ever so slightly. Then he remembered. He was a little late today; his ganglion was missing him, so his two front teeth, one top and one bottom gripped onto his tough piece of flesh on the inside of his mouth. He crunched and felt the twinge inside similar to crunching on a muesli bar without the health factor. It was addictive, but it nagged him every time. He hated it but he seemed compelled to oblige. Well, he thought, minor side effect of the operation, and continued crunching.

He turned from the window and went over to the fan heater he had positioned well in the middle of the room as if making it the centre of attention. Turning the switch from off to on without a second thought, he immediately felt better. Even before the heat hit him, he was reassured in a psychological way. He looked at the bedside digital clock which read 11:00 am. Without a second thought he ambled back into bed, feeling a little chilly. Outside the sun shone.

It had become so common now for John to feel cold; so

normal for him to feel this way. So much so that he had dismissed the thought in his mind of going to discuss with the doctor. He had no real problem, so why go to the doctor, he had said to himself on many occasion. Wrapping the blanket completely around himself, and even underneath himself, he snuggled into bed, increasing the level on the heater reluctantly, because it meant he had to get up again to switch the levels. Just a short nap he thought to himself. He was asleep in minutes, the humming of the heater helping to hypnotise him to sleep.

His dream was one he'd had before but not for a while. This recurring dream he had no control over. In his completely white world surrounded by snow he noticed the lonely tree in the distance. Clearly the kind of tree shaped by cold, it was brown and leafless, almost lifeless. It didn't look particularly friendly or inviting and John had still not figured out why he was looking at it. But as it was his recurring dream it became puzzlingly warm to him and he welcomed the dream. There was nothing else there except that tree and the snow so the tree itself took centre stage. Looking a little closer he thought the tree could easily be upside down. In fact, it looked more like tree roots than a trunk and branches. He had the feeling he had been there before.

He'd slept for an hour, though it seemed much longer. The dream had become so vivid now, he'd seen it so many times. It had become a reality to him now and he often puzzled over it. What had woken him was in fact an incredible headache just over his left eye. Maybe it was a migraine, but he saw no stars nor felt any nausea. Regardless, he just needed it to go away, and it must have been a bad one to wake him from that welcoming dream.

It had been a while since he had experienced such a bad headache and it was that which did send him to the doctors, the headaches not the cold feeling that he had pigeonholed somewhere hidden in his mind. The doctor guessed it was a regular headache, prescribed the usual paracetamol, and sent him on his way. He got up reluctantly, took some tablets and tried to ignore away the pain.

Then he noticed a twitch over his left eye was back. Not a nervous twitch, just an antagonistic one. This also came and went at will to harass John. He lay back in bed, not tired by sleep but by thoughts that were molesting his mind. Sometimes he wished he could have his old life back; live with the risk of heart failure, but without the fears and chagrin that consumed him now. Confusion continued to spoil his mind as he lay staring upward at the ceiling, eye twitching occasionally.

Outside the sun shone boastfully. It was quite simply a lovely day, no doubt about that.

30. SPIDER

Yes, it was a real super day, sun blazing down and a very light breeze. These days were rare in Lancashire, so on a day like this people boasted. Weather forecasters spoke for once with a smile on their faces. High pressure dominated and the breeze was minimal. Yet John was not a weather forecaster; he shivered in his bed, the fan heater still churning out false rays of hope; a plethora of warmth during a most unprecedented time. It was no good, he thought, reaching over to switch on the light. Trying to shake himself back to normality he shook aggressively. It wasn't like a fever or temperature he felt as he once again tried to convince himself to go visit the doctor. Following on from his internal wrangling's he decided he would call the doctor later.

Amidst his contemplative plans to visit the doctor he noticed a black mark on the wall. Squinting for better vision he noticed it move a little. The flat was generally okay in terms of furniture and decorations, enough for a single resident at least, though it had seen better days.

Living alone, and male as well, daily house cleaning chores often went by the miss and it had been a while since he had cleaned anything. After his separation from Kate he wanted a place fairly near to town for convenience, though when we talk about town, it was a very small town, almost like a village where most people new each other or at least knew of each other.

This flat had been the second place he had visited and it was just fine. It was all he needed and his relatively well-paid role at Comfort Upholstery left him with more than enough money to survive. This flat was really more than he needed for the rest of his miserable life. Initially, John had kept the place in good shape but more recently it had been left to clean itself. His army discipline had initially ensured he plan and look after things, but since the operation he had become a little undisciplined. Despite knowing this he had not done much about it.

Have a look, buddy. Have a closer look, it could be tasty. You won't regret it; I guarantee you that.

The black mark, on closer inspection was a house spider, maybe a little unusual to be found on a hot summer's day with no moisture in sight. Maybe it wanted to get out of the sun? It was quite big for a house spider, huge long and thin legs. It must have a desired destination but just watching it, John thought it really was lost in his flat.

Occasional quick movements followed statue-like stillness, and vice versa. Quick steps and no steps, almost ballet-esque across the bedroom wall. Ironically there were previous victim's silhouettes shadowed on the walls of his bedroom; enough to spread fear into any approaching arachnid. John had never really thought about it, but if you looked closely you could see the odd skeleton of a fly, spider or moth remaining as evidence on the walls. But you would have to look close though and put the jigsaw of the exoskeleton back together to figure it out.

John obviously didn't care too much. To him it was just a minor affair. The long-legged inspect tiptoed across the ballet dancer's morgue; an unfortunate spotlight already had eyes on it.

John got out of bed for a closer look, simple curiosity at this stage. He had forgotten about how cold he felt for a moment, the buzz of the fan heater pumping out layers of hot air. He was really perplexed by the insect dancing in the spotlight, mainly because it was so large, especially its long thin legs.

John was less than an arm's length away from the little creature as it froze perfectly still right there in front of him. Reminiscent of a chameleon in the dessert but unable to change colour, the spider tried to hide in the markings of the wall; not good. The wall was mainly white; the spider was black. It still did not move, like a mannequin in a fashion shop it was a statue on the bedroom wall. With its long legs and black dress, it was well positioned for its own little catwalk. Maybe it was waiting for human eyes to vanish. By now John was eye to eye with the challenger in this fabricated faceoff.

John's twitch had halted, for a few moments at least right about the time when he met his challenger on the wall. Who would twitch first? The spider stood like a painting on a wall. John stood waiting to see if he would twitch first, almost admiring the painting. There was a stalemate.

John unfolded his arms and began to lengthen his sweaty palm towards the spider. Opening his palm almost gave his fingers the shape of a spider itself; challenger, meet challenger; or had it become ballroom dancing? His fingers darkened over the challenger. He only had five legs to the challengers eight!

Then panic in the black corner. The spider, ever so impetuously responded to the touch of damp and hot human skin. It scampered, it scurried, it screamed for its life. Was it a low blow? In the panic John's stuttering hand had only flailed, managed to touch the spider, harmed to such a degree that it fell on the floor. Unfortunately for the spider the floor was cream coloured, though as it had not been cleaned for a while it had become a dirty cream colour. It scrambled for any kind of safety, long legs everywhere, but the long legs adding to its speed. John tried hastily to coordinate the whereabouts of the insect.

'There you are you little bas…' he said aloud but not finishing his sentence to himself and of course to the spider. It was now running across the floor; a streaker on a football pitch, following no planned course, just running knowing time is short. John thought about plunging a slipper down right on top to get the job done. But he knew, in a strange, almost ethereal way that it was not right to do this.

He stretched down, creaking his throat muscles as he did this. This time in a scooping motion he lowered his right hand, successfully lifting up the frantic insect. His wrist closed carefully, then his other one also. He now held the insect like a butterfly in his hands, ensuring it could not escape. If it went to the judges now it would be a unanimous decision.

He hurried over to the kitchen, his prize possession in both hands. With great versatility he used his elbow and both sides to lift a long glass from the kitchen sink area. It was a very delicate task, especially with the long legs of the spider tickling his palms. Like an old man now, he struggled into the living room.

He struggled because in his hands he was clutching his prey, and under his arm he had a tentative grasp on a drinking glass.

It looked like he was praying now, a mantis ready to devour. Bending, he placed the glass on the table, upside down, then he sat down on the sofa. It was the sofa he would call a 2X without even thinking; the sofa he had got half price from his workplace. One of the perks of the job. He was still dressed in pyjamas and his green sweater.

The bell rang to signal the end of the round. His next challenge was to somehow manage to get the spider how he wanted. He felt like Tom Cruise on one of his missions. The bell rang again. John's fight was far from over. He lowered his hands onto the table near to the glass, still upside down. Then he opened his hands with the care of a saint letting out peace and good feeling to the world. The spider leapt free, almost making it to freedom, even after a knockdown in the early rounds. But John quickly grasped the tall glass and planted it down over the fleeing spider. In the process John snapped down over two of the spider's long legs and broke them instantaneously. A few stains of liquid lined the glass rim and the table. The spider's broken legs lay still and wasted as the insect itself still used instinct to try and escape from this glass prison.

Throughout all of this, John was getting a wonderful childish pleasure that he had not even realised. He had completely forgot about his twitch, ganglion, headache and even fevered coldness. The spider hobbled now inside the glass as John stared, mesmerised by the disjointed creature dying right in front of him. But, like a determined boxer, he continued to pound into his opponent. Then John began a verbal sparring battle with the insect.

'Not so big now are you, Spiderman?' he began. 'Come on up the glass my hero, that's right, keep trying to get free you dirty critter.' It was like verbal torture, very peculiar as well. I mean, who in their right mind would talk, never mind verbally challenge a trapped insect inside a glass, maybe only David Attenborough on drugs; absolutely incredible. 'You're a hairy creature, aren't you? Come to invade my privacy? This is my house, not yours. And besides, you're taking my heat, which I paid for. Look at you, you can't even walk straight.' Obviously, it could not walk straight, it had just had two legs amputated.

Finish him, buddy. Do yourself a favour. You know what I mean, buddy.

And John thought he hear the old familiar jingle of the jester's hat.

The fight was coming to an end, and it was by now it was clear who was in control. John placed his hand over the cup. He quickly lifted it. The damaged insect tried to scramble out. 'She loves me; she loves me NOT!' At the word NOT, the glass pounded down again, on a third leg. It crunched off so easily like a thin matchstick, as dark liquid was let free. Even then the insect tried to fight on. You've gotta admire the courage, despite John's unflinching desire to torture.

Up rose the rim of the glass once again. So too, did the spider, ambling in any direction. This time louder, 'She loves me, she loves me NOT!' Slam.

The glass thudded down on the helpless captive, now with only one working leg left. John's aggression on the last pound-ing had actually impaired two more legs. His eyes now wide and excited, John grinned a kind of enchanted grin. It hardly moved now. A breeze would probably have moved it more that it could by its own living facets. It was pretty much defeated, mercy please...

Not quite the hand of God, but the hand of John it was who picked up the glass now in his right hand. He flung it up in the air with confidence, simply to flip it over. It was now the correct way up in his hand. He stared down for some moments at the dying insect. It moved only in fractions now. Then he spoke. 'Ring-a-ring o' roses, a pocket full of posies, A-tishoo! A-tishoo! They all fall DOWN,' and the spider was crushed under the flat base of the glass as John splat down harshly. He hammered the glass down onto the table on top of the spider synchronised with the word 'DOWN.' The body of the spider squashed as dark liquid bled out.

John had slammed the glass with so much force that the glass too shattered in his hand, firing parts all around the room.

It was a unanimous decision.

31. GLASS

It was clearly not normal to act in this sadistic way he thought to himself as he went to the bathroom. Why did he torture and dismember that long legged spider in such a way? He never saw himself as that kind of person.

He was an army man and always stuck to the law. Disciplined yes, but not torturous. Maybe the heat got to me, he thought shaking his head in disbelief, his hand held high to ensure the blood did not drip too much. The smashing of the glass on the helpless spider had sent shards of glass all over the place. Fragments of glass had cut his hand; maybe the spider had the last laugh after all, at least made it a points decision.

His headache had cleared. This, at least made him feel happier.

32. DAGGER

It was Sunday. It was the day before he was due to go back to work. He wasn't really looking forward to it though as he was still not feeling a hundred percent, though he hoped this may come from going back to a little normality.

A couple of weeks had passed since John had won the fight with the spider, and of course it was another day of John feeling cold. It had seemed to get a little better recently, but now it was back as strong as ever. For John it was his new normal, though it was extremely odd and to be honest, not normal. Some days were worse than others. On those days he wouldn't even bother getting up.

What few visitors did come had also noted his odd reactions and gave curious comments or responses. Simon seemed a bit concerned, suggesting he go back to the quack again for another opinion. It was an idea he had run by himself a million times but never got around to taking a stand.

John had not mentioned the headaches or the ganglion to Simon, but Simon had noticed John's left eye twitch sometimes.

He put it down to just a stress reaction or adjustment. It was just that sometimes John described that cold feeling with so much enthusiasm that it felt like a constant fever with ripples of cold blood flowing through the body... as if thousands of cold pins are piercing all over the body. Simon could just hear the words resonate when he would say 'I just don't feel like the same person I was before.' In those words, Simon felt not only resonance, but also reflection, a reflection of his own grave condition.

This was what concerned Simon the most; it was what motivated him to at least consider going back to get a judgement from the doctor. In the back of his mind John thought it was pointless going to the doctor. He found it a trivial thing, but at the same time he was fearful that he would find out something he would not want to hear. Thus, he just delayed and delayed, putting off and putting off.

'You've no idea what it's like, Simon, when you're having a bath in hot water and shivering, dreading coming out. I can't understand it. When you put off even going outside in summer cause of the discomfort that goes with it. It's like winter all year round out there for me. The temperature just makes no difference. Can you believe that, Simon?' Of course, Simon couldn't believe it but was intrigued. Intrigued by how or why it had happened and especially how it could be possible.

Simon was also captivated by what, if anything triggered it like a switch. Bottom line from Simon's point of view was that John must at least go and see what the doctor would have to say about it.

'Dr. Rajesh is good, isn't he? Is he your doc, John?'

'No, we always used Dr. Munir. He's pretty good, little guy

with a warm way of speaking to you. I just didn't want to waste his time though. Sometimes though he does seem a little busy, overburdened.' Both doctors were Asian.

'Not many British doctors left are there, John?' asked Simon.

'Not unless Rajesh and Munir have wrangled a citizenship out of us.' It was a rather pompous view, maybe his military roots coming to the fore. In all honesty, John knew that Dr. Munir was a great doctor. It was just that certain prejudices were hard to lay down to rest. Also, John didn't know how to handle a visit to the doctor. How would he react if John walked in and said, 'Yes doctor, I have this ganglion that has been in my mouth for a month. I keep getting headaches, and this twitch, oh that twitch, it drives me crazy. Oh, also I feel as cold as hell all the time.' The best doctor in the world wouldn't know what to say to that.

How could John walk in and spout these symptoms? As cold as hell, even though hell was not at all cold. How would the doctor react? How could he react? Part of the problem was John's secretive nature, almost bashful. He had only spoken to Simon about these issues, and even then, had only passed on half of the story. How could he talk to anyone about his little rendezvous with the little Chinese hyperactive lady and the fighting with subsequent dismantling of the spider? These were out of bounds. It was psychiatrist material.

'Well,' the doc would ponder, 'what do you think it is?' That would be the problem going to a psychiatrist. You end up answering the question yourself. They should have a banner up on the front of their door...

BECOME YOUR OWN DOCTOR FOR FREE

Just answer your own questions as truthfully as you can and

you could make it!

'Well anyway, Simon, I don't intend to go back to the doctors unless I'm really desperate. I'm starting work tomorrow and want to see if this will fix things. I'm hopeful things will all go well and this conversation will be a thing of the past.'

Yes, that's right, buddy, you start work again tomorrow. Good luck, you'll need it. Pass on my regards to your favourite boss, buddy.

'Like with the operation?' craftily questioned Simon. It was a like a dagger in the heart. Simon had been thinking about this but was reluctant to have to say it. Only someone close could twist that kind of implement into someone's heart. But it had merit and a place like all things have places. He was clearly a little concerned for John who was not himself. It went silent, a painful truthful and lengthy silence, pretty much ensuring John got enough emotional time to take a look at himself.

After the meeting with Simon he decided that he would seriously consider a visit to Dr. Munir's surgery.

33. GRANULE

Outside it was still summer, it was still Sunday and it was still the eve of his return back to work. It was a baking afternoon for Lancashire, at twenty-eight degrees, and that was about as hot as it got.

George, a work colleague, had offered to pick up John and drop him off for some time just to help him settle in as smoothly as possible. It was a little out of the way for George but it was only a temporary thing. John planned to be back driving in a few weeks based on medical advice. Besides, George was himself was a little odd character and John did not want to outstay his welcome. George 'Granule' Graham was considered by the whole company as a little eccentric, but at the same time a harmless cheerful guy.

'Granule' Graham was a funny looking guy, similar in appearance to Kramer from 'Seinfeld' but with a beard. He adorned a scruffy look, a little bit quirky and odd. He too had become part of the Comfort Upholstery furniture; had been there so long.

He, and his wife, had two kids, and by his general appearance and openness you would imagine him being a pretty good dad and humorous husband. Like his superior Roger, he also had a very thick Lancashire accent, so obvious that one sentence would give away a lot of his background, and in fact shape his character to onlookers.

His brown, undyed hair and equally brown beard bordering bushy, distinguished him, especially that beard. Take away his beard and he was Kramer. With his beard he was George 'Granule' Graham. He was tall too, and somewhat gangly, not that he especially watched his weight, just that he had a pretty good metabolism.

Whilst being a gentleman, he still had the potential to be stern and frank. He pretty much got on with everyone, but everyone looked and thought about George with this view of eccentricity so ended up distancing themselves from him. It helped that he was so down to earth in himself and the way he dealt with others. In many ways he was this humble person born to work at Comfort Upholstery all his life.

His family followed suit with him, dressing a little odd, with no care for fashion. George and his family just wanted to be George and his family, and no one was going to change that. But because of his oddities people often kept a mental distance from him, and the Graham's as a family. To him, work was for the workplace and family to remain in the family. That blue parker he always wore. It was as if he slept in it because whenever he came into work, he would have it on. For as long as John could remember, he had never seen George wear any other coat.

Regardless, 'Granule' Graham was still a nice, harmless man

just doing what he needed to do and with honesty. He was more honest than most, more friendly that a lot and more humorous than the majority at Comfort Upholstery. For these reasons alone he proved his worth and value at Comfort Upholstery.

But there was one thing which really amazed John about 'Granule' Graham. One thing which was very strange. As unbelievable as a magician. George drank coffee. This wasn't the odd thing. He drank coffee from a regular mug, but always preferred dissolving coffee, rather than percolator coffee. That in itself was a little odd but not the oddest thing about 'Granule' Graham.

What was odd was that George, when brewing coffee always put in one granule of dissolving coffee in his cup. Not two or three granules of coffee, or even half a granule, but one. And for sure you would know about it in case by mistake you happened to put in an extra granule? You sure would. Many had been and gone, having put in two granules as a trivial error. Well, it for sure would be the last time you would make that error. It would not be classed as a trivial error by George. It was a guarantee that the next cup made would always be perfect. George made sure of that, because he enjoyed his coffee that much, if you could call it that.

There were times when people tried it on; colleagues who had been there a while sometimes trying to test him, in patience and in his powers of tasting. John had tried a few times putting two granules in on purpose. 'Let's see his powers of taste, the weirdo,' John would whisper to himself.

John, on one occasion, had carefully handpicked one medium sized grain of Nescafe from the jar, and then sneaked in an extra one. How can someone tell the difference? 'Look at the tiny size of the grains,' he murmured to himself. The granule was about the size of a pinhead. He then filled the cup and stirred as normal, and watched the water change, but only very slightly to a pale shade of yellow. He was sure there was no visible difference. It seemed like he was dissolving two huge cubes into a cup. Of course, George noticed immediately.

'This coffee's too strong,' argued George in haste, a faint glisten of weak coffee shining on his upper lip. 'Did yer make this, John? It's unlike yer, John.'

The man is a magician. How else could he have guessed? Don't let him think he knows what you did, Johnny. No guilty looks, Johnny, he's testing you. He'll read your mind, Johnny. Don't look him in the eye. You know it makes sense, buddy.

And it really stressed John, as he tried his hardest to hide the fact that he had in fact intentionally added two granules.

'It's just the same as usual, George,' lied John. 'One granule, the way you like it.' John was lying through his teeth; he knew it and the quizzical doubtful face of George 'Granule' Graham was evident and putting more pressure on him.

He knows you're lying, Johnny. Think about the oceans and the sound of waves smoothly easing home again. Whatever you do, don't think about coffee. He's a wizard! He dresses like one too. He has special talents! Not from this world. He's not like me or you, buddy.

Then George looked deeply at John, and John was visually paralyzed. He just looked straight back as if found out. Piercing x-ray eyes gunned down John like a nuclear missile homing in. Like Superman with x-ray vision John thought George was looking straight through him into his mind. Perhaps he was. And like Lex Luther, John was scouring his mind for lead-like covers for his eyes. It was all only a second, nothing more.

George took another sip, testing the water further.

He's homing in, Johnny. He's getting warmer. The blue sea, Johnny. Waves smoothly relaxing you, buddy. A precious refreshing breeze on a summer's day. You know the score, buddy.

Then another tentative sip and he looked pessimistically down into his cup as if even noticing the colour was a little too dark. In all honesty the liquid was almost clear.

He's a gypsy, Johnny. Gypsies make curses, better start praying, or own up, buddy.

Then, almost nonchalantly, George turned and headed back to his desk to continue with his day. He did not utter another word, just a slight pensive look on his face. John was unsure what to think, but could remember the last look on George's face as he turned. It was a grin to suggest he knew it all, knew the secrets of John's mind but was letting it go this time.

He cursed you, Johnny. You saw that look he gave you? I saw it. You're doomed buddy. Admit it now while you can. Call him back before it's too late. Don't be foolish.

John just turned and headed back his way as if the duel was over, done. He was trying to listen out for the sound of waves smoothly brushing through the ocean but instead could only see thunder clouds forming in the distance.

And George 'Granule' Graham was going to come to pick John up in the morning for his return back to normality. What a way to return back to normality he thought.

34. CAT

All through Sunday, John was not feeling too good. He felt on edge, like he'd forgotten to do something. A nagging feeling of unfinished business pending. His ganglion was pulsating today and his twitch dancing irritably. His coldness was as alive as ever. He convinced himself it was a strange kind of tension he was feeling because of going back to work in the morning (or at least the journey in with 'Granule' Graham).

It's not every day you begin work again after major heart surgery. That much was very true. John had gone through a very challenging time over the past few years. Maybe it wasn't the operation? Maybe the divorce had more to do with his emotional state? He had always been more popular with Kate at his side, even though he had always been a relaxed, easy going man himself. She had the attraction though that captured others, very vocal and garrulous, social and entertaining. Maybe that was why he felt additional awkwardness at going back to work tomorrow, she would be there.

All the windows were closed. The heater was on. Yet all John could feel was cold, fevered cold. But he had no fever, he had checked on many occasions. He almost wished he did have. At least that would have given him some explanation. Why else would he test his own temperature, if not in hope of some reason for this madness?

He felt like he was going for an interview all over again so many years later. It sure was a big step forward for him but knew there was only one tough way to go, forward. Leaving the heaters on and putting on another sweater, he donned his shoes then added his donkey jacket and left his home. He needed some air. He needed to get out. So, he did.

The sun influenced air did not hit John. Although approaching dusk, it was still a very warm day, perhaps even a heat wave in its early stages. The sunset did produce a kind of natural quietness; a relaxed sense of calm. Hope for John and a good omen. It did not necessarily feel like that to him though as he walked through the heated streets overdressed. Onlookers casted quizzical glances, looking almost in trances, speechless and grasping for answers.

It didn't help John, whose initial hope from the tranquillity of the sunset had been neutralised by human views. But what else would you expect? You go out for an afternoon stroll in the joys of June, finding John here, dressed fit for the dullest of Decembers.

Yes, he was feeling this coldness, and yes, he was crunching away on his ganglion, but in a way, he was enjoying his walk. It was at least some time away from the depression he felt at home and that was enough for now.

As he continued down Manchester Road, he passed a local

factory, a metals factory, one of the most profitable in the town that had changed hands so many times over the years. The town, the very small town, was known for a large shoe company and a travel agent, both that had over the years attained national fame. Both, over the years, had experienced the vicissitudes of business. Both were still standing. It was more of a national curiosity though, adding minor portance to the little town of Haslingden.

Most people in the town seemed happy enough; most had not ventured far out from its reaches as though the ends of the world were here. But, aside from the rolling hills and undulating valleys the place itself was somewhat limited.

The sun was setting quickly and it was definitely getting cooler. It didn't really affect John that much as he was already feeling cold. He'd been walking now about fifteen minutes and despite his reluctance he knew it was doing him some good, well at least he had convinced himself of this. If he was going to go back to work tomorrow, he would need to look and feel a little more like he was a part of this world. So far, he hadn't really had that feeling since leaving the hospital. It was up to him to make that leap back into humanity. Time for him to feel like a new man in a positive way. Time for him to live again and stop simply existing.

He approached a steep sloping road at the back of town and remembered the walks with Kate through these streets. They used to walk so often down these same streets and he was sure they must have loved each other at some point. At least he did anyway.

If he was to be completely honest, he still did love her in some ways, missing her often. Sometimes he still woke up and expected to see her near him. John supposed she must have loved him to marry him, it was just, that after that divorce, he was not sure. The hurt leaves stains of doubt on the best of people. At times John even asked himself why she would have divorced him.

We all make mistakes, Johnny. She did, didn't she, buddy? She married you didn't she!!

'Oh, shut up!' John said aloud, but not too loud. Anyway, after sunset in Haslingden very few ventured out to these parts. No one was around to hear the domestic argument with his other half.

Look at yourself, Johnny, just take a look. You're dressed like an Eskimo in summer. You don't talk to anyone except me. You're living in this world you know?

He had a quick look at himself. He could not deny it, but still tried to deny his conscience. If he felt cold what could he do? Yes, it was a problem, but he had learned to live with it, or at least thought he had. The road itself was steep and a little tiring for John as he was still recovering and hadn't been exercising for a while. It was a little bit like his road to recovery.

To his left lay farmland, now empty. To his right, houses filled with insignificants passing their time the best way they could. Some were preparing to go out, others preparing for a night in. John noticed a light turn off, a bathroom light. Whoever was coming from the toilet must be feeling better now John concluded to himself, hopefully like I do when I get home, he continued.

Thinking about reaching home made him think about 'Granule' Graham again. John was not looking forward to tomorrow morning and the journey back to normality with his abnormal friend. It's like knowing your finals are coming and really fearing the worst; a grim reluctance to face the future. So much so that John had tried hard not to think about it. That, coupled with the simple fact that working life was now back on the agenda for tomorrow really put the butterflies inside John's interfered stomach. Tomorrow was his new big day.

The hilly road tested him as he contemplated tomorrow. Sweat now sparkled on the outside of this man quite literally freezing on the inside as Venus began to glow above. The challenge of life was quite a quest, sometimes making death more of a goal. At least he was turning back to normality, or a form of it he thought auspiciously, nearing the top of the road.

Just as things are going well life comes along and takes a turn in an unexpected direction and turns life upside down. And the sweat turns to sour. Just when you forget about problems and the complexities of life, you can guarantee one will come along and smack you in the face. Just when you think life is peachy, the jester comes out and blows a raspberry in your face.

Nearly there thought John breathing much more heavily now. The top of this road was only fifty meters away now.

He cursed you, Johnny. You not remember? When you put two grains of coffee in, Johnny? One of the worst things you could ever have done that was. You're gonna pay, buddy. And you start tomorrow. You start tomorrow, buddy. Oh Johnny, and you know what? You'll be lucky if you even pay the interest off. You'll be paying for a very long time. The sins you do one by one you pay for two by two, buddy.

Then he could hear Roger's huge, almost nefarious bark, though there was nothing chicken about it.

'Yer do a thing like that again and yer'll be out, do yer hear me, John?' Close to the crossroad now thought John. But this time Rogers's voice had taken on another guise. It was the face of Aunty Sheila grinning with those teeth... Oh those teeth. Grinning and speaking in that way only she could, chilled and knowing, in full control. That croaky Lancashire accent that had full control of the situation from such an unhealthy set of lungs. It was a voice that spread fear, especially for John and his past association.

Now it just seemed like yesterday and he was in her house again, young in appearance but old in heart. Confused, yet knowing how it went. He could smell smoke all around him, asphyxiating him, drowning him.

'Yer'll be out next time, don't think I wouldn't do it, Winters,' spoke the image of Aunty Sheila in a combination of voices; a mix of Roger and Aunty Sheila.

John stuttered to the top of the hill, to the crossroad, still a little confused. Yet, making to the top, he let out a huge sigh of relief, not only because of the difficulty in getting there, but also the mental torture he had just been through... as the jester's cap jingled and the door closed into the darkness.

John stood at the crossroad looking around, a collection of thoughts from his past getting misty with the present glimpses of Graham still persisting. He certainly was caught between the tigers, wondering where he had been and where he was going. Either side, it didn't feel pretty now to John.

Blurred images faded as John's heavy breathing subsided, giving way to the real image to his left. The graveyard, and home to his parents who had died tragically many years ago. How he wished they were here to make some sense of these erratic feelings and his behaviour as of late. How he wished he could go back in time to find them waiting, understanding and able to warm him up. A faint tear mixed into his drying sweat as he looked up and asked those mental questions maybe only parents were designed to answer and by default were already knowing of the answers. How he wished he could go back in time when he had no stress from life and strife.

He wasn't much aware of the time when his parents died. He was in fact only ten at the time. For John it was a time of confusion. He had pretty much forgotten that period of time, or maybe it was too far back. It was strange that he had blocked the whole episode from his mind.

John, himself was in the car at the time. It was never fully explained to John how he managed to escape the car crash with no major injuries, or maybe he had been unable to explain it to others. Though his parents had been wearing seatbelts, his parents at the front had died on impact. Maybe he was saved by the front seat stopping his impact into anything other than the back of the driver's seat? Ironically, he was the only one not wearing a seatbelt.

Following the car crash, the conclusion from the analysts was that they had the belts to the side and were in fact not wearing them correctly. The car had gone straight into the wall at about sixty mph, much higher than the allowed limit. The parents had smashed into the window, splitting their heads open. The impact killed them, and John had blocked pretty much all recollection. The car was badly written off, but strangely the crash had managed to save a life as well as take life, even though it had been written off by the newly orphaned John.

He had never seen it that way though; as a saving of his life. Would anyone? When you lose your parents as a ten-year-old boy you're not exactly going to be ecstatic at being alive; the pain not ever going away. All recollections though had been washed away. All he could remember of his youth was the harsh time he spent at Aunty Sheila's.

It was dark now. The sun had inevitably lowered itself into the southern hemisphere. The moon had become more and more prominent, taking the stage from the sun in the darkening sky.

It was still very mild. John though, was of course feeling chilly, in fact increasingly so. Trying to wrap up more, he decided to take a short cut across the park. Opened over a hundred and fifty years ago, Victoria Park was always welcoming to John. He had spent plenty of his early youth swinging on the swings and riding on the roundabout. It was a welcome sight tonight, would save him at least ten minutes on his journey back home. Nevertheless, it was always a dark and lonely place at night and he remembered often being warned from going there in his youth after sunset. If the dogs don't get you, the rapists will.

The park comprised of an ever youthful, although somewhat dilapidated playground, with a slide, roundabout, climbing frame and of course, swings. The climbing frame had been a more recent addition. Further afield were a bowling green, old unused tennis courts and a clock tower commemorating the opening in fact by Queen Victoria herself.

Over the years the clock face had become more and more

dishevelled, with only cosmetic surgery keeping it respectable. The tennis courts though were hardly recognizable as such. Built on cement they had not stood the test of time, with tufts of grass and weeds growing out from within the courts. You could say they were now a combination of hard and grass court.

At this time, it was always empty, naturally, but this time it did not deter John. He had always wanted to take the short cut, simply to save time, especially this time when he was starting to feel greater impatience and cold right down to his bones. He went past the playground, just making out the images of juvenile pleasure, wondering how small these had all become from his original impression as a child; small not just physically but also mentally. The slide was hardly worthy to be called a slide it was so small now to John.

He was feeling a shivering coldness all too familiar through his body and it was overpowering. Though fully clothed, he felt a naked coldness that made the hairs on his body stand up in search of heat. The ganglion in his mouth began to throb like a fresh bruise inside him. Biting would follow, he knew that, but how far would it go, only time would tell. The twitch over his left eye danced like a child in a playground. And his headache seemed to split him in two. He was not feeling good and needed to get home quick.

Then his mind was distracted; a movement to his right. To his right were some bushes, though not that thick. It was just a hedge at the edge of the path he was walking down. It was a movement wasn't it? Looking deeper into the hedge he found nothing. It must have been the wind. The park was in an open location and Haslingden often had breezy days.

Then again, the rustle. He wasn't in the mood for hide and seek, even though he was in the park. Clear evidence in front of his eyes, the leaves were moving, but not naturally. He stopped, glued himself to the spot like a musical statue without the music. Then out it jumped. I spy with my little eye…

The cat jumped out in front of him appearing not scared at all, though it stopped and stared straight at John and the reflection of the moon shone in its eyes. John repaid the complement. They continued as if it was some kind of staring competition. Then the cat opened its mouth and let out a roar. Well, to the cat it was a roar anyway. To a human it was just a loud screech, nothing beyond that, the warning noise an excited cat would make. Then, it kind of grimaced or smiled, it was hard to tell. It was the kind of expression a cat would make if some food was stuck in the wrong place, a fishbone maybe. Equally, the kind of face a cat would make if trying to challenge and show sarcastic anger. The cat turned around like a model on the catwalk, elegantly and confidently down onto the grass.

It had startled John, even frightened him, unsure for some seconds what on earth had hid in the bushes. He needed to act quick as he was shivering with cold and his ganglion was pulsating like it had its own heart. Without thinking John gathered pace then dived like a rugby centre back for the legs of the forward. This time though, the forward was in fact the ferocious little feline.

The cat hardly noticed. John came to a thud on the ground, hurling himself but not even thinking about that. He grabbed at the cat's body, flailing and grasping. As John touched down, he managed a firm grip over the cat's slim and soft body. He felt the backbone like a thin hard wafer in a water bed. He sank his hands to get the best grip possible.

Paws scratched, scraped. Movements jarred. Madness jolted. Eyes scrambled. Arms and legs flailed. Sweat dripped onto a swooshing tail. High pitch voices, groans emanated. Rustles from trees responded. Twigs twitched then torn. Leaves left their homes. Claws etched red lines of anger; veins of desperation. Blood effortlessly dripped from the backs of his hands as the cat screeched like a getaway car; but there was no getting away this time.

With greater urgency John grasped hard with one hand on the cat's body, the other jerkily clasping the cats two front paws. Then he felt a bit more relaxed. The cat continued to screech and panic like it was being fried alive. Head jolting back and forth, eyes occasionally glistening with a distant light. An occasional glistening three-dimensional glow of a coloured torch. When eyes met, there was moment of terror each could see in each other's eyes. Or was it a moment of reflection?

'This kitty got claws,' John said to no one hastily, looking straight into the cat's eyes. The cat's eyes reflected back. 'You're a tough one, aren't you?' He continued casting glances for proof of his efforts, his own hands now dripping in parts with blood. Due to the darkness and very faint light the liquid on John's hand could well have been water, but John knew it wasn't. From the pain alone John knew that.

He shook the cat angrily, screaming at it like an enraged father does to a guilty son. 'You came out here to shit me up. You're not gonna do that again?' His pressure increased on the cat's body. He was still feeling cold. Then, maybe the cat, still shaking in unison with John's own body, seemed to beg for remorse. John could see that in the feline's eyes. Again, maybe it was a reflection. But still it continued to fight, fighting for survival in a way any nonhuman always does. It also seemed to be shaking its head sideways in a No-No fashion, maybe begging for mercy. Then John felt it begin to relax, feeling softer in his hands as he got better control.

No mercy, Johnny, you must complete your job. No good half-done, buddy.

John's coldness was simmering, his ganglion had relaxed a little and his twitch was drowsy. Keeping his solid grip on the body of the cat with his right hand he moved his left from the grip on the two front paws. Automatically the legs began to scratch out again but John was now unconcerned with these minor disturbances.

He gripped hard with both hands and pushed the cat's neck down as hard as he could whilst squeezing the cat's body as forcefully as he could possibly dream of doing. He was shaking tremendously, partly with effort and partly with a force he did not recognise. The cat struggled, yes, but it all seemed irrelevant to John's control. John was sweating like crazy.

A vague and whispered whimper preceded the cracking sound of many bones from the cat's body. Kerplunk. The insides of the poor feline had given way. The cat's paws stopped scratching at air and skin into a feather-like spray of a kitten playing with wool. Then it stopped. John was not content. He grunted to himself, tears flowing down his cheeks and teeth grinding like a pestle on mortar.

The helpless cat was motionless now. John moved both hands to the cat's neck this time. He bit hard with his teeth and squeezed hard on the cat's neck. What little life remained inside the cat left with this final push. John squeezed so hard as tears continued down his face. A groan of freedom escaped John as he looked up to the sky in victory and confusion.

Without a second thought, he stuffed the dead cat inside his coat and scurried home.

35. OIL

Once home, and still stunned (though not as much as the cat), John plucked the dead animal out of his jacket like a magician does a rabbit out of a hat. Without thinking John plonked the dead cat down on the living room table. If he was thinking more logically, he would have gone straight to the kitchen, but seemingly he wasn't.

He sank himself onto the single seater, the 1X as he would call it, and stared at the cat. What now, he thought looking straight through it like a zombie? Its dead, open eyes stared back; reflections of a time gone by. John really could not believe what had just happened. He knew what he had done, at least that much he knew, but didn't know how and why.

Confused thoughts glittered his stained mind. Mixed images of the evening spat abuse at him. Scenes catapulted into his mind like a cacophony of chaos.

After an encore of headshakes, he sighed heavily, threw is coat onto the other chair, and began walking around the room. More specifically, he was circling the table which had become the temporary resting place for the dead cat. Imitating a shark circling its food, he continued around the table unable to think straight in a kind of ritualistic sacrificial march.

Round and round he went on his own private playground roundabout.

Ring-a-ring o' roses, a pocket full of posies, A-tishoo! A-tishoo! They all fall DOWN.

Like a mad man in a mad place the nursery rhyme came to his mind; he just kept thinking and thinking of the rhyme, repeating it to himself.

Ring-a-ring o' roses, a pocket full of posies, A-tishoo! A-tishoo! They all fall DOWN.

Ring-a-ring o' roses, a pocket full of posies, A-tishoo! A-tishoo! They all fall DOWN.

The smell of the cat was now apparent to John, not only in the room but on his clothes, especially having stuffed it inside his jacket. Very slowly, he was coming to his senses. A stale, garbage-like smell suggesting, when alive, the cat had spent most of its life homeless; eau de chat.

Just ridding the streets of the homeless, eh buddy? Still no excuse to do that to it. You'll burn for that, Johnny. But all for the best, buddy, all for the best.

John had no reply. Maybe I deserve to burn for this thought John, feeling sorry for himself but a little pity as it was his own self under the microscope.

Too late to be sorry now, Johnny. Look at the poor creature. It's not moving, buddy. Not moved for the last half hour. Don't expect it to move in the next half either do you, buddy? Jingle, jingle.

Head bowed ceremoniously; John went into the small store he had. From there he searched and eventually found an old

Puma holdall. It had not been used for quite some time, so appropriately it too possessed a stale smell, this time from lack of use. He picked up the bag and gave it a slap. Dust bounced off, onto boxes and tins of food. Stretching it to air it, he crossed back to the table, the cat still motionless, like a slab on a butchers table. John, the slaughterer, rounded on the cat again, but with no knife in his hand.

Only a small amount of sweat now lined his face. Also, there was something else he just realised. He felt no shivers, no coldness or bodily twitches. Or maybe he was just so engrossed to even think about his ailments. That of the cat was far more immediate. Maybe the adrenaline had taken over. Rather reluctantly John picked the dead cat up by its leg and placed it into the dusty holdall. It was a bit like prodding a monkey in a cage.

For some reason he did now not want to touch the 'diseased' animal; like it was contagious or maybe it evoked unwanted memories. He was casually omitting the fact that some time earlier he had not only been touching the same animal, but was practically crushing it to death. I suppose you put it down to a change in mental state. He certainly seemed mental a few hours ago, that's for sure.

Squeezing the lifeless animal into the base of the bag was a bit of an unhappy chore for John. Using pincer-like fingers he had successfully stuffed the cat into the bag. Ironically, the Puma bag had a similar looking black cat on the front. A customised bag mused John, not really seeing the funny side.

Don't let the cat out of the bag, buddy. Don't let the cat out of the bag. Not a good idea for the world to find out what's in there. Jingle, jingle.

Feeling kind of miserable and disgusted, John zipped up the

holdall. Now the bag lay on the table, right in the middle, the same place the cat was before, even though in reality it still was there. But it didn't feel right. John could still smell the dead cat; could imagine it inside staring at him. Worse still, he could see the logo of the leaping black cat striding so confidently.

Maybe the smell was what had remained on his fingers form the murder, playing on his mind. Or maybe the smell was simply the fact that this dead creature had been in the room for this length of time. It was possible also of course, that the smell was the smell playing on his mind, torturing his thoughts? That stale smell of dirt and the outside; of old clothes not used for months. The smell would not leave John's mind or his home.

With continued reluctance and disenchantment John scoured his cupboards, not really knowing what he was looking for. He scoured for something to clean his room and mind. Scoured for something to free his chains of guilt and embarrassment.

It was all he could think of. Not particularly inspiring or imaginative, but John picked the small bottle from the small cupboard. The small cupboard was home to all kinds of medicines and seldom used goods.

Returning back to the room the smell hit him in fresh waves, part realistically and part semiconsciously, knowing what was on the table. The leaping black cat. He really did not want to have to open the holdall at all, but knew he would have to. First though, he unscrewed the top of the bottle and had a good read of the label. 'Youkillthepus Oil,' it read. Then his eyes shot back quickly at the words as if he had read it wrong. This time it said 'Eucalyptus Oil'. He shook his head in confusion. Blinking rapidly, he made sure by reading again and again. 'Eucalyptus Oil'. A sigh of relief, maybe the smell was playing tricks with his mind.

It was all he had that he thought would do the trick. He only really needed to fool his own mind. He was also sure that if this didn't remove the pungent odour, nothing would. Problem was, part of the problem was that the smell was also locked inside his mind. Maybe he needed to drink the potion as well. He took a whiff of the open bottle, quickly jerking back, a compulsive reaction. It was very strong and cleared his nostrils out immediately. Like a breath of fresh air, it rejuvenated him, seemingly filling his lungs with a fresh dose of oxygen, or at least it seemed that way. He couldn't help smiling to himself after a second intake of this new oxygenated eucalyptus air.

Then, in his own time, his own hand took the small bottle and sprayed it all over the holdall like holy water over a baby. Unsparingly and unstealthily, he threw droplets into and around the bag in an almost religious act of self-amelioration. Baptizing the cat with eucalyptus oil to death he whispered his own sermon. 'Please, please go away that foul, foul smell. Please leave me and go to hell.' He also wanted the smell to dissipate with that smell he was exorcising. Knowing it wouldn't be easy he had to at least try.

All he could smell now was an overwhelming strong minty smell of eucalyptus oil, overpowering, all over the place. Feeling a little victorious and relieved, he threw the almost empty bottle into the bag with the cat, scrambled the zip closed and without really thinking, strode back into the storeroom.

It was the elongated panic that had ensured he simply put the cat in the old holdall and then baptise it with eucalyptus oil. It wasn't exactly well planned or thought out though. The confusion that gripped him ensured he didn't simply, as one would expect, put the dead cat in the bin for the bin men to take out in the morning. That would have been the actions of a rational man; something he was not at the moment.

So, in his store John had put his dead cat. The stray black cat that had crossed paths with the wrong walker. Of course, John did not think of it that way. He was still mixed up in the confusion of the evenings events he had taken part in and the inexperienced clean-up process that had ensued. John hadn't even realised that throughout all of these events; the attack on the cat, then its kidnapping; the stuffing of the cat in the bag and the final blessing and final burial in the storeroom. Throughout all of these bizarre acts John had not even thought about his headache, his ganglion or twitch and especially the coldness that he always felt.

Why would he think about those things, especially as they had abated, temporarily at least? Feeling overwhelmed by the the challenges of the evening, John Winters departed to bed for one of the better night's sleep he had experienced in a long time, even with bouts of restlessness from the night's adventures.

36. BABY

Despite a degree of calm, John's night had some visions of the cat. He went to see his doctor in one dream that night. 'Hi Doc, I just attacked a black cat, took her home, stuffed her into a holdall, soaked the bag with eucalyptus oil then put the bag back in my store. Do you have anything for me?'

'No medicine, just treatment, John,' as the doctor motioned to his colleagues outside to bring in a straitjacket. Four guards came in to restrain John as he was sedated then forced aggressively into the jacket; the jacket of course was bathed in eucalyptus oil. The aggression woke him up feeling hot rather than cold this time.

Soon he found sleep again. And he saw his own dream this time; what had become his favourite dream. He was in the huge white expanse, white snow, cold snow. It was whiteness as far as the eye could see. The snow had the fresh, just fallen appearance, with an untouched texture. In the distance was a lonely tree, a thick and solid trunk with occasional finger-like branches emanating from the trunk. The tree stood in isolation, almost paralyzed by its position; by its fixed position barricaded in by snow.

John found himself walking in the snow quite a distance from the tree, surrounded by snow. It seemed to have just stopped snowing, as he crunched heavily underfoot, the way only fresh snow does. John walked slowly through the snow finding walking in it quite tiring. It was so deep.

The tree looked so helpless and alone out there. It looked cold, bare, powerless and unprotected. Strangled dark fingers grasped upwards, as it pleading for the sun's help. The branches groped up higher and higher, still probing for a piece of prominence pie. Unlikely though, the canopy of cloud that cascaded above would allow little or nothing through. The white sheet that blanketed above pretty much would keep anything above asleep or in check, not least the sun's heat.

As he approached the stranded oak tree, unclothed of leaves, he caught the sound of something. A low scream, a cry, a moan, very high in pitch but faint. Then it became clearer because he was getting closer. It sounded familiar. It was a baby crying. A very innocent and untainted sound; unrefined and unrehearsed; often uncontrollable but not totally crazy.

As the infant came into view John noticed it was naked. Naked in this fresh snow! No wonder it was crying thought John. But to be honest, despite all the snow surrounding him, John himself did not feel the coldness. It was as if his own nerve ends were themselves paralyzed.

John came nearer to attempt to comfort the child. He just wanted to help. He lowered his arms to pick up the infant, getting lower and lower. The baby had stopped crying now, maybe alarmed by the onlooker. As he placed his hands under the baby, he was suddenly hit by it. The baby was cold, freezing cold, like a block of ice. How could it cry then? How could it move then?

Then suddenly a great moan as a cry escaped from the child...

37. ALARM

It was the buzzer downstairs from the door of his apartment that coincided with the wails of the baby in his dream. More importantly it was 7:30 am and he was supposed to be going back to work this morning. To add to this George 'Granule' Graham was probably at the door, coming to pick him up for work.

'Oh Shit,' whispered John looking at his clock; the clock whose alarm seemingly didn't work. He watched his clock click ever closer to 7:31 am and stumbled out of bed in a sluggish and torpid manner. With increased alertness, he woke himself up and gathered his way to the entrance. He opened the door and met the not so welcoming stare of 'Granule' Graham. George simply looked and pointed at his watch, intentionally suggesting the problem at hand. It was as if they had been going in to work every day. He was not even trying to be hospitable as host to John in his rehabilitation. 'Granule' Graham seemed more bothered about reaching work on time than checking on the wellbeing of his work colleague. John, still in a lethargic state of mind was a little surprised at George's lack of compassion.

He was speechless, casting glances from George to his watch, and then back again. It took him a few seconds to realise that George was being deadly serious and needed him ready and out of the house. There were oddly no introductions or concerns for John's health, just straight down to business.

'I'm sorry George, I just must have slept through the alarm. You know, being the first day back and all.' He even added a yawn just for good measure. He lied about the alarm as he had never even set it last night. He actually had no real intention or desire of going into work today. He had just become downright lazy and the challenges of last night and the cat were still fresh in his mind.

As if right on cue George gave an exaggerated sniff, then tried to peer inside the apartment. 'What's that smell? Yer smell that... that strange minty smell, John? Do yer smell that, John?'

'Oh George, I got this new air freshener, I think Summer Mint or something... err it was on offer at Boots so I thought I'd give it a try. Maybe I better leave off on the offers next time.' John laughed to hide his guilt and gave quite a good alternative story to the real one, being impressed by his own inventiveness.

'Oh, okay, John.' There was still a little doubt inside George, as he continued to sniff randomly.

Youkillthepus... Youkillthepus... Youkillthepus... don't forget that.

John hadn't forgot, and that was what was hurting his conscience the most. In his mind he couldn't rid his thoughts of that black cat in motion, then motionless on his living room table. That was the nail in the coffin. That was what had eroded away any chance of him even putting his alarm on. His mind was in bits and picking up the pieces was next on his list, but he was still planning how to begin. There was a jigsaw of pieces he had to contend with. He knew he wasn't ready to recommence work, not just yet.

'I'm sorry George, but can you please tell the folks that I'm not quite up to coming in yet. I'm still not feeling well enough. I'm thinking of going back to see the doctor first. Sorry to drag you out here this morning, I hope you understand?'

Go to the doctor? And say what? That you just killed a cat and pumped it to death with eucalyptus oil? Wake up, buddy, wake up. I thought you were feeling fine now? See the ganglion, it's gone, Johnny. Check if you like. Your twitch is no more, buddy, and you're not feeling cold, are you?

It was true. All of those things seemed ok somehow after a very long time. Despite the tiredness and the emotional mess he was in, he was actually feeling a little better.

'It's fine, John, but yer could have told me earlier. I have gone out of my way here to come to pick yer up from home.'

'I know, George. I appreciate your help and coming over today. I was hoping to be fit enough but really don't feel like I could manage all that stuff at the moment. I don't know, maybe the operation has taken more out of me than I thought.'

'All right, John. Do yer need anything? Food, shopping, that kind of thing? Yer don't look too good actually.'

Who does after the night you've just had?

'Thanks George, and sorry again. I'll be fine. I'll call Roger later. Maybe it's the heat?' That was a bit of deception from John, although at the moment he was not feeling cold at all. 'I'll make you a coffee when I get back in to the office, George.'

That was John's little joke as both parties knew how fussy George's drinking tastes were. They both laughed knowingly.

He's a wizard, Johnny, don't try to be clever now. Look at him, he's just being nice, but don't get the wrong side of him. He's a magician, buddy.

'Okay then, John, I better be off. They'll wonder what happened at work if I don't get their myself soon. I'll let Roger know and hope yer get better and back to yer usual self soon. I'm sure yer'll be fine once yer've been to the docs. Hey, I'll be waiting for that coffee, man.'

'Yep, thanks, George.' But George was already gone. Relief combined with increased tiredness engulfed John now. I minor hurdle had been jumped. More major was this wall blocking his mind, with the cat steaming away in his store. He hobbled back to bed, hoping to forget about cats, work and 'Granule' Graham.

38. EXCUSES

Later that day John did wake up again. Emotionally he was on a much more level playing field. As promised, he decided to phone up his manager Roger to formalise the reasons for his absence from work today. It was never something he looked forward to, talking to Roger, but it was a situation he had put himself into. Now, he had to get out of it, the hard way.

It was his second try at contacting Roger, having tried a little earlier, but only succeeded in finding his voicemail. He had resisted in leaving a voicemail, did not feel it right to leave a message and wanted to explain properly. Hearing the intimidating tones of Roger requesting a message was even more disconcerting to John. That was not the way John wanted to, or was going to speak to Roger today. Knowing 'Granule' Graham, the message to Roger would not have been a positive one. George was the type to jump to conclusions to easily, filling in the blanks wherever he wanted. God only knew what tale he had wagged in Roger's face.

And thus, John rang up Roger for a second time. He wanted

to speak in person to his manager. 'Roger Alliston,' answered John's manager.

'Hello Roger, it, it's err John here.' John was a little unsure of himself, a little apprehensive because of the situation he was in. It was a situation he was in solely because of himself and his own silly actions. Somehow, he had convinced himself it was not all his own fault. This made him feel a little better about things, about himself.

'I err, I err tried to call you earlier Roger but you were not in maybe? Maybe erm, you were busy, Roger?' John stuttered his way through the sentence.

'I was out ter office for a minute, John. How are yer now? Weren't yer meant to be coming back into office today?' It was more of an inquisitive and calm Roger today, rather than the more well-known Roger that was rude most of the time. But still he had that Lancastrian assertiveness that would not beat around the bush. And Roger knew good and proper that John was supposed to be in the office today. It was just his style to ask in his own way. The calm before the storm?

'Yeah, sorry, Roger. I err, was planning to come in today. I don't know. Well, I felt not too good last night and was up most of the night with headaches and pains. I'm err, not too sure what it is. So, I have made another appointment with my doctor.' John was doing pretty well making it all up as he was going along. He was even starting to convince himself. And that reminded him. He really did need to make an appointment with the doctor. He wasn't completely sure what he was going to say but he'd have to think of something.

He had realised more and more a different side of himself over the past few weeks. A more secretive, almost sneaky trait he never knew he had, when cornered. 'I know I've had a lot of time off recently, Roger, hmmm, but, but, I intend to begin back in again soon. I'd just like to see what the doctor thinks, whether these side effects are expected.' John knew Roger probably wasn't even listening; was probably checking dispatch invoices or preparing month end reports, or even picking his nose. He knew that Roger was more concerned about a day's profits than even a lifetime of complications for him. He was speaking to a man who knew work and no play.

'Okay John, I've another call on the line. Good luck at the docs, and hope to see yer soon. People are beginning to think that yer aren't coming back yer know? I expect yer quite bored at home all the time too. Keep yer chin up and come back soon. Anyway, bye for now.' Then the line abruptly went dead.

'Bye Rog…' began John as he too fell to the dead phone line. People were just numbers to Roger, but today he had been strangely polite.

A few things played on John's mind. Firstly, why had Roger said that some people were wondering if he would be coming back? Was it part of Roger's plan to get rid of him? Why was he so nice to him? And I suppose most odd, why did he continuously refer to him as John? Roger always called him Winters, with a familiar lack of respect. John could not remember Roger ever calling him by his first name before. A few things played on his mind as he looked at the dead phone on the table, in a similar position to where the dead cat was last night.

John then took the giant step; he made his appointment with the doctor.

39. WHISKER

The next day John went to see the doctor. He had succeeded in making an appointment, and was fortunate, especially after asking for a same day appointment. He was hoping for a magic pill from his doctor, and soon things would all be back to normal once again.

It was cloudless and sunny in Lancashire with a gentle breeze you prayed for on hot days, just enough to pollinate the verdure. The peripheral hum of local factories expelling pollution with productivity, a solution for economically challenged lives. Twenty-four hours a day, the perpetual drone escaped from those factory walls. Twenty-four hours a day, shift workers shifted like clouds traversing in the sky, waiting to move on. Twenty-four hours a day, cards clicked like the tick tock of a grandfather.

Hay fever heaven blossomed, pollen counting higher and higher, giving way to a sentence of sneezes, sniffles and snorting. Car windows down today or A/C machines conditioning the way. Sun roofs open all day, till sunset has its say. From dawn till dust t-shirts adorn, and more than often shorts are worn. It was a wonderful day. For Lancashire it was looking like the best summer for years. Weathermen were now supermen, heroes with smiles on their faces.

The day was perfect. Well it would have been had John not needed to go to the doctor.

'John Winters?' the receptionist spoke inquisitively. Automatically, John realised it was his turn. A wait of twenty minutes to see his doctor was not too bad at all. He, and many others had experienced much worse. Maybe luck was on his side and things were going to change for the better. A collection of antiquated pointless magazines sat impatiently on the side table in the waiting room. Woman… Hello; it was like a one-word conversation interchange.

John had decided what to say and what not to say. Danger areas like the cat and spider or recent bus journeys he had taken would naturally have to be out of bounds, but John knew he had to get his message and feelings across correctly or he may end up never going to work again.

'Please, Mr. Winters, sit down,' Dr. Rajan said perfunctorily. At the same time the doctor was tapping the keys of his IBM keyboard in a very nontechnical way; the changing face of the workplace. Whether you were a technician or even a lawyer, the desktop PC had become second nature. Of course, John sat down near to the doctor.

Dr. Rajan was his local GP who had been following up with John since his operation. He had been fully briefed with all the test results and in his opinion, things were all fine. 'How have you been, John, since your operation? Have you settled back into your new life?'

New life. Tell him about your NEW LIFE, buddy. You know what I mean? Tell him, Johnny. Don't leave out the juicy bits. Jingle, jingle.

'I don't feel myself, doctor. You know, I had planned to come for some time, just kept putting it off. I still feel very uncomfortable, not myself. I feel a bit like a man who has been wearing a watch all his life then all of a sudden has it taken away from him. What I'm trying to say is that I feel a bit like, I mean a lot like, erm, unsure of myself, like I don't recognise myself. Does that make any sense?' John was opening up a little for sure, but had to keep some prudent secrets to himself. He wanted to get across his emotions without appearing too desperate. 'I don't know if you've had patients in the same situation as me?'

As John spoke, he looked down at his sweater. It was the same one he wore two days ago. More specifically, the night of the cat. John's eyes focused more eagerly on his sweater now and he instantly recognised what it was. A cat's whisker. Thick, long, black and prominent if one was to look at John's grey hairs verses this black one. Something odd and not matching. As if suspecting the doctor was onto the case or at least would be soon John surreptitiously picked the hair from his sweater.

Youkillthepus... Youkillthepus... Youkillthepus
You hadn't forgotten had you, buddy?

Instead of simply flicking the whisker onto the doctor's floor, he kept hold of it in his right hand, as if it was evidence, he did not want to let go of. It probably looked odder, but John just didn't want to take any chances however small. And he grasped it like a child does a toy. He would not let it go, not for a while at least, so he nursed it.

In the back of his mind was Dr. Rajan's vinyl carpeted floor, and that it was white. The thick black whisker would stand out a mile. So, John kept hold of it; some kind of evidence. But in all honesty how would it stand out a mile? A single hair on a regular tainted floor? How many dozens of hairs must actually build up over a day?

But it still could stand out you know, Johnny.
Even if there is a one percent chance, it COULD, still stand out.
Youkillthepus.

By now John really didn't feel like staying much longer, even though his appointment had not even properly begun yet. The whisker, the poisoned whisker, it had polluted his mind. Like a poisoned dart from a frog, it had already entered his bloodstream. The more he tried to hide it, the more abnormal it looked. And Dr. Rajan had noticed a concealment in John, an oddness, unlike the John that he knew. Maybe John was hiding more than the whisker; the cat, the spider, the girl. Dr. Rajan looked at John with more inquisitive and concentrated eyes, cat's eyes?

The unease finally departed with the whisker, as it glided to the floor, the vinyl floor. 'Well,' croaked the doctor clearing his throat 'people react differently from all sorts of operations, especially one as serious as yours. Sometimes patients feel worse for months, some become health or exercise freaks. It is a lifestyle change, sometimes more so than a midlife crisis that we can go through. So, don't worry too much if you're getting tired or still having palpations. Don't worry too much if you're having trouble sleeping or not eating properly, it has been a big shock to your system. Don't even worry if you're losing weight or having hot flushes. We all deal with things differently, even if the things we have to deal with are the same.'

John was all ears, especially when it came to the last bit. From a medical point of view the doctor was pretty much covering everything that could happen, maybe trying to cover himself. But John was not bothered. He was there to take solace from the words that related to him.

The doctor continued, 'John, I'm no genius. We don't even know if a heart operation is always the best thing for angina. We just go with our best judgement, a call we make based on experience and knowledge. We are normally correct in our judgement; we go based on what the book tells us. Like I said, we are usually right, just that sometimes recovery takes a little longer for some, that's just life. We'll give you some more time off as sick leave, I think that will be for the best.'

Usually ends up right, thought John. He didn't like that from the doctor's words. Usually is not good enough for me, especially the emotions and actions he was going through at the moment. And exactly how long is 'longer for some' he thought.

After mentioning that he was having a lot of trouble sleeping at night John was eventually prescribed amphetamines. Dr. Rajan had noticed John's fumbling around nervously earlier and general unease in him. That was why he prescribed amphetamines, to ease his mind and relax him and get him a good night's rest.

Without mentioning the real issues in his life, John had presented some of his fears. He just hoped that when the doctor had mentioned the hot flushes, it could also include cold bouts. He hoped this potion would work because he knew for sure Roger would not wait much longer for his return, at least patiently anyway.

In the back of his mind the jester turned and shut the door behind him, the bell on his hat jingling quietly. Before leaving he drank some milk and wiped his mouth with enjoyment, only to display a moustache full of whiskers.

You're gutless, Johnny, can't speak the truth, not even for a second. You think you can hide me away, buddy?

Youkillthepus... Youkillthepus... Youkillthepus

40. STORY TIME

It was a better day for John. The amphetamines must have worked. Although he had become accustomed to his own company his day was made more auspicious by the visit of Simon, who John did enjoy the company of. Simon Wayburn was always welcome at John's, especially on a day that John felt a bit more like his old self.

John's welcome was really sincere and friendly like a doormat with those eternal words 'WELCOME' stamped on. John had a sense of a new lease of life, now again feeling like a new man, this time more recognizable.

He swung open the curtains and with equal liberation flung open the windows, though being restricted from living in an apartment. Fortunately, he had even gone to the trouble of tidying up the place. Thus, and coincidentally Simon's welcoming was made that bit more welcoming. He had even cleared out the cat from his storeroom that had been a weight from his shoulders, a blot from his mind that he would have to work hard to erase.

He felt better. No cold flushes or headaches, no ganglion or uncomfortableness. The drugs did work this time, he thought, and how glad he was that he had taken that leap and visited the doctor. Simon had been to see him a few times pre and post his operation. He was probably the only one person who had really showed genuine allegiance to his friend who had undergone this major operation. Yes, they had met often when he had been married to Kate, but Simon had kept up appearances with John where many had ended them after the divorce. So, where Simon had met him and Kate more often before the separation, they had grown closer since. Not necessarily by physical visits but by that enemy, difficulty.

They had similar personalities, he and Simon, both quiet and non-confrontational, almost bashful. Both had their problems. John with his divorce which was followed up with his operation. Simon, on the other hand with his skin problems a lifelong difficulty; eczema, pruritus, but on a whole different level. From a young age it had plagued him, an uninvited guest that just kept knocking at his door. It had become so bad at times that the aftereffects of his scratching showed up as blotches and sores, with blood and puss the end result. It was as severe and inflamed as imaginable.

Simon placed a bunch of grapes nonchalantly down on the table. It was Simon in a nutshell, resisting any desire to show himself as anything other than who he really was. No show or over politeness, no comment or card. They may even have been eaten inside the brown paper bag, who knows. Despite John's own anomalistic tendencies, he still found it a bit too straightforward of Simon to just dump some grapes in a bag on the table for him.

As Simon whispered something inaudible and pointed at the bag, John slightly embarrassingly grunted 'Thanks' in return. John's embarrassment though, would have been far less had it not been for Simon's tattered presentation of the grapes even with wetness still visible. Wetness, either from the grapes very recently being taken out of the fridge or from some damaged grapes seeping their liquid through the bag.

And John couldn't be sure if they were part eaten. John wouldn't put it past Simon. That was just the kind of guy he was, no frills. They did look partly eaten to be honest. But John could care less, he was probably not going to eat all of them anyway. More important was that his friend since childhood had remained his friend and was one of the few who continued to provide him company. Others had left him as his wife had. 'So, how've you been, John?' he said sitting down.

'Oh, a little better, Simon. I did plan to go back to work this week, then on Monday I felt like terrible again. You know, headaches, cold flushes and I think just adjusting to things. I've had memory lapses and sometimes don't feel like myself. You know what I mean?' At this point John was not opening up about the truth of things. There was a wall in his mind that he held up on the controversial episodes that he had recently been through.

Youkillthepus, Johnny.

He sure did. And he was still trying to work out why and how he could have done such a thing. Simon didn't know what he meant, though with his own illness he sure understood the physical frustrations that can affect you emotionally. 'Yeah, I'm sure it will just take a while to get back to normal,' still hiding his thoughts.

Then to avoid an uncomfortable silence John jumped in 'But I must say, I feel better at the moment. Maybe things are turning.'

'I expect so,' muttered Simon. 'You know life has a tendency to throw unexpected things at you. Sometimes when you think it can't get worse, it does. Life's a killer you know, John. I've had so many arguments with life, John, just that sometimes it just doesn't listen. Sometimes you wish you could just start again, maybe come back as a dog or something. But that's all for another day. All this chatter probably making you feel worse.' And John could relate to every word. He knew what Simon was referring to; his lifetime of skin problems, so visible and never abating.

Then John began to tell Simon his little secret, partly because Simon was an easy listener who never came with any qualms or prior opinionated views. He had also known Simon long enough to realise who he really was dealing with. It just seemed the right time as well. Simon's frank analysis had stirred John's emotions.

'You know why I didn't go to work on Monday?' Simon nodded his head the wrong way. 'Well, I'll tell you, Simon.' Then John began again, in graphic, almost sadistic detail, the story of the black cat John had killed, christened with eucalyptus oil. He also opened up on his previous endeavours, the Chinese girl and the spider.

And as John spoke, Simon listened. And as Simon listened, John spoke. It was like a remedy for John, better than any pain killers or blanket he could be given. He felt a weight being lifted off his back, releasing his hunches; lifting, with every word. He felt more and more exempt from guilt with every word.

More and more relieved of guilt with every nod of the head from Simon. John needed this. Any chords of tension were just being plucked away like a chicken's feathers. And that plexus of stress and pain that he felt for so long just seemed to be clearing now. Every time he exhaled these truths about his dire confessions, he got stronger and stronger.

He replaced his mask of guilt with a face of innocence. And in an addictive, almost alluring way, he couldn't resist that even more elaborate description to orchestrate his play on the stage of life.

But was he wrong? Maybe, maybe not. Doesn't a confessor feel better after confessing at church? Doesn't a child gain some kind of intrinsic happiness from owning up? Isn't honesty, however late, the best policy? Simon certainly thought so, even if the black cat didn't.

He listened to John conscientiously, like a child, every word meaning something. Simon didn't say much. He never did. But he took it all in like an addict does the needle. He wanted every last drop. And John gave it to him, even the bits John made up, more through forgetfulness rather than intention. 'I remember diving full length and grasping full length to get the neck of the cat. I'm not proud of it but you know, I just felt compelled to do it. You must think I'm a real looney tunes or something, Simon?'

'Well, it's clearly a bit odd but hey, it's only a cat. How many times have you seen a dead cat or something on the ground or field? You know it's so common. Maybe that's why they have so many lives?' John was a little shocked by Simon's comments, again trying to see the lighter side. '… and, and, and how many times do you drive home and see dead foxes or even hedgehogs on the roadside? I know I do.' It seemed like Simon was trying to make John feel better, maybe a little less awkward. He was trying to almost justify John's actions and exempt his mind of this guilt and tension he clearly had. Thus far he was doing a good job, even convincing himself that it really wasn't a big deal.

'Anyway, did it struggle, the black cat?'

'Yes of course.' Then John showed the faint lines on his hands like thin veins, healing but clearly visible. 'I don't need to tell you how this happened' spoke John holding up slightly trembling hands like a sparring boxer. Wounds and scars in stripes like naughts and crosses boards were painted on John's hands.

It would be lying to say that Simon was amazed by the image of John's tainted hands. He had noticed them earlier but had not the jigsaw pieces to put a story together. Consequently, he let out and audible phew of air in accentuated amazement; more to feed John's desire of astonishment rather than his own shock and awe.

If the truth be told, Simon could uncover any area of his body to display much more painful areas from his years of extreme eczema. Due to its obvious visibility it was no secret, but it was a condition he had always tried to hide from public viewing as much as possible. And his was no temporary scratch or scar, it was a lifetime punishment on a grand scale. That was why, in the audible phew he let out, there was a degree of forced exaggeration.

'It took me some seconds I think to really get control and strangle the cat, but I don't know why I felt relieved at the end of it. Like a warm glow fed right through me. Must seem odd to you I know, but this is why I keep thinking I'm going a little mad. It's why I felt I needed to discuss with you, so that you can give me your view of what you think of me.' As John spoke his fists gesticulated the grasping of a neck and his teeth ground together harshly. He was clearly emotionally involved by his re-enactment.

Simon meanwhile, was equally entertained as well as a little concerned, but only a little. His face grew with excitement at times and alertness at others with every act. His eyes widened more with every word and even his palms sweated with involvement. But he couldn't help thinking that if John only knew of his own story and the day to day struggles, he had to go through, well it would have put a different complexion on things. His own war with his body had turned him into an internal exile, not knowing at times how he would get to the next day.

And Simon could associate with John feeling better after the killing. For him too, after every scratching session, there would be a moment of relief; relief after taking a hit, knowing though that next time the punishment would come back harder and stronger. It was the private life of Simon that had become a permanent reality of pain.

Simon fidgeted and itched as he always did. His unsmooth facial features providing evidence. It was clearly visible he had skin problems. It was an unwelcome friend he had lived with all his life. A genetic disorder that he had learned to live with. It was his private problem for everyone to see.

As long as he could remember he had lived with this itch. Some days were better than others and other days were less bad. But one thing was for sure, there were very few carefree days for Simon Wayburn. He'd tried a plethora of creams, cortisones and steroids with flamboyance, sometimes going a bit too far trying to fix the issue. His skin often glowed with a greasy complexion, emanating from texture after texture of skin cream.

The itch always had the last word; it didn't matter much lotion was pasted on. It was the glue that always stuck to Simon. Always hanging onto his mind as much as his body. Even today there was evidence of itching that had caused the skin to break and a combination of puss and blood to escape. Blotches of this discharge lay visible on Simon's arms, though to him it was a sign of normality. His condition was his little friend; a friend that clung to him heartily.

41. FRIENDS

Weeks passed as time ambled slowly by. Life continued in an odd way for John. More cats met death. More cold days followed by better ones for him, and it seemed his old friend Simon was visiting him more often. Abnormality had become more of a normality. His eccentric lifestyle was now his centric way of life.

Summer was at its peak in the north west of England. Normally Lancashire was reluctant to greet the warm embrace of summer. Seldom was heat and humidity a friend of these parts. But today an old family friend not normally seen that often.

It was hot outside and even more so inside, a day when the buzz of pedestal fans was common place, to compete with that of insects. Once in a while this happened and retailers would inevitably sell out of fans of all types. Ironically this peak in sales would always be a bit of a false dawn as the supposed heat wave would only normally last a few days, then it was all over and the glum weather would return to bite.

Automatically, John opened a window, despite the fact that he didn't actually feel hot. It was just an old habit, natural reaction to the shine outside, maybe in hope. The smell of summer entered with the oxygen. It was uplifting and promising, promising with the optimism of solar power. Yet for John it was only short lived. He still felt regular chills despite the explosion of a very good summer this year. Powerful rays bombed down, pleasing depressed minds, radiating beacons of light in a way only nature could.

Ninety-three million miles away it was just another day in the life of the sun, but those blasts of hydrogen heaped uncontrollable blasts of heat onto the lands and hearts of the north west of England.

Meanwhile, John only felt momentary satisfaction, tortured by chills and numbing apprehension. Even before he would sleep there would be dread of the day to follow. He almost expected the next day to be worse than the last, especially if the last had been more bearable. He simply feared the worst. His operation was supposed to have been his cure; it only had become a trigger for an engulfing demolition of his mind and torture of his body.

He had given up on doctors; having frequented them many times. His demented mind ran his day now, and the sun had become a kind of laughing enemy, with a hat on. Just reaching the end of the day was a victory, especially if it went trouble-free.

His one saving grace had been his friend Simon; his friend who had spent hours listening and offering friendly advice. He had been the only one John had been willing to share his often-graphic experiences with. Not only did Simon listen well, but he also clearly felt now for John, in a way almost in synchronicity with him. His visits were now often every other day, and both waited in anticipation for their next meeting. John would often have another adventure to tell to excite and enthral Simon with.

From John's side there was a reassurance that he had not gone mad, despite regularly prowling the streets and fields for domesticated animals to decapitate gruesomely. Sometimes he had ventured out further to the hills of Rossendale to search for more challenging creatures. Foxes, hedgehogs, squirrels all lay out there waiting for the insatiable hands of John Winters.

Nothing would shock Simon. Not now, after weeks of explicit detail. Often John's hands and clothes would have the tell-tale signs for days after and on occasion Simon would be more than willing to help out with disposing of the remnants and helping to clean or dispose of the overly used clothing.

By now the apartment was a real mess. Pungent odours plagued his home, a home where he had to keep the storeroom closed most of the time to avoid an unbelievable odious smell from consuming everything. It was a home almost anyone would be reluctant to call home, sometimes more like a farm or zoo. Yet he and Simon spent so much time there now in thought and contemplation.

There were times when John was not sure about Simon. Why he had become so enamoured by the incidents that ruled John's life now. Maybe Simon got some kind of sadistic or voyeuristic satisfaction. In many ways John did think of Simon sometimes as worse than himself, almost encouraging the onslaught of his darker half. Those were just minor thoughts John had. Always rewarding to John was the acceptance that he had a friend, a good friend willing to listen, advise, understand in a way no one else ever had.

And that was all. John had struggled through day after day in his own isolated world as a prisoner inside his own body, living day by day, surviving and happy just to get to the next morning, an internal exile. It was his new life since the operation. The doctors had promised him he would feel like a new man after the operation. They had not been wrong.

42. LETTER

John received a letter in the morning. The morning which was bringing along a fresher climate. The switchover to autumn was on show as a wind was developing outside; a wind possessing a slightly cooler tinge to it. Still, whilst it had been mild of late it seemed things were beginning to change, like they had to. The first fresh leaves had begun to blanket the floor as seasonal fluctuations took effect. Lifeless veins adorned those poor leaves that had departed from their homes. The strong verdure was just starting to show the signs of defeat as per God's command.

When he looked at the letter, the front and then back of it, he nodded to himself part suspecting, part quizzical. He first read the back of the letter. It was from Comfort Upholstery. His mind wondered what it could be, but he had some ideas and thoughts. He squirted around with various ideas, knowing that the only way to find out would be to open it.

I might as well open it, he thought. Maybe it's a bonus letter, or a welcoming back letter? It could be a get well soon letter?

Maybe it got delayed in the post? Yes, Comfort Upholstery, they must still need me. I have given them so many years and taken so much from Roger to last a lifetime. Maybe it's a form to fill in for a change in policy or for my years of service? It could be details of my pension scheme, maybe a statement? Yes, it must be that. Could be related to my sick pay or to the long-term illness? Yes, I expect they are informing me of the legalities of long-term sick pay. Could be a million and one things he concluded.

I may have had my rough times with Roger but at the end of the day we've been through a lot together. I'm sure Punch even loved Judy. John massaged the sides of the envelope. He slowly tapped the edges of the envelope on his living room table, haunting himself with the tension and uncertainty.

A brown whisker tipped over the table side and onto the floor. He quizzed himself with the realistic and unrealistic scenarios, even trying to sneak a look inside at the contents without opening it. Torturing himself with the possibilities, he gazed at the window. At least the autumn sun is shining he thought, even though his mood never was.

Don't do it, Johnny. Put it straight in the bin. Pretend the letter never came. You know what to do, buddy. Jingle, jingle.

He continued to tap the envelope on the table, mind fidgeting for answers, but only finding more questions. He also had some junk mail that gave his mind some breathing space. 'Zoom Zoom Taxis', one flyer said, 'Your local, whether home or away'. It was a local taxi firm bombarding useless advertising. At least to John it was useless. Even if I was going to use a taxi, I would use an online one. They are cheaper and easier to use, though he did not use taxi's or rarely.

John drove his mind back to the ever encroaching and inevitable collision with the much-handled envelope from Comfort Upholstery. Comfort Upholstery had been a pretty big part of his life. There'd been bad times of course, yet John had become part of the furniture, or thought he had. There'd been hairdryer moments as Roger had often released his anger using John as a punching bag. But John, absorbing the abuse, must have made the allegiance that much stronger. They couldn't think of firing me, could they? There he said it, another permutation that he had been so reluctant to consider.

After a lifetime thinking of what the letter could be, he nonchalantly threw it in the bin, intentionally not opening it, just, I suppose to leave the psychological door open.

Good work, buddy. You know it makes sense. You did the right thing, you really did. No doubts, buddy. Move on, onto better and brighter things. Stick with jingles and you'll be fine, buddy.

43. LEAVES

A multitude of colours now glittered the landscape; autumn in full flow. Richness glowed on the ground as gold and silver shades adorned below like treasures awaiting discovery. It was not a time for people to be reserved, but a time for crispy leaves to dance a song for freedom since their release. Shades of red also carpeted the land, not to mention the expected green leaves envious of their counterparts. Some areas denser than others, blankets cushioning the bedrock, sheet after sheet.

Autumn, traditionally a season of reflection before the onset of the harsh and inevitable winter, lay in wait for John as he stumbled through the difficulties that had pressured him.

So, what happened to John? Well, he had continued over the months, the autumn months, shreds of tattered leaves dripping from the sweat he gave off. He had adapted, tried to adjust to the challenges he was posed.

The colours of his life had changed, as he tried to forge a world of sense from his afflictions. Some illnesses are visible to others, some are hidden. Some are emotionally destructive or controlled. For John, he was still figuring it out and figuring that it was a harder equation that he had ever envisaged.

Crisp under foot, walkers would crunch leaves below. Children would play youthfully, games for sometimes easy to please minds. Games as simple as to amass as many leaves as possible or to make as loud a sound as possible. Well, for John it sometimes became an obstacle as he tried and tried to remain as hidden as possible in the streets of Haslingden.

His image had changed tremendously since his operation now; hardly recognizable from the person he once was. His dishevelled look fashioned out of his desire only to exist for the moment. His lengthening beard was a sign of the times for him, greying more and more each day. His weight too, that had lowered, as if removing signs of life from his body to his face. His friend, isolation, was always there by his side. His only other friend, Simon held no reservations though, and was still sympathetic day and night. To be honest this had kept John going, the support of his friend.

It was tough living day to day for John, an almost primitive fight for survival amongst the jungle of confusion in which he fought. There was no one there to welcome him back into life or greet him with open arms from his jungle. His contact with the open world had grown more and more limited. It had been like taking step after step deeper into a cave, deeper, knowing there was no way back; no point retracing your steps.

The only way to freedom was to keep walking and climbing now into the darkness with the eventual hope of some light becoming visible. It had been a gradual affair. First, his declining relationship with his wife that had led to the darkening inevitability of divorce. Then the health fear that had led him to an operational destiny pushing him further into his abyss. His abyss was abysmal. It was a blackness that had very few silver linings, only poisoned veins and icy arteries.

Then the lifestyle he had grown into. A hermit's life of foraging around for hope and warmth in a quagmire of difficulties. An animal-like instinct of searching around the streets like natures garbage collector just doing the thing that had become natural to him. Then, as if he was natures voyeur, Simon had lapped up the latest news cutting that John could dish up in an autobiographical deluge of vomit.

The final nail in John's emotional coffin had been him losing his job. The letter that he had been so reluctant to open, for obvious reasons, despite providing numerous positive reasons for the letter from his employer, or former one.

Whilst initially choosing not to even open the letter, John had, I suppose, hoped for the best. Hoped for the best but in the back of his mind, feared the worst. There had been no planning to his madness, just a hope upon hope that he would have been given even more compassion. Truth was that he had been given many chances and opportunities to show his desire, each time refusing to show a willingness, and eventually Roger and his gang had given up on him. It had been a further shedding of his hope in an already desolate and dying existence he found himself in.

What did we agree, Johnny? To bin the letter, right. Why don't you ever listen to me, buddy. Well, you want to learn the hard way, you always do. There are no winners in that war, buddy. See how much worse you feel now, buddy. Next time take heed, buddy.

So, the months dragged for John. The best thing you could say was that he at least was surviving; surviving the coldness in his mind and body by whatever animalistic desires he could muster. And with each victim he found, whether cat, rat or even smaller, his internal torture was kept in check. This was his only source of salvation. But for how long?

He remembered opening the letter from Comfort. At the time he was a little nervous, not sure what to expect, or even what to hope for; eventually knowing the truth. No one wants to lose their job and he was normal in that sense, but when he had opened that letter and revealed all, there was also a strange sense of relief. He took the contents of the letter very casually, as if he knew it was coming.

As weeks passed, he hadn't even brought himself to begin searching for other opportunities. His emotional state had dissuaded him.

The termination letter noted that, whilst he had been a key part of Comfort Upholstery over the past fifteen years, recent issues had led the company to severe ties with him. The company had tried to call him many times over the past few months but, as John himself knew well, he would never answer their calls or return them. For that reason, he could not be, and was not, too surprised when he read the letter.

You knew they were like that, buddy. Stick by me next time and I'll keep you clean. Jingle, jingle.

He was now living off the months of generous pay they had agreed to pay him for the years of work and was fortunate that the company had agreed to pay him for three additional months, feeling compassion for him recently going through his life changing operation. But they only knew the half of it.

44. SNOW

It really was bitterly cold. More time had passed. Much more time. You could say for John it had been much more time than for you and I. It was perhaps normal for northern England but it seemed a colder snap than usual. Despite being in the grip of winter the last few weeks had seen sub-zero conditions; icicles in the morning which had become uncommon since the chatter of global warming had placed its vice-like grip over the earth.

There had been many sceptics of this global warming and today John was one of them. He would physically shiver under his covers, despite leaving whatever heating he could do so to keep as warm as possible. The bite of clear nights and even clearer days was punishing to John. There was no sense of normality anymore; every day was a new normal, he had just grown used to it; he prayed for abnormalities.

This morning was harder for him. He had been suffering mentally as much as physically with his condition. It was a battle of the mind, will and heart, not to mention his bones that felt like blocks of ice. The trips to the doctors, there had been many, had proved useless.

He had been and explained all the physical aspects of his condition, but left out the sensitive parts like the numerous cats that he had mauled to their deaths and pretty much any creature he could find to torture just to ease his pain. Somehow, he had figured out this link between his condition and the pleasure he took from abusing these creatures. It had been a correlation but he just found it so hard to come to terms with.

With only half of the story, doctors, and especially Dr. Rajan was left a little puzzled that the aftereffects from his heart operation had lasted so long. He had started to question himself now and even his skills as a competent doctor. But looking at it from another perspective what could John have done? If he had gone in to the docs and told him the truth that he can't help killing creatures to feed his body and release the cold from his bones. How would any doctor have reacted? He had no real choice in his actions.

'Global warming?' he whispered to himself poignantly, cynically. A wry smile found its way onto his face and then left as he sat up in his igloo for a while. As he had got older, he had struggled to sleep much in the morning. He often now found himself looking at the ceiling trying to make out images in his mind. Hence, it was lunchtime as he creaked out of bed. The last thing he wanted to do was get up from his comforting bed; comforting because there was at least a small amount of body heat still lingering under the covers.

Outside it was stiff with winters edge. It had been snowing for the past few days on and off, and the rains had not yet come as it was still very cold. Trees, having lost most signs of green were only left with fragments, leaning in the direction of the sun, hoping for some mercy from nature. Forks of life barely sprouting from branches like desperate fingers in the frost. Desperate twigs grasped the air for life, dreaming of a distant surprise.

It was biting cold. To some it would be depressingly dull, to others fresh and fulfilling. There was a lot of white outside, many parts layered with fresh snow. John wasn't much of a George Winston fan but if only he looked out of the window and listened to 'Carol of the Bells'.

The family of trees in the distance glistened with frost and perhaps fear of life, unknowing of the spring that lay in the distant future. They looked similar to each other but were in some way different. The all grieved for the same light form, had the same hopes and dreams. They all begged for water, yet when it had come in the form of snow and ice, they were not so cheerful. They had adapted but it was harsh and even with the sun's limited help, life was a challenge to them.

As he stood and stared out of the window, John felt colder, if that could be possible. In some ways it made him want to look away, but in another way the artistic majesty of nature kept him glued. Look don't touch, he thought to himself.

The sun was bright now in the sky as the clouds had cleared. It was a crisp blueness that now met his eyes. What could be better he sardonically wondered, then shook his head in disbelief with his emotions. Pangs of reality sent shivers down his spine and he visibly shuddered with cold. Yet he had no fever as the doctors had correctly pronounced on numerous occasions. 'Drink lots of liquids, soups, herbal tea, John. Not too much caffeine though,' they would repeat to him mechanically. It never made a blind bit of difference. His chills had persisted just like he had expected, just like the doctors said would not happen.

Not too much caffeine though! Polite crap! He thought as he donned his sweater hoping for a temperature miracle. To John, the world was against him, the doctors and especially the weather. This was his world, his depression; outside the window what he looked into was another world. This world inside his mind and his flat, the other outside of this window. It did look more appetizing outside, but for John, the security of his four walls was all that he aspired for. The sun was out but far out. It looked close but with zero degrees out there it did not feel that close at all. Though nine minutes away it did feel much further and this winter it seemed a hopelessly long nine minutes away.

The reflections on the deceptive rooftops gave hope, not only to John but also to wildlife, trees and the once upon a time verdure. How many more times would the window to the world deceive John and those of his kind? The more he looked outside his window the brighter it looked. Each blinking of an eye gave a ray of hope to beleaguered minds, blinded sometimes by the sun and at other times by the endless days of deception.

John's bony body reluctantly headed towards the shower, especially so as he was feeling so chilled already. Entering was sure to be a killer, particularly the first few seconds. In his case, probably the whole experience was one he was not looking forward to but it had been three days since his last shower so had little choice.

The floor was cool on his feet in the bathroom, now he wished he had a bath mat. He put it down to a combination of laziness and not being very domesticated, though it had not been the first time he found himself complaining over his bathroom floor.

The skeleton under the thin skin which clothed him had become more and more visible over the months. His emaciated body now a shadow of his former self. Life's toil had taken a piece of John leaving him hopeless and hapless. His natural instinct was keeping him going now along this path that he had no clue about.

His life had become a jigsaw with missing pieces.

45. BOY

Simon thrashed at the door. It made John flinch in his chair mainly because it was so quiet and he was sat embracing his own company. He often sat watching a switched off television. This was one of those occasions. He was day dreaming as usual into his former life and hopes that now felt well buried beneath the permafrost.

'I'm comin', I'm comin',' he returned, partly to himself and partly to the one behind the door. He creaked up as fast as he could towards the door, occasional shivers emanating from his aging body. It wasn't just his body that creaked; the floorboards had seen better days and they chorused with the bones in his body. Cracks creaked from his joints as squeaks spat from beneath his feet. It was not pleasant but part of the inevitability of growing old quicker than planned.

'Come in, Simon, come in.' John spoke up even before opening up fully to see who it was. It had to be Simon as he was the only one who ever came around nowadays. It was a little bit of a grumpy welcome. You could have expected a more welcoming reception from John, especially as there were so few avenues of embrace for him from any outsiders. Strangely, Simon was somewhat enthusiastic despite John's cooling desire to meet his old friend. Simon was still happy and relieved and not in the slightest bit tormented by John's repetitive lack of interest in his visits.

Simon's short, almost furtive height was probably his most striking feature twinned of course with his eczema. So, Simon himself had not been free of life's little complications, or big one's too. At present his eczema had been making his life a misery, inflaming with excessive dryness in the atmosphere which was one of the features of the dry, crisp wintery days they were in at the moment.

In a while John settled to his visitor, offered a drink and some digestive biscuits. It was too early to drink anything stronger. After a few unpleasant pleasantries John again opened up on what had happened to him a few days ago. This was of course on the top of the list of things that interested Simon of late and the reason for his impatience at the door. At first John felt self-conscious but as time passed, John's unease again turned to ease, as he opened up to Simon about his strange turn of events; strange, yes, but strange had become his middle name.

It was a few days ago when John had ventured out into his local town for basic necessities. It had been a trip that had become more and more uncommon over recent months. Having been brought up in this town he of course knew it like the back of his hand.

At the corner of the main street was his local public house where he used to go often. If he was to go in now everyone would look at him in shock not only as he had not been in for so long but also mainly due to his increasingly sloven appearance. He had become unrecognizable from the old John Winters they all once knew.

The pet shop where he used to window shop as a child had never lost its charm, though over the years it had certainly lost a lot of customers as locals had either lost their love of domesticated pets or had chosen to travel to larger chains for their pet shopping.

John could never have imagined that the same child, as a child, who was enamoured by the fish and cats and hamsters, would end up making a hobby out of assaulting them in his later years. Somehow old Jim Borman had kept the place running, turning it into part of the town's makeup; part of the furniture in the same way occasional stray cats were seen out and about in the streets. John, in his own lonely perversity had ironically hardly ever made any purchases from there, despite his ever-increasing association with his feline friends.

Old Jim did consider it odd that John had been in so many times but never bought anything, or hardly ever. And, over the past few months he had noticed John had been in more often. He wasn't complaining just raising an eyebrow in confusion.

The corner chippy also had good custom, this time more paying customers, though curry houses, dotted around town had eaten away at much of the town's appetite. It had not been easy to digest for the other eateries, but certainly Pakistani and Indian takeaways had certainly consumed a lot of local interest over the past twenty years. Yet, the corner chippy was still standing, still living, still keeping the flag of the greatness of Britain flying.

Paul's Dry Cleaners had been around for as long as the

earth had been spinning, or at least it seemed that way. Paul Roberts used to have a toffee shop across the road but as times got somewhat financially unhealthy with the advent of bigger supermarkets, Paul had seen the light, cleaning up his act and moving across the road both physically and in business type. It had proved a good move as ever-present Paul had kept things ticking over nicely.

Paul himself was a fat, now aging man, into his early sixties. He had always been part of the town and John remembered going to his toffee shop decades ago, when John himself was fairly young. Even back then John remembered a young Paul being well overweight.

John managed to buy bread, milk, apples, some woolly gloves and a box of latex gloves. Repulsive to John was that he had paid ten pence for a thin plastic bag. It was the price to pay for so-called global warming but to John it seemed a drop in the ocean, especially as most of the rest of the world didn't seem to give a damn about climate change. He of course referred to the developing world given unfair leniency. To John, by definition climate naturally changed over time and this example being set by the UK and other European nations was nothing more than social marketing of their own nations; a trend for the trendy.

John generally kept his hands in his pockets as he shopped nowadays, hands scratched with the side effects of close contact with nonconforming feline friends and foes. Thus, the explanation for the various sets of gloves he had purchased. The wintry weather was reason enough to buy woolly gloves but John had ulterior motives.

The local discount shop sold pretty much everything you would want. Even a psychopath would find his hearts desires in the local discount shop. 'Shop 4 1 & Shop 4 All' was the complicated slogan. It certainly worked with John, although he was the one and only one in his flat so it didn't really impact him. For many, especially new folk, they would be seen staring at the shop sign for a long time trying to decipher the shops code name. On success, a wry frustrated smile would rebound off their faces like they had just solved a Sudoku puzzle.

As he impatiently set off back home, he felt his usual but more severe shivers. Well wrapped up, he felt a combination of sweat and cold with unease. His neck itched frantically; his old ganglion that seemed to have temporarily disappeared was back and raring to go. It started to pulsate inside his mouth, inside his head, like an internal core sore. It was horribly distracting to him and completely intractable.

He found himself twitching and grinning to himself, the twitching in fact causing him to grin convulsively. His grinning was also partly caused by his efforts made in crunching to ameliorate the situation. It was not working. He winced and grimaced and smiled like an insane clown.

Gotta grin, buddy, gotta grin. Chew good and strong, buddy, good and strong.

Other commuters saw him, and for a second, but only a second, gave him a second stare. He would often only get a short stare rather than a prolonged one due to the fact that eccentricity had become pretty much second nature in society; a little bit like passing a homeless person on the street. After a while it becomes part of normal life, despite the fact that on face value someone sleeping on the street for year upon year can be considered nothing normal whatsoever. A momentary uncomfortableness, maybe some guilt, then back to being consumed by life's marketing and greed.

A few abnormal soft groans also escaped from John's lips, partly due to the cold and partly his urgency to get home. Squeaks coming from him pressing and crunching his ganglion were released. His blood pressure was rising as he went down a side street for a short cut home. It was a short cut he was well familiar with so to him it was not really a short cut; it was his regular way home.

His steps quickened in an irritable way as he was angered by something but didn't know what. There was something pricking his mind but he couldn't figure what. He was in a bad mood but had no idea why he was in a bad mood.

He felt pretty alone as he strode hastily along like a solitary shell, inconsolable. He had already become a recluse in any case, this I suppose was part of the package. So perhaps it was understandable. Down the lane he noticed someone else in the distance walking slowly along in absolutely no rush; a stark contrast to himself. It was just a passing glance towards the distant walker. John just wanted to get home and out of this cold.

The lane sloped downwards, Charles Lane, named after the King himself; executed for treason whilst himself being in power! It was pretty slippery (not just for Charles), as he walked briskly onwards, partly due to the downwards slope. Mainly though, it was slippery because of the icy surface layering the ground.

It had hardly gone above zero so the road had not fully recovered from the frosty night. It had been a frosty night that had given way to a frosty and clear day; a day so clear it was hiding nothing, not even clouds. Bare and innocent, no hidden surprises.

It was rare in the Rossendale Valley to get such a morning, portentous for the day ahead. Empty trees clothed the road, with nothing to hide. Trees leafless and even they themselves unclothed during this bitterly cold day. Pure blue sky above, a sea of emptiness, guarding nothing from the day ahead. Yet still birds chirped freely and without fear; or maybe calling for help? They sang a song of freedom. It was like the sky was all there was above, nothing beyond. Even the roads seemed empty. One thing not empty was John's ten pence plastic bag, the bag that really irked John. His ten pence bag swung in his hand, happily laughing at him with the fact that it had cost him ten pence!

Occasional crackles under feet as remnants of the night's frost clutched to the ground. The crunching of autumn leaves under foot; cracking mini frozen ponds of frozen water. Although John was freezing cold, he did get an addictive satisfaction from splintering ice under his feet, almost childish. Finding a fresh untouched patch of ice always seemed to gleam some satisfaction for him. It also made him think that maybe if he went and crushed all the ice on the ground it would make it warmer as there would be less ice outside. It was a stupid thought from a fractured mind; a strange logic that he was even considering.

Sometimes old leaves, hardened with ice, cracked and white with crystals of frost lay dead and motionless on the ground; now saddened to have been divorced from their parental trees nearby. Their separation causing them untold stress and concern. Frozen branches were also not pleased, having laid bare their clothing, lying dead and naked on the ground.

As John crunched his way along the lane the figure in the

distance grew closer. It was partly due to the fact that John was travelling with this urgency but also as the walker was just going along unperturbed. As he got closer, he noticed it was a young boy, probably about eleven years old. John crunched on his ganglion and simultaneously on leaves below; the biting in his mouth given an extra sound effect.

He was walking with increased urgency now down the lane, made easier by the fact that it was a downward slope. In walking so impatiently he was even risking slipping on the glassy surface below. Get a grip John! Occasionally he did slip, just managing each time to stop himself from falling.

It seemed inevitable at some point he would fall, but somehow his balance remained. The surface and temperature was making his feet numb now as well, though he could care less. Like an ice skater from hell, John continued down his hill.

The walking boy was now probably thirty feet away. John recognised the boy, had seen him around town a few times, though not enough to know his name or whereabouts. He remembered seeing him once in the local pet shop, window shopping from the inside as most boys did. The boy turned around, his sixth sense noticing eyes were on him. It was just a quick glance then he turned back unconcerned. What helped was that John instantly looked away at the same time intentionally, to avoid undue suspicion.

Yes, eyes were on him, but he took no notice. Just another of the local residents. John slowed down instinctively, pretending to look in a different direction. Moments later he continued down the lane; down the slippery slope as the boy led him on his way.

John was now not far away as the ganglion harassed and

tortured him. He automatically continued biting away inside his mouth as he tasted blood. Having caressed it for so long and so hard he found it could not keep up with the pressure and then sweet liquid grew on his tongue. It didn't seem to bother him though, as he spat blood onto the icy ground. It wasn't thick or heavy blood, just saliva mixed with it forming diluted blood but producing a slightly odd taste in his mouth. The taste was familiar all the same. The blood did not dissuade John in any way as he could not resist biting out of tension and preoccupation. His mind had already forgot that he had punctured a hole in his mouth.

John's heart was reverberating now much stronger yet it felt cold as he continued to occasionally shiver uncontrollably. Maybe the shiver was born of nervousness, or was it excitement? His journey was closing to an end he thought to himself as he saw the end of the lane in the distance.

Twenty feet separated the pair now as the boy made another glance over his shoulder, still trying not to make it obvious that he was nervous about something.

They were so close now that John could almost smell the warm breath of the boy in front; warm and comforting, nothing John had been familiar with for a long time. Soothing and welcoming, feelings that he had forgotten the meaning of. All John himself had now was ice in his veins, blending in well with his environment like a cool chameleon.

Occasional shards of ice cracked under foot but only for John. The boy on the other hand was now too self-conscious and careful to tread on any ice, resembling eggshells to him. He had become extremely careful not to cause any disturbance that might rock the boat. Yet John himself, clumsy and maladroit, continued to bound on, slipping occasionally with impatience.

By now they could possibly even hear each other's breathing as there was just a few feet between them. The boy considered turning around to ask what he wanted. It had become so obvious to him that he was being followed. John meanwhile, had only one track on his mind… and it wasn't a ballad. They approached a junction down the lane, both pretty oblivious now of their surroundings.

John took his cold, cold hands from his slightly warmer jacket, reluctantly yet necessarily. He was virtually ready to pounce; to dive forward. This was no cat though. He was still sliding around like a drunkard trying to act normal; hands sometimes flailing up and down.

Then, just at that final moment a blue Ford Focus came across, skidding in a similar uncontrollable manner to John, almost jerking and shivering, stuttering its way into John's path. It could have been a disaster. Instead it was a close call as it slid into the side, grazing John initially, who felt like it had driven right through him. He ended up on the bonnet of the car. For a second, he seemed to splat on the windscreen.

There was a portion of a second when John and the driver stared at each other in disbelief and confusion with just a layer of glass between them. It was a pregnant pause that seemed to last longer than child birth. It clearly had the potential for much more pain also, like a freeze frame picture, frozen in John's mind; an icicle with a drop of water hanging and ready to fall but never quite doing so; a teardrop of anguish.

That pregnant pause which would not stop. Like a speech therapist trying their life out to get the patient to release the words but failing every time. It lasted forever, all for nothing.

Like a policeman pointing a gun at the known assailant, forever contemplating whether to blow out the brains or let the convict fester for fifty years in prison. It was an eternity and beyond.

Then John shot back as the driver's head simultaneously spun back, similar to two like poles of a magnet. Thankfully the car was going slowly across the junction so John just limped up off the ground as the driver jumped out of the car to see what damage had been done. These incidents are often the driver's fault. In this case, the slippery surface and John's erratic behaviour had something to say for the incident. John's impatience had brought this upon himself.

'Sorry, are you, are you ok?' apologised the driver urgently. 'I really didn't err, see you. You seemed to come from nowhere.' John was just getting back to his feet, dusting himself down.

'It's ok, it's ok' replied John, almost dismissive and ignoring the driver's questions. 'I'm fine,' he continued brushing himself off and trying so hard not to slip on the glassy floor. His ten pence bag, that treasured piece of plastic that had harassed his mind for so long, lay on the ground. Apples began rolling down the lane, a little whitened by the burst plastic milk carton. John instinctively looked at them rolling down the lane not really caring for losing them, or even the ten pence bag that once cantankerously argued with his mind.

Then John remembered and realised where he was, looked around and there was no sign of the boy he had been following. The driver, of course, was very confused. Confused by John's appearance, and evasive responses, as if nothing had happened; as if he got hit by cars for a living. But John had already set off in search of the boy, not his groceries. Sadly, he could see no one else around him.

Still shivering and cold, John Winters turned to go down the hilly road to his apartment, crunching his ganglion angrily inside his mouth.

***

And all the while Simon listened, fully absorbed and fully understanding and fully saddened by what had happened. As John narrated the whole story to his friend, he noticed him fidgeting continuously, partly in excitement and partly due to the fact that his itchy skin was really flaming up. As such, John was not fully sure if Simon was really gripped by the story or if it was simply him suffering from his skin condition. Either way, John got a satisfaction from releasing his private story out into the public.

46. BARK

John awoke in tears, face soaked with a mixture of perspiration and teardrops, matted to his face. There was probably a good supply of saliva apparent too. In his dream that single solo tree stood shedding its leaves in isolation. The bright whiteness was blinding, paradoxically blocking out any clarity. Yet with time his eyes would automatically adjust to the surroundings.

In the distance the bare tree bled shards of bark, desolate and disconsolate. There was wind, wind which helped to disperse the flaky dying shreds of the tree in a multitude of directions. It was extremely cold too; nothing visible actually adding to or causing this but, somehow, it was pretty chilly. There was no sign of other life at all, just barren and deserted land which dominated. There was a dew that caused a slippery feel. Was it morning or sunset now? It was not clear to him.

The wind blew; it blew with passion. At times the tree swung a little, but like a palm tree in a desert it was in no mood to capitulate. It just kept losing skin, brown flakes of skin. From a distance the debris could have been bran flakes, though they were not very appetizing. They also resembled living creatures, black and brown moths, as if confused by the plethora of light. If moths love the light so much why don't come out during the day when it is brightest?

Shards of brown corn flakes flew high and low, butterflies confused, an imbroglio of nature. Despite the skin of the naked tree being torn and ripped apart, the tree itself never changed, never felt the aftereffects or devastation of losing its shell. It just stayed intact even though swaying occasionally with the wind; sometimes a billowing wind.

Moths everywhere, blowing, flying, coerced into life. Even a faint buzz emanated from them as they disappeared into the distance. But as they left others came and at the same time the trees branches seemed to cry out in sadness. It was like the sadness of a mother losing a child as their offspring blew away, far away.

The rain began to fall in a gentle pitter patter, almost rhythmic at first; heavy drops of cold water splashing then expanding on the white ground and on anything around. The debris from the frantically panicked butterfly tree was not spared. Blobs of rainwater hit plasters of tree bark, forcing transparent blood to drip; their wounds only temporary as they flew away in search of treatment. Acid-like drops of poison injured their outer brown skin. It seemed as if steam was emanating from their lacerated skins.

From the tree too, it seemed as though acid induced steam was escaping, soon becoming invisible in the condensing air. The rain got heavier as was expected. It appeared to be of greater penetration, potency and purpose. One huge drop of water came into focus as it crashed onto a lame flake of bark. It crashed into it then...

47. DRIP

John awoke in a rush, as panic and trepidation overtook him. It was the heart of winter. Cold sweat or a dream come true? In reflex his hand went to his face and brow as if preferring to check if his face was still there? It was more likely though that he was just seeing how drenched he actually was. It was not good news.

Despite what he had hoped, John was not only drowned in sweat from top to toe, he was also feeling extremely cold and rightly so as it was sub-zero outside. He didn't know if he should wrap up more to avoid the cold or waft the blanket to somehow ameliorate his perspiration. It was a no-win scenario.

He remembered his old boss used to moan about dwindling sofa sales. Roger would often go on and on complaining about his, his... no win scenario. 'John, we can't win. Can yer try and at least find a way to improve sales? Sales are down but we can't afford to invest more in marketing or promotions cause we can't afford it! Can't yer do something, John?' John regularly had no answers. He thought that half of the time these questions were rhetorical; just the supervisor's frustrations boiling out. He would just casually listen to the verbiage.

'If yer want to keep yer job and me mine yer better find a bloody way to improve sales,' Roger would spit at him with disdain. Well, now as his job was no more John could only smile to himself as he metaphorically smiled at Roger, with huge satisfaction.

'I'll try my best, Roger,' John would mechanically reply, knowing they were often empty words.

John shook his head. How much rubbish he had taken from Roger? Still, it had been a job, it had been a job. He could have kept nodding to the same tune but had also grown fed up with the work, and his emotional state gave him the necessary impetus to simply stay away and wait for the inevitable.

On the other hand, was any job better than the festering state he was in now, and what he was going through? Maybe better than the existence he was living through now? For some the jury may be out but for John, well, he just didn't care much now for Comfort Upholstery.

During his random thoughts John never realised until just now that there were occasional drops of water dripping from the ceiling onto his bed, on the side pillow. This, it seemed, had added to the perspiration on him, or maybe it was all of it? The drip, then thud of the droplets John only noticed after placing his hand on the side pillow.

It was not what he needed right now, not at all, especially after feeling so cold. Cold drops of water confusing his sweating body. His was a heartbeat already drained of hope, the drops resonated like the beat of a heart, his heart. He was feeling beaten, heart beaten. Cold water, ice water, on a sizzling saucepan of distress, cooking up more and more tension. The thud seemed to pound heavier and heavier, draining life, whilst the pounding sounds deafened already blocked ears. It was only once he actually noticed the drops that John couldn't get the sound out of his head.

Casually John drifted off to the bathroom, partly to relieve himself but more importantly to return with a medium sized blue coloured tub to place on the pillow next to him. At least it should reduce the already soaked pillow from getting even more saturated.

Despite it working, and the bed now not getting more drenched with water, an even louder thud now began from the plastic tub next to him. Sadly, for the tub, despite lying on the neighbouring pillow, it could not even think of resting due to the constant thud on its originally dry base. Not a moment of peace for the poor tub that had been disturbed from its resting place.

The thudding drip eventually hypnotised himself back to sleep and away from the coldness of consciousness.

48. CUTLERY

John creaked himself up from his cold, cold position. It had been a comfortable position inside his welcoming blankets despite the fact that his sheets had not been changed for weeks. The pleasures of bachelor life. Living solo had given him justification not to look after himself or his home. Keeping himself warm was his priority nowadays.

It had been snowing but the dreary depressing raindrops were like tears from above, adding to the disheartening outlook, not a good portent for the rest of the day. The freezing snow was turning slushy as the rains took command. Not that John was too tech savvy, but he checked his phone to see the weather for the day and near future. It was expected to be dryer later. At least the terrible weather would depart even if his sombre mood may linger longer.

He made an omelette, spoiling himself from the normal tea and biscuit breakfast that normally welcomed him into the day. Dirty dishes lay strewn all over his living room, with a greater concentration on the dinner table. He was just surviving with a few remaining plates and little cutlery now, disregard for the cutlery around the house.

As he ate, he remembered the visit yesterday from Simon. Simon had shown a strangely overfriendly nature as of late, though John was not complaining. John had detailed the some-what private sordid details and strange tendencies that he had been carrying out over the past few months.

Simon listened with great eagerness, almost willing him on to the next scene. His own furtiveness was always on high alert during these chats, itching uncontrollably, almost searching for new places to scratch as he always fell into the temptation. Often times he had no control over his eczema and at times it seemed as if he was actually enjoying himself. When being told of the exploits of John he would often nod in agreement and a strange understanding of John's actions.

Whilst John often felt embarrassment and disgust with himself, Simon was a little different and never visibly displayed any disgust or anxiety like John himself often felt. He just listened more attentively each time, like a rabbit on hearing movement in a field, he was attentive. It all seemed strange and voyeuristic; this only spurred John on further.

Maybe Simon was just trying to ease his friend through this tough time, a kind of rehabilitation? Or maybe Simon was trying to appear overly interested? John couldn't figure it out. Couldn't figure out the mind of Simon and the motives for his concerted attentiveness. All John knew for sure though, was that he needed Simon for his own survival and salvation.

Now John was staring into the cold tea in his cup, wondering about Simon. They both had their problems, both like brothers attacked by the cruelties of life. Biscuits had been dipped and eaten, and his omelette lay half eaten and cold. The heater was on but neither omelette nor John could remain warm. He picked another digestive and sat back in his 1X.

Today he felt unease, a little like yesterday. Biting his lower lip, he took turns at giving the biscuit a spin in his tea, occasionally dropping soggy bits into the cold tea. It helped to prove even more John's turn towards carelessness. And it was no fun, even to himself, dipping a biscuit into cold tea.

With a creaky sigh he rose to prepare for another day of boredom. His bed complemented his sigh with a creak of its own as he slowly released a spring in the aging mattress. He was tired now, despite his body being satisfied by a partial night's rest. He was cold and weary as he rose for another battle.

Feeling continual exhaustion, his start to the day was even more challenging than yesterday. Like a bird that missed its flight and had to spend its winter in the cold, John felt increasingly uneasy. The toil of winter, dragging your feet through deep snow, fresh and soft. It all helped, in John's case to make his heart sink deeper and deeper. The crushing of snow beneath hard feet, like the crunching of John's ganglion, his ears reverberating like reams of paper thudding on top of each other. Cracking bones, high and low pitch. Life's toil had taken John to his limit.

49. CHIPPY

John Winters put on his heavy jacket, black and thick, now smelling dank and odious. It was taken from the equally odious unpleasant back room of unwashed clothes. Cat hairs glittered the jacket, though the naked eye could consider them to be of human decent, especially if one had a beard as John now did.

A constellation of cat hairs shimmered in the moonlight, shining through the window, though John could care less. His heavy donkey jacket, disguised as wool stank of oldness, stale, as his hands stammered their way through the sleeves. Heavy and thick though it was, it did not ease the shivers of John Winters.

His equally fake woolly hat then found its way onto his slightly thinning head as an episode of goosebumps overtook him. For his age he still had a good head of hair, but there were signs of age beginning to show. The original brown had become a combination of bronze and grey as was normal with a man into his fifties. Rubbing his arms and body, John tried to move his arms around quickly to increase circulation to alleviate the goosebumps, knowing it was not their last visit tonight.

The cheap wooden door thumped as it shut. John then reinforced it with an extra pull to make sure it locked correctly. It wasn't a very welcoming chilly evening, but as usual the sky in Lancashire would change very quickly as clouds were already forming in the distance.

His heart had been beating heavily all day; it had seemed to deteriorate as the day had progressed. Yesterday had been bad, but tonight there was an extra weight of burden that seemed to be pressuring him; a deep chill that was way down in his bones.

He was headed for the town's corner chippy that always had been popular with the locals and even with the new generation of immigrants that had increasingly engulfed the country. Did it make John a racist that he often wanted less immigrants in the country, or a crackdown on those coming in? Regardless, it always seemed to anger John.

There were a few teenagers already in the chippy as John entered. They turned to look at John, and the smell that emanated from him. They were actually looking more at the smell rather than John himself; it was so strong. Usually there could also have been reason for a second look, but the distantly old smell of dampness hit the button.

The three youngsters from the Asian subcontinent looked at each other secretly, casting downwards glances. They all grinned a little as they moved back to give John more space. If John did realise all eyes were subconsciously on him, he hid it well, completely unperturbed and oblivious of his appearance. They exchanged some non-English words, waiting for John to order, then went back to the front of the shop to wait for their order.

All this was going on while John was privately angering himself with ideas of hate towards immigrants and with wonder as to why the government had not put a halt to such a high influx of foreigners. 'Fish an' chips… an' an' gravy ppplease.' John stuttered his way through his order.

'No problem sir,' replied the white assistant behind the counter. John wondered if the assistant Lisa had the same thoughts as he regarding the foreigners. Lisa had been working there so long but tonight even she looked at John with a faint surprise as she took his order. Because of the others in the chippy she declined to open up a conversation with John but in all honesty, she looked at John with concern having known him for so many years of visits to their chippy.

He looked into her eyes trying to teleport his questions. Lost in translation, she was more caught up by the stench and odd appearance of John rather than any political ramblings.

The three boys got their takeaways and a few seconds later John got his. As they left, they shook hands and split up to head their own ways. John put his freezing hands into his warmer pockets after wrapping the chips bag around his wrist. Coincidently he set off in the same direction as one of the immigrants. Warmer air escaped from John's mouth into the coldness of the world outside. It seemed more apparent to him from his own mouth than others as he shivered down the street.

The clear frosty night had conceded to enveloping cloud as droplets of cold rain just began to fall. At least it might raise the temperature a little, though John didn't notice any change in temperature. It was still very light rain, as the clouds developed further, darkening the sky. The droplets began to resonate on already damp ground and growth, adding more depression into already sombre surroundings.

John tried to wrap himself up more as his chip bag got more and more soggy. His hair infested heavy black jacket was getting heavier with moisture. Whiskers shimmered like a plague of shiny worms under streetlamp illumination, parasites unto his jacket now.

The immigrant walked his way home with very limited care. More attention was being paid to the social media sites on his mobile as he blindly walked home. Being after 9:00 pm in Haslingden meant the roads were pretty much clear of most traffic fortunately, because he was not paying much attention to where he was walking. The sites on the internet were more important to him than the sites on the streets; this was no Google Map.

John's chip bag swung rapidly as he strode, full of life and energy; occasional white whiskers touching and sticking to his plastic bag. His urgency was not that his food was getting cold or that he was getting wet. Moreover, it was the usual chills sending him quicker down the street to get home faster.

He approached Victoria Park, his usual short cut which coincidently was also being used by the immigrant. The huge clock tower in the distance marking its entrance was nearby. Trees like skeletons bordered the park, fingers welcoming customers, pulling them in. Old and crooked fingers pointed upwards and to the side, or were they a plexus of lifeless veins? Sometimes hands pointed in the other direction, and at other times cold arteries, lifeless and forlorn. Go back, the bony skeleton hands proclaimed. The evening cold was still there, but encroaching rains were thawing away at the battling frost. The last throws of winter colliding with the wetness of the blossoming future.

It seemed the park was empty but for the immigrant and John, sounds only of nature warning the two. Moaning sounds from the wind interacting with the trees and the rain, interplaying with any surface. The scuttling sounds of rats and cats jumbled up amongst the disturbing cacophony of nature became unrecognizable. Or maybe it was simply the wind? Branches swayed one way then the next, nature's organization in a disorganised way.

The rain was heavy now, smacking onto bare branches and soggy leaves, old dying leaves. It was a mixture of rain and snow, but it was still cold as the droplets crackled onto the sodden leaves and thudded onto hard grass.

John continued along his familiar path as his ganglion began to throb. His response was to crunch into the sides of his mouth with his canines. The warm familiar feeling as fresh blood oozed from his mouth into his tongue. He spat out instinctively partly as a reflux and partly as he didn't like the taste. Part of him was angry also that he had once again fallen for the temptations of the ganglion.

Crunch, crunch, crunch, crunch for you...

Gotta Chew, Johnny, Gotta Chew...

Chew to be free, Johnny. Chew to let the juices flow. Chew for you, Johnny. Chew to ease the pain and warm your soul, buddy...
Jingle, jingle.

The jesters cap jingled quietly in the distance.

A mixture of saliva and blood looked back at John, disguised as a black patch on the already dark grass. He couldn't help himself as he took another chunk from the inside of his mouth. It was irresistible yet painful as he continued walking, the immigrant not too far in the distance. John's outline in the darkness took a jerk forward as he took that chunk; like some creature going for an attack with its vicious teeth trying to lock onto its prey.

Striding along powerfully he didn't care too much where he was walking as the rain picked up. His coat was now heavy with moisture and his thick woolly hat was getting more and more saturated.

Drops now formed and escaped from his hat as they hit the ground like sweat from a boxer's brow, but this was cold and rainy. The scenario was not what John had hoped for, especially as there was no rain in the pipeline when he had set off.

He was extremely close to the immigrant now who seemed to be taking the same way home as John. It was a popular shortcut for many. John's cold hands locked into his pockets in what had become a lifelong ambition to keep warm, woolly gloves only partially helping as he gripped the implement in his jacket pocket.

He was shaking, cold, yet sweating, as his blood felt like it was frozen in the watery surroundings. The twitch just over his right eye danced like a beatbox machine, vibrating to the sound of its music. It was uncontrollable even as John, frustrated with it, tried to stretch his face and widen his eyes in an attempt to cure himself of the twitch and the sounds from inside his head.

The black hair was visible on the immigrant's head in the distance. Everything looked black in the darkness so maybe he was mistaken. As he passed by a streetlamp nearby in the park, John thought he could make out that the hair was curly at the ends of the locks. The hair glistened as he passed by some lighting. Lighting though was rare, as they navigated the slopes of the park. As expected after 9:00 pm there were very few frequenters of the park, especially on a cold and rainy night.

John's hands shuffled in his pockets for the correct grip as he crunched some more with urgency on his inner cheek. Down the muddy path they went, along the border of the park, trees intertwined with the edges of the path swaying uncontrollably. Sweat and rain continued to develop on John's brow, despite him feeling usually and unnaturally cold. Because it was cold, one could be confused into thinking John was feeling cold due to the weather, but he himself knew better.

His plastic bag of fish and chips swung rapidly as ever side to side like a child on a swing. His mind slid from thought to thought about his condition and how he had deteriorated so fast into this recluse. He went around and around in circles asking himself these questions, knowing deep down it had all been a result of a botch up of some kind during his operation. At least in pondering the cause he gave himself a chance. He did sometimes manage to control his emotions, but only sometimes.

And his friend Simon, yes, his friend Simon. Without Simon, John really did not know where he would be. Simon had been so supportive, even too supportive. And John sometimes asked himself why? Why? Especially as Simon had so much going on, spending a lifetime sentence with his itch.

Simon's own life had been a disaster, but seemingly had made the most of things and it gave John hope and motivation to get through. Maybe that was the reason for Simon being so understanding? Maybe he didn't want others to have to suffer the way he had all his life? John could relate to that and it seemed the most plausible reason why. John banked that thought and carried on. Seemed the most likely calculation; the only thing that added up.

A sigh escaped him as he headed home, heart beating heavily in a mixture of pulsations and palpations as he was in touching distance.

Then he took his hand out of his pocket with an urgency as a few cat hairs got stuck to his gloves, drops of water falling. He raised his hand to head level and then drove the cleaver down in haste on the neck of the man. It was a good clean strike into the side of the neck, immediately rupturing and abundance of nerves. He continued a second, then a third time, ensuring job was done properly. Dark liquid spewed out inevitably. The man squirmed uncontrollably, hysterically, on the muddy path, his own knife now on the floor next to him. The once muddy path was becoming muddier. John put his own sweaty knife back into his pocket.

In the meantime, the immigrant had fled in panic, terror and confusion. He had somehow escaped as a pool of blood was forming near the man squirming on the floor.

The man squirming on the floor looked up overcome with helplessness. He looked up into the now calmer eyes on John Winters. Winters looked back, looked back with a new calmness despite still breathing heavily. John looked deep into the eyes of the one who had spent so much time with him.

On the muddy floor, Simon Wayburn squirmed like a dying cat, muted screams like that of a whimpering cat forced themselves out of him.

When Simon realised it was John, his eyes widened, shock and confusion overwhelming him, but no words. The strength for words was not there, nor what to say.

For John, a sense of relief covered him as he put his hands back into pockets and took the long road back to recovery.